FORGIVE *Us Our* TRESPASSES

Also by Rev. Penny Stephens

Till Death Us Do Part

FORGIVE *Us Our* TRESPASSES

Reverend
PENNY STEPHENS

QUERCUS

First published in Great Britain in 2026 by Quercus

Part of John Murray Group

A CIP catalogue record for this book is available from the British Library

HB ISBN 978 1 52944 147 5
EBOOK ISBN 978 1 52944 149 9

Typeset in Bembo by CC Book Production

Printed and bound in Great Britain by Clays Ltd, Elcograf S.p.A

MIX
Paper | Supporting responsible forestry
FSC® C104740
FSC www.fsc.org

Papers used by Quercus are from well-managed forests and other responsible sources.

Quercus
Carmelite House
50 Victoria Embankment
London EC4Y 0DZ

John Murray Group
Part of Hodder & Stoughton Limited
An Hachette UK company

The authorised representative in the EEA is Hachette Ireland,
8 Castlecourt Centre, Dublin 15, D15 XTP3, Ireland (email: info@hbgi.ie)

For my nieces and nephews, with lots of love –
Ed, Matt, Andy, Hannah, Helen, Phil, Clare, Karen,
Rachel, Rebecca, Jerome and Sharmila.

CHAPTER 1

Victoria's Journal

It's glorious here. I didn't realise how much I needed this. The sea stretches on forever – but you can see big ships in the distance sometimes, too. I hadn't thought of Cornwall being on a trading route, but I guess it makes sense. Didn't wreckers and smugglers operate from here? *Poldark* and *Jamaica Inn* and all that.

The retreat starts tomorrow, but I've been exploring by myself today. I drove down through Mullion to Poldhu Cove, then up the other side of the bay and on past the golf course. The sea is soothing, and all the greens of the landscape, too. It's good to be here, although some residual sadness is always with me. Marriage over, husband gone. The golfers looked silly in their garish outfits above the bay. The husband played here once, too, I think. The ex.

It's time for a reset. Time to really let go of him and the whole sorry mess. Coming away gives that opportunity. I might go to Falmouth for a haircut – get a new look. It's time for new clothes and there are plenty of great shops there. Time for big decisions, too.

But more of what I want later. This is Cornwall. This is now. A reset. Time to rest and to revitalise.

Fresh journal pages are so inviting. I like the cover of this new one. I won't be too precious about it, just write what I feel. It's bliss to have time here, and to chill.

I'm off to find a glass of something and to watch the sun go down over the sea. No scrolling, no work of any kind. Just here. Me. And Lucy, arriving tomorrow. And the others on the retreat. I hope they're interesting. No weirdos, please

CHAPTER 2

A Year Later

Reverend Clare Brakespear dropped her children at school and drove on to visit All Saints' Church, in Tudeley. She had a lot to do that May morning in readying her own Kent parish for her week's absence, and she wanted time to herself before finishing her list of tasks.

It was unusual to be invited to facilitate the 'Refresh and Renew' event, which was advertised as being in part a holiday and in part a restorative retreat for the participants. It was being held at a smart hotel, and in Cornwall, not even in Clare's own diocese.

The organisers thought she had the pastoral experience to cope with the sensitivities of this gathering after the tragedy that had befallen the event the previous year, and Clare always loved time in Cornwall. Her archdeacon had encouraged her to accept the invitation, and it had been cleared with Truro that she could exercise ministry in their patch. It wasn't a Church event, though. People of very varied beliefs and lifestyles would be staying at the hotel and participating, and her job was to care for them all.

This morning's snatched interlude at Tudeley's church was a gift. Over the years, Clare had visited in different seasons, the daylight varying and the famous stained-glass windows always slightly changing, too. Every time she came, she saw something afresh.

Marc Chagall had designed the windows in memory of a young woman who died at sea. He used deep blues in the east window, the colours of the water encircling her body as she lay suspended amongst the swirling depths. Also depicted were things that had been precious to her – a horse, her childhood home, members of her family now grieving for her – all etched in the glass. An angel seemed to help her move upwards, towards a smiling, youthful Jesus, who welcomed her beyond the grave. A rainbow curved over them, in a covenant of love.

Clare sat and looked at the familiar images and prepared herself for the time in Cornwall. She pondered the mystery of the woman who had gone missing there while on the retreat a year before. Prayed for her, and for all who grieved for her. Victoria had simply disappeared. It was possible she had fallen, or drowned at sea, but there were only theories about what had happened, no one knew.

The window before Clare invited lament, recognised sorrow. It depicted a personal tragedy, the loss of a woman who was loved.

Other windows depicted the beauty of the moon, stars, animals and birds with joyful enthusiasm. To Clare's right, the designs were less literal, forming a kaleidoscope of yellows and golds, with symbols of hope and of life beyond death. Outlines of candles were hinted at, amongst some butterflies and the shapes of angels' wings. The brightly coloured shafts of light coming through these windows fell across the darkened church interior.

No one knew whether Victoria had died or whether she had been taken somewhere against her will. Perhaps she had simply chosen to leave her former life.

Clare thought about her, and prepared for this year's retreat.

CHAPTER 3

'She went missing on the Friday.'

Clare took in the troubled look on the man's face as he shook his head at the painful memories of a year ago.

'I'm so sorry,' she said.

They stood together in the Morva Hotel's windswept car park, with its sea view. It had been a long drive from Kent to Cornwall, and Clare hadn't expected to be accosted the moment she stepped out of her car.

The man had introduced himself as Jeremy, the hotel's events manager. He was bulky, perhaps in his mid-fifties, and he sported a swirlingly patterned shirt. Clare thought its firework colours rather overwhelmed his faded khaki trousers and battered trainers. He seemed quite casually dressed for a member of staff at a pricey establishment, and Clare wondered if this relaxed Cornish vibe was something the hotel sought to promote.

'Victoria's sister raised the alarm,' Jeremy continued. 'She was rather dramatic, and, to my regret, I admit I was slow to realise the seriousness of the situation.'

'Yes,' Clare agreed, wanting to ease his distress. 'It's often difficult to recognise a tragedy in the moment.'

'Exactly. Things seemed normal – yet, a year later, we've still got no idea what happened to our guest.' Jeremy seemed to brace himself, pulling his shoulders back and injecting a note of cheeriness into his voice and manner. 'Still, we must carry on. Thank you again, Clare, for coming to lead our "Refresh and Renew" retreat this year – we do appreciate it.'

Clare nodded her head in acknowledgment as a car with a rooftop box and a couple of bikes on a rack attached to the back nosed its way into the car park. It came to rest with its bonnet pointed seawards, and the couple inside sat motionless. Probably savouring the view and that moment of arrival after a long journey, Clare surmised.

It was a magnificent setting. The clifftop hotel curved along the ridge and seemed to be layered, descending the slope in tiers, like an iced cake. Stone-slabbed steps led from the car park down to lawns, which were invitingly terraced, with a clear view of the open sea, which glistened in the sunlight.

Clare smiled. She had been unsure what to expect when she agreed to lead the Morva's annual retreat, but the location, at least, was beautiful. Last year's disappearance of a guest made hosting the event again a point of sensitivity for the hotel. It would go ahead – they needed the money – but, with a police investigation into the disappearance still technically active, they wanted to ensure they had a facilitator who could provide pastoral care in difficult circumstances. With her previous experience of caring for people during a murder investigation, Clare had been the hotel's unlikely answer.

'Let's get you sorted.' The events manager seemed propelled

by this other car's arrival to offer Clare a more hospitable welcome, and urged her inside.

At reception stood a young woman with a mass of curly hair. Clare was excited and surprised to see her working there.

'Rachel! You look so smart!'

'Clare – how are you? How are the family?' Rachel looked delighted and reached out her hands in welcome.

'Well, they'll be furious when they hear that I've met up with you before they even arrive!'

Jeremy looked quizzically at her, so Clare explained, hastily: 'Rachel works at the stables where my children ride every year. My husband's bringing them down at the end of the week, when their half-term begins.'

'I see. Well, Rachel, we're delighted that Clare is assisting with our annual "Refresh and Renew" event.' His voice had turned unexpectedly formal. Clare suspected he wanted to remind Rachel of their professional roles. 'I'll take those copies of the schedule with me, now, thank you.'

'It's lovely to find you here.' Clare smiled as the young woman handed a stack of paper over to Jeremy. 'I knew you worked at the inn, but I didn't know about your hotel job, too.'

'Needs must,' Rachel said shortly, perhaps in reaction to being put in her place by Jeremy. Then, her face brightened, and she spoke warmly again. 'We've a new pony for Anna to try. He's a bit of a handful – we call him the pocket rocket – but she'll love him. He's got plenty of zip.'

Clare tried to look pleased at the prospect of her daughter

riding an uncontrollable missile, but thought she probably only managed an expression of benign queasiness.

'Perhaps I can show you round the hotel,' Jeremy interjected, betraying little interest in this exchange of equine news. 'You can see the rooms set aside for the retreat gatherings, Clare.'

'Sure, thank you. See you later, Rachel.' Clare smiled resignedly at her, raising her eyebrows. Rachel raised hers in return, both women in tacit agreement that this older man needed to feel that he was in charge of proceedings.

Across the passageway from reception, a pair of glass double doors had been thrown wide open. Jeremy led Clare through them and into an inviting lounge and bar, where huge sofas and potted plants were dotted about artfully. On the far side of the room, an enormous window stretched from floor to ceiling, providing a panoramic view of the gardens and the sea beyond. On the other side, a polished bar glistened.

'Quite a vista,' Jeremy declared as they walked through the upper part of the lounge and down some wooden stairs flanked by two stone lions. Here, several more large chairs were scattered across the pale timber floor, interspersed with coffee tables and other seats, each positioned to make the most of the view.

'This room is of course available to all the retreat participants, as well as our other guests. Speaking of which,' muttered Jeremy, coming to a halt. 'We have an early arrival.' He inclined his head towards a woman in jeans and a striped shirt. 'Sorry – I should have said.'

The woman sat on a large wicker chair, a magazine clutched

tightly in her hands, which, presumably, she had been reading before they entered. Now, she was frowning at the two of them.

Clare moved towards her, hand outstretched, keen to alleviate the tense expression that clouded the woman's face.

'Hello! I'm Clare,' she said, conscious of Jeremy hovering beside her anxiously.

'This is Lucy Mackie. I'm delighted to introduce you,' he said. He had plastered a smile across his face and there was a forced geniality to the way he spoke, quickly and loudly. 'Reverend Clare is one of our retreat facilitators.' He paused before lowering his voice and continuing in a more sombre tone: 'It's so courageous of you to return, Ms Mackie. I'm so glad you felt able to do so.' He turned to Clare again and dropped his voice still further. 'I'm sorry to tell you that Lucy was with us a year ago, in very difficult circumstances.'

Lucy stood up to grasp Clare's hand. Her eyes were deep brown and she had an intense stare, which she returned, now, to Jeremy. 'I'd say that "difficult circumstances" is a bit of an understatement, don't you think, Jeremy?' Her voice was clipped. 'My sister, Vic, went missing last May at this retreat. I don't suppose Jeremy told you about that, did he, Clare?'

'He did tell me, and I was very sorry to hear of it,' Clare replied, as at the same time Jeremy offered, 'Can I get you both a drink?' It seemed that his response to the slightly awkward turn in the conversation was to ignore it completely and return to his ill-judged gusto.

With a small incline of her head, Lucy accepted, and as Jeremy bustled off, the two women turned to face each other.

'Let's sit,' Lucy suggested, and they settled themselves in two of the large rattan chairs.

'I'm very sorry to meet you in such sad circumstances, in a place which must hold so many memories for you,' Clare said, carefully.

As she did so, some of the tension on Lucy's face seemed to ease. She leaned over to pull out a plastic folder from a flowery fabric bag, which rested on the driftwood table beside her.

'Here she is – I'd like you to see her.' Lucy's voice was reverent, as she produced a photo of her sister. The woman had an arresting, gap-toothed smile, a sunned face and dishevelled hair. She looked joyous, beaming at the camera. This picture was very different from the more formal, sombre shots featured in news reports of her disappearance which Clare had seen online. Here, Victoria had a much livelier presence, in marked contrast to the suited professionalism of those press photos.

'She looks happy,' Clare commented, holding the picture with care.

'Yes, I like to think of her like that. I took this on holiday a few years back. My sister had a lot of pain in her life, but this wonderful capacity for fun, too. She was a free spirit.'

'And you came here together, last year?' Clare asked. She already knew the answer to this, but thought that Lucy wanted to talk.

'Yes, we shared a room. We always shared a bedroom growing up, so in some ways it felt like we were back to our teenaged selves again.' Lucy replaced the photo in the document folder.

'No one like a sister,' Clare agreed, thinking of how much she enjoyed uninterrupted time with her own siblings, and how seldom that seemed to happen these days. Though, time apart was something to be appreciated too – she knew how heated things could get with her siblings if they were cooped up together for too long.

'We'd become closer again,' Lucy confided, and leaned forward almost theatrically, 'since her husband left her – Michael. Vic was hit hard by that, as you can imagine. But, being here with me, she was happy. The sun shone last year, too. Not like today.'

On cue, a splatter of rain struck the huge window in front of them. Clouds now crowded the sky, scudding across the view and darkening the sea. Clare was taken aback by the speed of the change. Although she had often experienced the rapid shifts in weather here on the Lizard Peninsula, on Cornwall's southernmost tip, the suddenness of such a squall was still disorientating. With such changeability, a day's plans could be upended in a moment, the mood of cheer and optimism transformed to a fractious scurry for shelter and a search for somewhere to dry sodden clothing and warm chilled limbs.

'Our last days together were happy, despite everything. That brings me comfort,' Lucy reminisced, idly stroking the bag containing the folder and photo.

'I'm glad to hear that,' Clare said.

The conversation became more general as Jeremy rejoined them. He commented on the change in the weather, and the brighter forecast for later in the afternoon. As he continued,

Clare saw Lucy's cheeks flame and her expression shift into something like stunned disbelief.

Clare glanced upwards to see what had caught Lucy's eye. Above them, just beyond the wooden steps and by the bar, stood a man wearing a long raincoat.

'Jeremy,' Lucy said sharply, cutting short Jeremy's deliberations on sea air temperatures and wind speeds. 'Is a Michael Armstrong staying at the hotel?'

The events manager looked uneasy and ran his hands through his greying hair.

'Yes, I believe so,' he replied. He cleared his throat nervously, disconcerted by Lucy's piercing look. 'Well, that is, he is – in fact – attending the retreat too,' he stuttered.

'Well, that will add a certain *je ne sais quoi* to the proceedings, Clare,' Lucy added, turning away from Jeremy to speak to Clare alone, pointedly ignoring the events manager's presence. 'That man was Vic's husband. They split a few months before she disappeared. Goodness only knows why he's here. And attending the retreat, too. He's tried to get in touch with me a few times, saying he feels badly about how he treated Vic, but I'm not remotely interested in his regrets. I stopped replying a long time ago.'

'That sounds very difficult,' Clare said.

'You probably think I should feel differently, forgive and forget and all that,' Lucy continued. 'But he'll get no absolution from me, despite the sorrowing penitent act.'

'Righto, of course,' Jeremy blundered. 'That's completely understandable. I hope any awkwardness in you both being participants won't mar your experience as a retreatant,

Ms Mackie. And that you'll be able to make the most of the Cornish beauty, the sea air and the opportunity for a personal "deep clean", so to speak, which this "Refresh and Renew" time offers.'

Clare itched to tell Jeremy to shut up. And the look that crossed Lucy's face told her she obviously wasn't the only one to feel that way. Instead, the grieving sister gathered up her bag and excused herself, walking quickly out through a glass door on to the paved area of the terrace outside. Clare watched as Lucy walked the length of the terrace, ducking her head to protect her face from the rain. Clearly, she wanted to make her escape from the garrulous events manager and was also eager to distance herself from her erstwhile brother-in-law.

It was weird that he had turned up, Clare thought, and she was unimpressed that she had been told nothing about this complication – or, indeed, that Victoria's sister would be attending. She had emailed Jeremy to ask for a list of attendees, but had received no response. This no longer seemed to be an accidental oversight. No wonder the events manager was agitated. What else had Jeremy not seen fit to mention to her?

The week had been advertised as a retreat holiday, with opportunities for guests to recharge themselves in the beautiful surroundings of the Morva Hotel. When her children had read this strapline, they asked whether people thought Clare was some kind of phone battery. Clare began to feel a sense of misgiving about the whole thing. The retreat seemed to hold unfinished business of the most profound sort.

She jolted when her phone pinged with a message: *How was your journey? Everything OK?*

It was her husband, David. Clare smiled at his concern. He had been uneasy about this trip because of Victoria's disappearance last year, but knew better than to try to dissuade Clare from going. Instead, he had confined himself to issuing random bits of advice about journey routes and being careful on cliff edges, as well as urging her to take note of tide timetables and weather forecasts. He would be even more perturbed if he knew that Victoria's sister and ex-husband had both turned up this year. He might be used to Clare landing in the thick of things, but that didn't stop him worrying about it.

'Be careful, Mum,' her daughter had counselled when Clare explained about the trip and the reason for her absence, which would be just before the children's summer half-term began.

'Why can't we come with you?' Tom was more plaintive.

'Because you don't finish school until the Friday, and I'll see you two and Dad then. The Carneys are arriving that evening, too. I'll book a ride for you all on Saturday, OK?'

'My turn to have the top bunk!' Tom announced.

'Half the week each,' Clare decreed, as she did every year.

'Who gets four nights?' Tom was quick off the mark. 'It's my turn.'

'Toss a coin for it.'

'Anna had four nights last year.'

This roused Anna from the examination of her phone.

'I didn't, did I, Mum?'

'Sorry, I can't remember. Ask Dad.' Lucky David, left to adjudicate.

'Dad will say to ask you,' Anna protested, and on this point, at least, the siblings agreed.

CHAPTER 4

'Would you like to see the other rooms? I'm happy to show you round,' Jeremy said, once Clare had put her phone away. 'And I can show you where you'll be staying, of course. You'll have a sea view.'

Her ears pricked up. A sea view?

'That's wonderful, thank you,' Clare replied. If there was a whirlpool bath and a big telly, she'd be in paradise.

'I'll show you the meeting rooms first – they're on the lower floor.'

He led her out of the lounge and along a carpeted corridor, past the loos and a spacious dining room and down a set of stairs to a second, smaller café area, where another set of French windows opened out on to a lower terrace.

Directly to the left was a room with a series of bay windows overlooking the garden and its expansive sea view. This meeting space held a circle of blue fabric-covered chairs in the middle, with more chairs stacked against the wall. It also had a glass-panelled door to the outside, and there were tables pushed against the back wall opposite it. Through the bay windows, Clare could see the rain beginning to clear.

Jeremy's phone rang. 'Excuse me,' he said, glancing at the screen briefly before walking back out to the foyer to take the call.

'Is this where the retreat meetings will be?' a tentative voice asked. Clare turned to see that a woman had walked into the room.

'Yes. Hello, welcome,' Clare said, smiling at the new arrival.

'Thank God for that.' The woman sighed and dropped a sizeable beige bag on to the floor. She wore a plum-coloured dress and was adorned with silver necklaces. Large, silver hooped earrings peeped out from her swathes of dark, glossy hair. 'I've just arrived and I can't quite believe I'm doing this. A retreat, I mean. The hotel looks great and the pool is huge, but who knows how woo-woo the activities might be. Sorry, maybe you come on a lot of these things? I wanted to try it, but I'm not sure what to expect.'

'Well, full disclosure, I'm not a regular either,' Clare replied. 'But I am leading the retreat this year. I'm Clare Brakespear. It's a pleasure to meet you.' She thought it best to let her role be known before the woman got herself into deep water.

'You? You look too normal to be leading.' The woman twisted one of the many silver rings on her fingers.

'Well, thanks, I guess.' Clare laughed. 'Do you know this area of Cornwall, then?' She wondered what a retreat leader was supposed to look like. Voluminous robes, maybe accessorised with a feathered cloak and wand?

'A little,' the woman said evasively, turning away.

'Well, here's a schedule.' Clare handed her one of the printouts that Jeremy had given her. 'You'll see we're having our first get-together in here, later this afternoon, followed by drinks and dinner.'

'OK, that's normal enough.' The woman smiled. 'I can cope with that. But what's an "Epilogue"? According to this –' she waved the schedule towards Clare and frowned uncertainly – 'they happen every night.'

'Yes, that's right,' Clare said. 'The Epilogue will be a time for us to reflect on how the day has gone, either in silence or with some music to listen to, and a reading or two – perhaps a poem or other spiritual writing. It's all quite relaxed. The goal is to give everyone space to process any thoughts or feelings, challenges you might be facing right now, that sort of thing,' she added, hoping to put the woman at ease.

'That's not too bad,' the woman said. 'That's what brought me here, really. The opportunity to get to grips with . . .' She paused, reluctant to continue.

Clare smiled encouragingly in response.

'Well, a few things that I'm finding quite painful, I suppose.'

'Exactly,' Clare said, wondering what the woman couldn't seem to bring herself to say. 'And, as in any group, there will probably be quite a mixture of people and circumstances.'

The woman simply nodded, before looking down at the schedule once more.

'Did you have any other questions?' Clare asked, after a few moments.

'I don't think, so . . .' she murmured, 'Perhaps, though . . . *Oh!*' An involuntary yelp left the woman's mouth, which seemed to startle her as much as it surprised Clare. She backed away from Clare, holding her hand over her mouth, eyes now fixed on something just beyond Clare's shoulder.

A man was standing outside, squinting through the glass door. It was the same man from earlier, Clare realised, and still wearing the long raincoat. Did this woman know him, too? Clare wondered. She seemed to be stunned into silence.

He pulled open the door and stepped inside, bringing a burst of air with him. Then, awareness seemed to dawn on his face.

'Pippa? What the . . . ? What are you doing here?'

'What am I doing here?' the woman echoed, laughing derisively. His question seemed to infuriate her; she crossed her arms over her chest and gave him a defiant look. 'I don't believe you have any right to ask what I'm doing here, or what I'm doing at all, these days. Do you, Michael?' she fired back at him.

Michael opened and closed his mouth, as if to say something, but no words came out. Before he could collect himself, Pippa shot him a look of disgust, snatched up her bag and hurried out towards the staircase up to reception. In her wake, an uncomfortable silence filled the room.

'Sorry, we've not had a chance to say hello properly,' Clare said, after a moment. She wanted to return to a more normal conversation. 'I'm Clare – I'm leading the retreat here, this year. It's good to meet you.'

'I'm Michael,' he said. As he stepped closer to her, Clare saw how weather-beaten his face seemed, and slightly grimy, too. He cocked his head at her, a curious look crossing his face. 'If you're leading the retreat, does that mean you're the person who sent those poems out to us?'

'Actually, that would be me,' a voice from behind Clare interjected at the same time as she nodded. Technically, Jeremy was right – the events manager *had* sent out the materials to the retreat participants ahead of this week. But it was Clare who'd selected them, and she suspected that was what Michael had meant.

'There's one I just can't get out of my head,' Michael said. '*Woman much missed, how you call to me, call to me.*' His voice caught at the end. 'That's right. Exactly right. My ex, Victoria, went missing at this retreat last year and I haven't been able to stop thinking about her. That poem – the Thomas Hardy one – says it all . . . How did you know?'

Before Clare could reply, Jeremy interrupted with gusto, tilting his head towards Michael as he did so.

'I know just how you feel. Hardy's poems are a reminder of painful times and the vagaries of fate, and of being separated from others, as I know. The isolation of loss, the loneliness which he describes . . . these are sensations which can feel all too familiar, and which resonate with my own experience.'

Will he ever stop? Clare thought, as Jeremy launched into a further monologue, ruminating on life's miseries – and his own, in particular – apparently with little regard for the man who had only just told them he had been married to the missing Victoria.

Michael simply ignored the verbal onslaught and held a hand up in farewell as he turned and left through the garden door, closing it gently behind him.

'Sorry – I panicked. I talk when I'm nervous,' Jeremy said.

Too right, Clare thought.

'I hadn't expected that so many people who knew Victoria would show up at the retreat this year,' Jeremy continued, as he hitched up his trousers and adjusted his belt, then clutched his hands together in front of his large stomach. 'To have her husband and her sister here at the same time . . . It's strange.'

Clare agreed – particularly as Victoria's husband had left her just before she'd gone missing. Of course, a bitter separation wouldn't necessarily preclude Michael feeling grief over Victoria's disappearance. After all, Hardy's own marriage had been poisoned by resentment and mutual antipathy for many years, only for him to mourn dramatically when his wife died, revisiting the sites of their courtship in Cornwall and writing agonised verses of lament.

The desolate poet might have yearned to hear her voice again, but, as Clare glanced at where Michael had stood, she wondered what Hardy's unhappy, embittered wife might have had to say to the husband who had neglected and despised her. Clare wondered how Michael had treated his ex, and what had brought him to the Morva.

CHAPTER 5

The final stop on Jeremy's hotel tour was Clare's room. After unpacking her things, she headed out to explore. The rain had stopped and, as she made her way through the hotel garden and towards the beach, she felt a sense of liberation. The footpath down to the cove dropped steeply, with occasional viewing points and benches strategically placed to enable people to rest and enjoy the view.

As she neared the beach itself, large stones bulged up from the ground and there was a narrow gulley with a scattering of pebbles in the middle of the path. Had Victoria walked or stumbled this way, on the night she disappeared? A year was a long time for there still to be no answers. Something grim must have happened to her, Clare thought. Unless Victoria had chosen to disappear for some reason, to escape from her life and leave it all behind.

Clare knew she was here to facilitate a retreat, not to get caught up in the sad events of the previous year. But that was unavoidable, now. With Michael and Lucy both in attendance, Victoria's disappearance would no doubt be brought up. It was odd and unsettling, she thought, that the two of them had decided to come this year. And who was Pippa? And why was there so much animosity between her and Michael?

Clare picked her way down, stopping briefly where the trail widened and a bench was placed on the grass verge.

'What the hell are you playing at?'

Clare started at the sound of the accusation and looked around.

'No excuses, I'm not interested,' a woman's voice spat. It was coming from Clare's left, behind a thick hedge that snaked down the incline and obscured her view of whoever was speaking.

'You've brought this bunch together, and I'm not happy about it. Not happy at all,' the woman continued. 'I've got pressure from suppliers, from every direction, and I need things to quieten. All you've done is stir things up – you've been playing with fire getting this lot together, and I know you're willing to stoke the flames, too.'

Clare stood rooted to the spot as the woman spoke. There was something riveting about the anger that rippled beneath her words. She hoped to hear more and was disappointed when the only noise that came from the other side of the hedge was the sound of footsteps leading up and back towards the hotel.

As Clare continued to make her way down to the beach, she mulled over the disturbing conversation. Overhead, seagulls flew languidly to and fro against a backdrop of massed clouds, and the sea had turned into a moody grey-green mix. She turned left and followed some steps down beside a stream trickling through the valley towards the sea. It led her to the head of the crescent-shaped beach, where a squat, flat-roofed building sat. It had an abandoned air; its windows were filthy and its graffitied yellow door was padlocked. There were no public amenities available here, Clare remembered.

She had come down here a couple of summers ago with her family to body board. The children had been shocked that there were no loos or café, and appalled when Clare suggested weeing in their wetsuits. They were also unimpressed by her remark that this was one way to keep warm. Embarrassing her children was one of the perks of responsible parenthood, like singing loudly in the car or cheering them on vociferously while standing beside a freezing football pitch to watch their matches. Clare was not one for exercise, nor for being cold. David did most of the dog walking, went for runs and regularly worked out at his office gym. He was healthy enough for both of them.

Clare smiled to herself as she reminisced about how David had entertained the children with tales of smuggling along this rugged coastline. Tom was enthusiastic about the idea that contraband could be transported up from the beach by quad bike, while Anna commented that packhorses would have been used, in years gone by.

Clare breathed deeply, returning to the present. There was a strong wind coming off the sea, and the rolling waves were swelling, their humps rising higher and growing fatter. The tide was out and ahead of her lay a wide stretch of sand nestled between large rocks at each end of the bay. Behind her, curved cliffs loomed overhead, their edges steep and sheer.

Invigorated by the salty air, Clare began to walk along the

shoreline, splashing in her boots as the water approached and receded.

Rounding a large rock at the base of the cliff, she came across a woman seated on some sort of plastic matting which had been spread across flatter stones. It was Lucy, the distraught sister. She was reading, a beaten paperback gripped tightly in her hands to withstand the breeze.

Suddenly, a thundering roar boomed overhead. The ferocity of the sound made the entire beach vibrate and both women looked up, startled. It was a fighter jet, engines shrieking as it swooped down low over the cliff face, before screeching off into the distance.

'What a noise!' Clare commented, somewhat redundantly, as Lucy looked at her. 'In such a peaceful spot, too.'

'It scared the life out of me,' Lucy replied. 'I was thinking of the sense of time and history here, and then that thing comes hurtling across the sky.'

'There's certainly lots of history,' Clare agreed, remembering the square building on the path and wondering what it might have been used for. Perhaps some of the D-Day landing-craft crews had been trained here.

'And centuries of wreckers and smugglers on these beaches,' Lucy remarked. 'I wonder where that plane came from?'

'There's a navy base near Helston – the air-sea rescue helicopters are based there.' Clare looked up again at the trail of smoke left behind by the plane. 'I saw them in action, once. Someone was winched up from the rocks further round the coast – I think they'd fallen and broken their leg. Accidents can happen very easily on these cliffs. The rescue was impressive.'

'That sounds scary,' Lucy said. 'Say . . . I don't suppose you'd like some company while you walk?' she asked. 'I could do with stretching my legs, if you're up for that?'

'Of course, that would be lovely.' Clare nodded, and Lucy stood to shake out her plastic mat, packing it into a capacious beach bag.

'I'm sorry to have left you and Jeremy so hastily,' Lucy said, after a few moments of companionable silence. She strode purposefully as she spoke, the pebbles and stones at the water's edge crunching beneath her feet. 'It was rude of me, but it was a shock, seeing Michael here.

'I didn't always hate him, you see. When he and Vic first got together, he made her happy. He seemed nice enough and even got on well with my husband. Sure, they got married a bit quickly, but they seemed fine.'

Lucy paused and looked out to the sea. She stooped to select a pebble and threw it towards the incoming waves. It fell short, and she resumed walking.

'But then everything imploded. It came out of nowhere, Clare. He left Vic, and she was devastated. There was no warning, everything had seemed just as usual. And now it's such a shock to see him here.'

'That sounds very tough,' Clare replied, as they continued along the shoreline, stepping over clumps of seaweed entangled with bits of driftwood and shards of plastic debris. 'And this all happened before you came here with your sister?'

'Yes.' Lucy brushed her hair back from her face. 'Vic wanted to put her life back together. I had some issues of my own to resolve too, so she suggested we go on this retreat. She was on the up, really optimistic about everything. There was even a new man on the horizon.'

'New man?' Clare was all ears. The press had made no mention of him.

'It sounded promising. *Very* new – I never even got to meet him and I think they'd only been out a few times.' Lucy sighed. 'I'd give anything to hear Vic tell me about him now.'

'Lucy, forgive my asking, but do you believe your sister is dead?' Clare's tone was gentle as she asked what she knew would be a difficult question.

Lucy seemed to appreciate her directness, moving her hair from her eyes again with an abrupt sweep of her hand. 'She must be. There's no other explanation. Vic would never break off contact like that. We were always in touch. Sending silly photos, whatever. You know how it is.'

Lucy now brushed tears from her eyes.

'Being here again brings back so many memories. We walked along this beach together. She seemed happy. We went over to Cadgwith.' Lucy touched her earrings, which were a striking shade of cobalt blue glass. 'She bought these for me. Today's the first time I've worn them since she disappeared.'

Two collie dogs hurtled down the path above the beach and careered past the women and straight into the water. The pair of them leapt acrobatically over the waves and ran helter-skelter in and out of the water, splashing up glittering arcs of spray. Clare marvelled at them, but Lucy continued talking, as if unaware of their arrival.

'Michael's hostile towards me, and I certainly am towards

him. I wanted you to know, as there could be difficulties if we're expected to do retreat stuff together.'

'Of course. I can't imagine how difficult this must be for you,' Clare said. 'You must feel free to come and go from any session as you please, Lucy. Everything in the programme is flexible and I want this retreat to be helpful for you.'

'Presumably giving Michael a smack in the teeth is beyond limits?' Lucy's bitter humour seemed to build a rapport between the women.

Clare smiled. 'Maybe write these feelings out, or punch a pillow, or yell at the sea instead,' she suggested.

'Vic used to write her feelings out.' Lucy smiled forlornly. 'She said it helped her sort out her thoughts. She did it most mornings. Not here, though. She knew me too well; I wouldn't have resisted snooping.'

The two of them fell into a comfortable silence. Gulls wheeled above them and one of the collies raced to fetch a stick which its owner, a boy wearing shorts and a hoodie, had thrown. The dog rolled over itself in its eagerness to reach it. Clare kept in step with her companion as they continued along the length of the cove.

CHAPTER 6

Victoria

This journal is a space for me to tell it like it is. Follow your gut, everyone tells me. So, what about those hairs on the back of my neck? I feel them, feel uneasy. Why do I feel watched?

Lucy's arriving today, and she'll set me straight. Sister power. I need sensible advice. I might message Jacks for some of that, too. They say that good fences make good neighbours, and she was great. Not nosy, but totally reliable about parcels, bin day and everything else. I've hardly seen her since she moved. It's time to get in touch – she has good judgement, in her no-nonsense way.

This sense of being watched comes and goes. Maybe I'm being neurotic. It's better to keep busy. I went to Atlantic Forge in Mullion and got a new wetsuit yesterday, part of the new me. I'll try it at Poldhu.

Michael was smug about his surfing prowess, but you need to be on the north coast for the big waves. Perhaps he'll be off there with Pippa this bank holiday on a surfing break, or a scuba trip somewhere more exotic. Maybe a shark or two will join them – let's hope so. But they'd be fine; things always go well for those two. There'll be no blood in the water – more's the pity.

I need to get him out of my head. An ex is an ex. Over and out.

I miss him. Even the surf bragging. Not the farting and snoring. Although, the flat is too quiet. At least there aren't any cereal bowls left out for the household fairy to put in the dishwasher. Presumably Pippa gets to perform household magic for him now, as well as bedroom gymnastics – she looks as if she'd be adept at those.

I wonder how she feels about residual bits of muesli clogging up the sink? Maybe she doesn't notice. I'm not sure she ever visits a kitchen or eats actual food. I bet she's got a capsule wardrobe and has alerts on her phone about whether it's time for another spinach face scrub. Wonder what sort of capsules she actually swallows? Ms Pippa, always pippity perfect. Or apparently so. Who knows what she's really like. There were some rumours.

This retreat is supposed to clear my head, and I'm going to make the most of it – spend time with Luce later today, and move on properly from Michael. Make space in my head and heart for the future.

I have a future. I will claim it. I will recover and move forward. I'll manifest it.

CHAPTER 7

With only an hour to go before the first session of the retreat began, Clare made her way back to the hotel's meeting room. She had a lot to do to ready the space for the participants and make it feel inviting and relaxed. She shifted some of the furniture and laid out brightly coloured tablecloths and filled the vases with yellow roses which she'd brought from home. On one table, she spread an array of pictures and books that people could browse through, if they chose.

Just as she was finishing her preparations and adjusting the background music on the speaker, she heard footsteps approaching. Clare turned to see the last person she was expecting walk through the door.

'Jackie,' Clare said. Jackie Carter, the DCI. Years ago, she had been in a relationship with Clare's husband, David. The two women had met for the first time last summer, when Clare had been caught up in a police investigation. A guest had been murdered at a wedding that Clare and her family were attending, and DCI Jackie had led the police team working on the case. Things had not gone smoothly, and the two women had been at odds to begin with, but eventually the culprit was brought to justice – and Clare had played a significant part in that.

'Sorry to surprise you,' Jackie began, looking around the room and taking stock of Clare's preparations.

'It's certainly unexpected,' was all the reply that Clare could muster, as she tried to compute the situation. 'Are you on holiday?' She stared at the policewoman, who was casually dressed in jeans and a T-shirt – not her usual garb. Her hair had grown out since the previous summer, from a pixie cut to a shoulder-length bob, and was now a more ordinary brown, as opposed to the bright blonde she had previously sported. Somehow, all of this served to make her less intimidating than Clare remembered. Then, Clare recalled the list of retreat participants Jeremy had finally given her and made the connection. 'Are you attending the retreat? Jacqueline Casey – is that you?'

'Yes, that's me,' Jackie said, looking self-conscious. 'I thought it would probably be best to go incognito, given the circumstances. Use a different surname, that sort of thing.'

'What do you mean?' Clare was indignant at being wrong-footed. 'Are you on some sort of undercover sting? Why the fake name?'

Jackie moved to take a seat, far from the door, and Clare sat next to her.

'I'm here on personal business, not police,' Jackie said quietly, but Clare knew Jackie was always police, whether or not she was on duty, just as Clare was always a priest, with or without her dog collar.

'I got a text, last year. From Victoria, the woman who went

missing here,' Jackie continued. 'She'd been a neighbour, a while back. A friend, actually. She said it would be good to catch up, and even sent a postcard, too. Who does that, these days?' Jackie seemed to be asking herself this, as well as Clare. 'The card was posted from here, but it had to be redirected because I'd moved since we were last in touch.'

'Did you reply?' Clare asked. She hoped she kept any note of reproach from her voice.

Jackie held her gaze. 'I forgot. I never replied to her text, and the card arrived much later. By then, I'd heard that she'd gone missing – it was a shock.'

'I'm sorry – that sounds awful,' Clare said. 'Do you think . . . I mean, was she trying to tell you something? Before she disappeared?'

'I don't know,' Jackie replied brusquely. 'When I heard what happened, I offered what information I could to the local team working on the case, but their communication with me was limited, to say the least.'

'That sounds frustrating.'

Jackie was all professionalism, but Clare could tell that, beneath the veneer, she was hurt. It sounded grim – to have been kept on the fringes of an investigation into a friend's disappearance and to have regrets over missing their last message.

'Devon and Cornwall have jurisdiction, of course –' Jackie's voice was studiedly neutral – 'but I've been following the case. What there has been of it, anyway. After all this time, with no significant progress, activity has dwindled.'

'Is that why you decided to come on this year's retreat?'

Clare asked. She was surprised – the DCI had been a real stickler for procedure during the murder investigation last summer. She didn't seem one to bypass protocol.

'It seemed as good an opportunity as any to see the site of her disappearance for myself, without treading on anyone's toes,' Jackie agreed. 'What brought you here?'

'I suppose I'm here because of Victoria, too,' Clare said. 'And because of what happened at the wedding last summer.'

'What do you mean?' Jackie tilted her head, curious.

'Well . . . the hotel wanted to run the retreat again this year, but after what happened last time the organisers were struggling to find someone who would take on the job. My archdeacon heard about their dilemma and suggested me for this role, as a sort of one-off. The organisers liked the idea – it's not a religious retreat, but they felt that the participants would benefit from having a vicar leading the sessions and that I'd be a safe pair of hands, whatever might come up, since the missing-person case was never closed.'

'I see,' Jackie said. 'How is the family, by the way? Your two young ones were brilliant last year – a credit to you.'

'Thanks.' Clare had her guard up – her family was off limits to her husband's former girlfriend. Then she relented. 'I suppose it's been challenging, after everything that happened. But we're doing OK. I'm pleased you got the conviction and that things worked out, in the end.'

'It was a real team effort – you helped us significantly with that investigation,' Jackie acknowledged. 'But don't quote me on that. When I heard you were leading the retreat, I wasn't sure you'd welcome me being here. But I thought I'd chance it . . . It's worth it, to be where Victoria was last seen. Not knowing what happened to her has been difficult.'

'So you *are* here to investigate?' Clare prodded.

'This isn't my patch and I'd never overstep,' Jackie replied crisply.

Clare noted how she clammed up at the insinuation and, realising that she'd hit a nerve, she stood up to return to her preparations. Turning around, she was surprised to see Jeremy standing silently in the doorway. She wondered how long he had been there, quietly watching the two of them. It was uncharacteristic when previously his movements had been as noisy as the patterns on his shirt.

'I'm so sorry to interrupt you, ladies,' the events manager said. 'I see you've sorted out the layout of the room, Clare. Is there anything else I can get for you? The kitchen will be bringing some jugs of water.' He stepped forward and addressed Jackie in a slightly exaggerated way: 'I don't think we've met?' He raised his eyebrows, interrogatively.

'Jackie Casey. I'm here for the retreat,' Jackie replied. She smiled at him, all innocent enthusiasm. 'What an incredible place you have here.'

Clare was surprised at Jackie's ease of demeanour. Not a single flicker of discomfort crossed the DCI's face when she used her false name, and she'd never seen Jackie so expressive or chatty.

'Do you come from Cornwall yourself? If I came from here, I don't think I'd ever leave,' Jackie continued.

'I'm an incomer. I've only been here a few years.' Jeremy

laughed heartily, although Clare didn't think he'd said anything funny.

'Oh, really? Have you worked at this hotel for a while?'

'Well, now, this is my fourth season, and we've been expanding our events programme year on year.' He faltered at Jackie's eager smile, then continued, 'I'm happy to work in such a beautiful location and with the excellent team here—'

'Rachel showed me your draft Christmas and New Year programme – it looks great,' Clare interrupted, feeling slightly sorry for the events manager, who looked uncomfortable for some reason. 'The Christmas murder-mystery night sounds fun; I'd love to come to that.'

'Aren't you rather busy with church services at that time of year?' Jackie queried.

But, before Clare could reply, a short woman with cropped and unusually bright turquoise hair entered, wheeling a trolley laden with jugs and glasses.

'Nadiya, thank you,' Jeremy said. 'Where would you like these, Clare?'

Jackie excused herself as Clare finalised arrangements. Jeremy began to help Nadiya unload her trolley on to a table by the window and promised to find a smaller table for Clare's speaker, close to her seat.

It would soon be time for the first session and Clare wanted everything to go as smoothly as possible, in the unusual circumstances. At least she could adjust the music volume, whatever else might be beyond her control.

CHAPTER 8

When Jackie returned to her hotel room, she thought about Jeremy, the events manager. It was odd how he had loitered in the doorway, and it piqued her interest that he had not only been eavesdropping, but had also seemed discomforted by questions about his past.

It was possible that Victoria had got herself mixed up in something untoward at the Morva Hotel, Jackie thought, as she unpacked her belongings methodically. She hung trousers, tops and jackets, arranging them according to their colour, and stowed her underwear in the appropriate drawer space. Hotels were certainly rife with potential for criminality as hotbeds for thieving and fraud, not to mention staff issues and failure to comply with employment law. The procurement and supply of illegal drugs happened in hospitality venues across the country, and Jackie knew that this area of Cornwall was no exception. Her own force, further along the coast, in Dorset, faced similar issues.

Even in this beautiful setting, nasty stuff lurked, she mused, as she admired the coastal view and watched a couple of ships in the far distance. Unfortunately, the local force had their hands full – in just the past few days, there had been a serious knife incident in St Austell and a murder in Exeter. They couldn't investigate everything properly – she knew that all too well.

Her interview with the police over Victoria's disappearance had been perfunctory – unsatisfying, even. They didn't seem to take Jackie seriously when she came forward with the information that Victoria had tried to reach out to her, days before she disappeared. But there must have been some reason Victoria had wanted to meet up, and Jackie felt sure that it held some relevance to the case.

It was disturbing how little she remembered of her former neighbour. Though the two women had been fond of each other, they had each been caught up in their own lives – although Lola, Jackie's fluffy and somewhat antisocial cat, had bonded with her neighbour. Lola would entwine herself around Victoria's legs, weaving a figure of eight and nudging at her with her head, her tail curling upwards in sinuous patterns against Victoria's dark trousers.

Lola was no more, and Jackie felt a pang of affection for her idiosyncratic pet, and for Victoria. Why hadn't she replied to her text?

Jackie cast her mind over the particulars of the case. Victoria and her sister, Lucy, had come to the Morva together to attend the retreat the previous year. The siblings had shared a room, probably not far from where Jackie was now. They'd had a sea view from theirs, too – she'd seen that in the police report.

Apparently, Lucy hadn't woken when Victoria left at some

point that night, and had been unconcerned by her absence in the morning too, assuming that Victoria had taken herself off for an early walk or swim. No alarm had been raised until well into the day – and, even then, only to a half-hearted degree. Victoria's handbag and phone were left in the hotel room, but her purse and hotel key card were missing, so presumably she had taken those with her. Her nightclothes were left behind, but a red dress and beach shoes were gone.

Could she have stumbled across some illegal activity, witnessing something which meant she had to be silenced? It was impossible to say. The hotel had no CCTV, nor had there been any evidence of suspicious vehicle movement in the surrounding area. Nor was there anything of note in Victoria's phone or email accounts, and she had confided no concerns to her sister or anyone else. She'd simply vanished.

If Victoria had chosen to leave her former life and begin anew, she had made an excellent job of it. Although her purse had gone, there had been no use made of her bank or credit cards. There was nothing.

The likeliest explanation had to be some kind of freak accident. A fall into the sea, perhaps – with a combination of tides and weather systems taking her body far from shore, or wedging her corpse somewhere still undiscovered, despite the searches by land and sea. Or a successful abduction. Horrible. Jackie wasn't one for prayer, but, if she had been, she'd have prayed that Victoria was spared that fate.

She looked out towards the horizon, where the grey blue of the afternoon sky rested on the deeper blue of the water beneath. Jackie always fought for justice, and she wanted to see perpetrators punished for their crimes. However unlikely it was that anything concrete would result from this trip, she wanted to atone for her earlier lapse in judgement and make the effort now. It was possible that someone had harmed Victoria – and, if so, the DCI was resolved to make sure they paid for it.

CHAPTER 9

The circle of chairs was ready in the meeting room, and Clare had put some upbeat Mozart on for the opening of 'Refresh and Renew'. Sunlight streamed in through the garden door and large windows, and the patterned tablecloths and bright flowers gave a sense of cheerful welcome, too.

Lucy, the missing woman's sister, was the first to arrive. She adjusted the position of her chair and asked Clare about her music choice. Then came a strikingly handsome young man with green eyes, who was wearing a T-shirt which announced, *Cleverly disguised as a responsible adult.*

An older, moustached man followed not long after, nodding at Heathcliff (as Clare had silently named Mr Ruggedly Handsome) as he took a seat next to him. The older man held a well-thumbed copy of Hardy's poems.

The room was warm, so Clare stood and opened the door to the garden to increase the air flow. A woman was walking with a toddler on the grass just beyond, slightly stooping, ready to catch the child, who was as unsteady as a ship on stormy seas, lurching this way and that in complete unpredictability.

When Clare returned to her position in the circle, she spotted a new arrival. A petite young woman had sat herself neatly, her espadrilled feet placed carefully together. Her hair was tucked behind her ears and she wore a wispy cotton sundress with a strawberry design and shoulder ties. Her head tilted as she looked around, her eyes bright with interest. Clare was reminded of a small robin, head cocked and inquisitive. The woman sneezed suddenly and quickly wiped her eyes and nose with a blue handkerchief.

'Excuse me – hay fever,' she said, pocketing the hanky with another swift movement.

Before Clare could greet her, Jeremy arrived and handed over a clipboard, keeping another one for himself and fine-tuning announcements with her about mealtimes and fire assembly points in case of emergency. Clare was sure Jeremy would have a high-vis jacket available to wear in such circumstances, although it was unlikely to be any brighter than his current luminous attire. He had changed his outfit and his shirt no longer featured fireworks; now, it was oranges and lemons in vivid abundance, which were splattered across a virulent mustard background, and he also sported cerise trousers. Clare's mother would have described the outfit as 'eye-catching'. Clare thought it was emetic.

Michael, Victoria's ex-husband, was next to walk in. Clare noticed how he deliberately sat as far as possible from Lucy, who resolutely avoided eye contact. He had washed his face, it seemed. The grime had gone, though his trousers still had splatters of mud on them.

Last to appear were Jackie and Pippa. Jackie had changed

into navy shorts and a crisply ironed scarlet-and-white striped T-shirt, giving her an efficient, nautical look. Pippa, on the other hand, now looked as if she had wandered in from a 1970s hippy trail. She wore a long batik skirt, tasselled cheesecloth top and jangly bangles, and her eyes were ringed with kohl. Clare almost expected to smell the heavy fragrance of joss sticks emanating from her.

At Pippa's arrival, Michael swore under his breath, causing Heathcliff to frown and turn, as if to rebuke him, but he stopped when he saw Michael's face. Pippa returned Michael's stare and gripped the back of her chair tightly. Clare could see her knuckles were held taut, their bones ridged and pale.

'Hello again, Michael,' she said, levelly. 'Hello, everyone. I'm Pippa. Sorry to be late.'

Jackie had seated herself as Pippa spoke, and now added, conversationally, 'If you're late, then so am I – hello, everyone.'

Clare was grateful that Jackie had defused the tension of the moment. The distrust between Lucy and Michael was already complicated enough, without this additional tension between Michael and Pippa. This combination of retreatants was a nightmare.

'Lovely to see you all,' she said. 'My name is Clare, and welcome to our "Refresh and Renew" retreat.'

CHAPTER 10

After Clare's welcome, Jeremy interrupted to give housekeeping notices. He bounced about with the jocular enthusiasm of someone announcing the winning numbers in a lottery draw, speaking at length and only interrupted by the petite woman in the sundress, who wanted to check the timings for breakfast.

Then Clare noticed that the handsome young man had raised his hand. He held it there until Jeremy noticed.

'A question?' he asked, somewhat unnecessarily.

'Yes, thanks.' Heathcliff had a courteous, deep voice. His bearded face was serious, belying the T-shirt slogan. His cheekbones were chiselled and his voice was like treacle. I really must get a grip and stop objectifying him, Clare thought.

'I wanted to ask about safety on the retreat,' he said, clearing his throat. 'Someone in the hotel bar mentioned that there had been some kind of mishap, or tragedy, last year. What's that all about, and should we be concerned?'

'I'll let Clare answer that.' Jeremy was suddenly magnanimous in leaving the floor to her.

Very helpful, Clare thought. She looked around to assess the room. At this question, Lucy's face had tightened with something like despair. Several others who had been lulled into a stupor by Jeremy's long speech jerked their heads upwards, suddenly interested. How much did each of them know about last year? Clare wondered. She must keep steady, for them all.

'Thank you for raising that. I'm very aware of the impact of last year's tragedy on different people, some of whom have been deeply affected by those events. We can address the difficulty of that on a personal and individual level during our time together,' Clare began.

At her words, Lucy dropped her head and Pippa looked at Clare with a mixed expression. Clare thought she detected fear, but there was something akin to hunger there, too, in her kohl-rimmed eyes – she seemed desperate to know what would be said.

'For those of us who may not be aware, one of the participants in the retreat held during May last year did go missing during their time here, I'm very sorry to say.'

'Her name was Victoria,' Lucy interrupted, her voice bitter. 'Or perhaps I should say her name *is* Victoria – but we all know she's dead.'

Lucy knew how to hold an audience's attention. She stood and swivelled her body slowly, her gaze engaging each of the group in turn, and finally alighting on Michael.

'As Vic's sister, I do have some idea of the grief she suffered in the final months of her life. Have you anything to add about that, Michael?'

Now, it was Clare's turn to interrupt.

'Hang on, let's pause it there,' she said, decisively. 'Lucy,

I suggest you and I talk more about this in private, but, for now, I'd like to explain a bit more about this retreat to the whole group, thank you.'

Much to her relief, Lucy sat.

Without delay, Clare distributed copies of the retreat schedule and launched into an outline of the aims of their time together.

'This retreat gives each of us an opportunity for rest and refreshment, time to reflect on aspects of life that might be especially challenging and to lament for any loss – whether of missed loved ones –' here, she dipped her head towards Lucy – 'or of relationships, hopes, perhaps a career, or whatever might be a loss, to any of us. The aim is to provide an opportunity to regroup, and to draw on whatever emotional or spiritual resources might be helpful to us in this extraordinary landscape, which so many people find to be a "thin place", where the everyday and the numinous are closely interwoven.'

She paused, raising her hand to indicate the garden in the late afternoon sunshine and the seascape beyond.

'It's important that, as well having time to enjoy our retreat activities, this is a break for everyone, too. We'll be able to visit local places together on this incredible peninsula. We'll go to Kynance Cove tomorrow and Cadgwith on Thursday. Jeremy can take us in the hotel minibus, for anyone who needs transport, or people can travel separately –' she managed not to look at anyone in particular as she said this – 'and, of course, everything's optional. Each of you must feel free to participate in sessions and excursions or not, just as feels best for you. We'll end each day with an Epilogue, here, at nine o'clock every evening.'

She alluded to the materials that everyone had already received, including the poems of lament, which she suggested might be a fruitful source of discussion and insight for some of them, but might not suit everyone.

'I liked the picture of a gateway,' the petite woman murmured to Lucy, who ignored her.

Now, it was time to return to the questions raised about Victoria. Clare put her hand in the pocket of her denim dress and briefly touched the wooden cross and wooden heart which she kept there.

'As Lucy explained,' she said, 'sadly, her sister, Victoria, went missing in the later stages of last year's retreat, and since then her whereabouts have been unknown.' Whereabouts? Since when did she use police speak, like Jackie? She ploughed on: 'For that reason, there are particular sensitivities around this year – especially for you, of course, Lucy –' Clare half bowed to her – 'and for others who had a connection with Victoria, such as Jeremy, our events manager here at the Morva,' she added, not wanting to out Jackie or anyone else, and being careful to avoid Michael's eye as she spoke. 'Jeremy coordinated things last year, too –' for some reason, Jeremy looked unhappy at this namecheck, rather than welcoming the attention – 'and it's great to have your expertise again this year.' She gestured towards him with her clipboard, but, instead of being mollified, Jeremy looked irritated to have been referenced further, scowling at Clare in a way which confused her. 'I suggest we have a moment to listen to some music, before we make our personal introductions. Perhaps we can share our names and what brought us to this retreat.'

As Clare turned to switch on the music, she caught sight of Jackie's half-smile and nod of encouragement. She hadn't anticipated seeing Jackie in this positive light, but her steadiness felt like a gift, given the tensions that simmered between the other participants. Somehow, they would get through this. And perhaps something good would come out of the retreat, despite last year's tragedy.

CHAPTER 11

Victoria

Luce and I skived off this morning's session – we went across to Coverack and had a coffee overlooking the harbour. We drove over the Goonhilly Downs, with those huge satellite dishes looming up amongst the wind farms. There's something bleak and strange about that landscape.

We're off to Cadgwith later.

Maybe I'll buy some baby shoes. A portent. A kind of promise to myself, that I mean to go ahead.

I'm thinking of going it alone as a parent. It feels so strange to have actually written that! And exciting. I've been realising what really matters, and what I truly want. And I want to be a mother, and to have a child. I'm not getting any younger, and you can choose a donor by catalogue. Like shoes. New man is great, but it's too soon with him, and involving someone so personally in this feels complicated. I'd rather go ahead without emotional strings, and partners don't always take kindly to playing second fiddle to a child. And maybe I'll meet someone else, anyway – there's plenty more fish in the sea. I've not told Lucy; it still feels private, precious.

It's almost mystical, the sense I have that I'll be a mother, however daunting that feels. It's a cherished secret, too early to tell. But I can already see this little one's face, already feel him or her cradled in my arms. I'm ready to buy them an ice cream at Coverack, or to take them to the seal sanctuary at Gweek. I'll be spending money on seal soft toys instead of getting my hair cut. I looked at the tiny children's wetsuits in Coverack this morning. This is real. I can't wait.

CHAPTER 12

'I'm Clare, as you know, and any excuse to come to Cornwall and I'm here,' she began. 'I lead various kinds of retreats – more often those with a specifically Christian focus and content, as I'm a vicar and have a parish in Kent. Occasionally, I'm involved in retreats of a more general nature, like this one, and I'm delighted to be with you at the Morva.'

She avoided any mention of how she'd been invited to lead this retreat because the investigation into Victoria's disappearance was, technically, still live. Nor did she explain quite how unusual participating in this kind of expensive 'wellness' business was for her, as an Anglican priest.

'Anyone else happy to introduce themselves?'

Jackie surprised her by speaking up. The DCI was proving herself a team player, Clare thought.

'I'm Jackie, and I don't know this area at all. I'm thinking about changing direction in my life and career, and this offered time out to think about that – and the dates fitted my schedule. My work doesn't give much time for a social life, so I'm looking forward to getting to know you all.' She smiled at each member of the group.

'What's your job?' asked the young woman in the strappy dress.

'I'm in manufacturing control and distribution,' Jackie replied. 'Endless spreadsheets and timelines – very busy and very dull. Time for a change.'

Nice one, Jackie, Clare thought. It was informative, but both vague and of zero interest to anyone. Little danger of any follow-up queries there.

'Would you like to go next?' Clare asked the young woman in the sundress. She had an alertness and energy about her, despite the sneezing.

'Sure. Perhaps like Jackie, my work is high pressure, but I'm freelance. I've worked as a wedding planner and events manager – much as you do, Jeremy.'

Jeremy was sitting on a chair placed slightly behind the others in the circle and had been focused on his phone. The mention of his name startled him. He rested his phone on his lap and returned his attention to the group.

The young woman continued, 'I'm sure you must host brilliant weddings here. I had a family bereavement and decided to take some time out. So, that's me.' She smiled and there was something brave about her friendliness.

'Thank you – and your name?' Clare asked, encouragingly.

'Sorry, yes. I'm Astrid.'

The older, moustached man followed on, introducing himself as Vincent and saying that he lived in Devizes. Ex-military, Clare thought. Or maybe not. He was succinct. His wife had booked him on this retreat; he wasn't sure why. Clare thought it would be unkind to conjecture, while wondering if his wife wanted the house to herself for a bit. Then Vincent said he had stayed here at the Morva several times before, and had enjoyed it, and added that he liked Hardy's poetry.

Michael was next. Would he mention his connection to Victoria? Clare wondered. No, he simply followed Vincent's brevity with a taciturn, 'I'm Michael and I wanted to be here.' And that was it, even though Jackie nodded encouragingly at him. No doubt Jackie already knew about Michael's connection to Victoria, Clare thought, noticing the way she had grown more alert as he spoke.

Heathcliff was more forthcoming: 'Hi, everyone. I'm Dan. I'm here for spiritual reasons. I'm a follower of Jesus.' Here, he looked at Clare almost accusingly, as he tapped the outline programme and continued with a reproachful air, 'I believed this was to be a Christian event, and hope that, by God's grace, there will be blessing here, even if this retreat isn't based on scripture, as I'd expected it to be, but on poetry instead.'

Clare looked on, silently. Clearly Heathcliff expected no reply. Or perhaps she should call him Luther, now, or Calvin. She could think of other possibilities, too. Come on, don't be so mean, she told herself.

'I'm sorry to hear about Victoria's death last year and am reminded that each of us, every one of us, must always be prepared to meet the Lord. Ready to come face to face with our maker and judge. Jesus warned us that death can come suddenly, like a thief in the night –' he was warming to his theme – 'or as to the rich farmer in the parable, who built larger and larger barns in which to store his wealth – and was shown to be a fool. His wealth meant nothing. Death awaited him that night.' He spoke in a voice laced with doom.

'Thank you, Dan,' Clare said crisply as he took a deep breath, managing to halt the sermon. She was less successful in masking her irritation at the young man's crassness. He was not so handsome now, as far as she was concerned. At least he'd expressed regret about Victoria, but using her supposed death as proselytising weaponry was gross. 'The retreat is for people of all beliefs and viewpoints,' she said, 'and we will be using a wide range of resources, which I hope will be helpful for everyone.'

'I don't think Victoria is dead.' The silver-ringed hands of the next person in the circle gestured towards Dan, who looked replete with self-satisfaction. 'Well, I don't think you can assume that, anyway,' Pippa continued. 'I never met her, but I heard a lot about her. Someone who was close to me loved her very much, once.'

Was that Lucy who snorted? At Pippa's words, the atmosphere in the room had changed. Astrid leaned forward slightly, as if to get a better view. Vincent moved his head to and fro, watching members of the group. Who needed Netflix when this degree of live drama was freely available? Once again, it struck Clare how odd it was that someone else who knew Victoria – albeit tangentially – had ended up at the retreat.

'I'm Pippa,' the woman continued. 'I'm not sure why I'm here, really. I felt drawn to come. Maybe as a mark of respect, I don't know. I've got changes in my life to process – spiritually, too, although I'm not a religious person. That's enough about me, really.'

'Thank you, Pippa.' Listening to herself, Clare wondered if this was how an AA facilitator sounded. Her words seemed formulaic. Hollow, even. But she wanted Pippa to find whatever help she needed on this retreat, preferably without too much distress or conflict arising from Michael's presence, and without adding to Lucy's grief.

'Jeremy, how about you?'

'Me?' He looked surprised. Did he not consider himself a participant? He jiggled his substantial body in his seat before embarking on his introduction: 'OK, right. I'm Jeremy, and I work here at the Morva Hotel, as you know. Maybe you don't know that *morva* means "blessed by the sea", which I think is rather lovely, don't you?'

It was indeed a lovely word, but Clare suspected that he was uncomfortable about talking very personally and was being deliberately evasive. Especially when he continued in the same vein.

'This is the Leven Room, and *leven* means "peace" in Cornish, which seems very appropriate, too, doesn't it? Amongst other things, I run our events programme – next week, we have a very busy schedule of children's activities for half-term, and this room will hold our daily family film showings, as well as our indoor crafts and games, if the weather is wet. I'm already planning our Christmas and New Year entertainments, and our romantic Valentine's Day specials for next year.' He elaborated further on the details of these, until eventually it seemed to occur to him that his listeners might not be fascinated by this slew of information, and his monologue dwindled to a halt.

Jeremy really was an expert in talking a lot and revealing little, Clare thought. 'Thanks, Jeremy – that's good to know,' she said, speaking with an upbeat tempo and avoiding Jackie's eye. She was suddenly afraid that she might laugh at this whole crazy situation, in an entirely inappropriate way.

'Well, we've got an hour or so before pre-dinner drinks will be served for us, in the bar area of the upstairs lounge, from six o'clock.' She was back into her stride again. 'Perhaps that gives an opportunity to stroll to the beach or to explore the hotel gardens, or even to have a dip in the pool, just as you prefer. Some of us have discovered the beach already.' She smiled at Lucy, hoping to help her feel more at ease.

'After dinner, we have time to ourselves, and we'll reconvene here at nine o'clock for our candlelit reflection to close the day together. And, of course, we'll have that evening Epilogue each day during our stay here. But you'll find all the timings on the sheets which Jeremy has kindly printed for us.' She paused for a beat, checking her notes. 'Anything else to add, Jeremy?'

The events manger was tapping on his phone, looking perplexed. 'Only that we have another participant due to arrive,' he said, his brow furrowed. 'Sorry, I'd forgotten and failed to add his name to the list. But I've just heard from Rachel and the reception team –' he waved his phone – 'that he's now here and has checked in, so we'll meet him later. I think that's everything.'

'Great – we look forward to that.' Clare wanted to keep the tone positive, and she looked round the circle with as much enthusiasm as she could muster. 'It's very good to have met you all. Thank you, everyone, and see you later!'

Was it good? She wanted to scamper to her room as speedily as she could, to ring David and regale him with details about the bizarre nature of this afternoon. She'd like a gin and tonic too, and chocolate. Lots of it. She was tired after the long day with its early start and numerous surprises. She wondered what David would make of Jackie being here, then suddenly wondered whether Jackie had been in touch to tell him. Stop that, Clare told herself. You're being ridiculous.

She took a deep breath as everyone slowly made their way out of the room. DCI Jackie Carter might be investigating Victoria's disappearance, but it was Clare's role to provide care for each retreat participant and opportunities for their spiritual refreshment. For everyone's sake, Clare wanted the retreat to go well.

CHAPTER 13

As Clare left the Leven Room, she saw that the clouds had dispersed from their previous clumped mass and the lowering sun now lit their undersides in shades of orange and gold. Lucy had stopped on the grass outside and stood looking at the glorious colours of sky and sea. Jackie stood beside her.

'However sad I am about my sister, this view is still amazing,' Lucy said, seeming to address both women. She sighed and stretched her arms out theatrically, before wrapping them around her torso to hug herself.

'Thanks for that, Clare. What was the last music you put on?'

'I wondered that, too,' Jackie said. 'I'd expected whistling pan pipes, but that was much better.'

'It was lovely,' Astrid said, joining them.

Clare hadn't realised that the young woman was nearby. She now wore a cherry-red cardigan over her sundress, its colour emphasising her red-rimmed eyes. This virulent hay fever was grim, and Clare felt sorry for her.

Astrid moved closer to Victoria's bereaved sister and lowered her voice: 'Lucy, I wanted to say how sorry I am to hear of your loss.'

'Thanks. "Loss" is a strange word.' Lucy shrugged. 'People use it when a bunch of keys goes missing. Or when someone's dead. It's an appropriate word to use about my sister, though – she is lost to me. Vanished. Not knowing how or why, it's hard.'

'Yes,' Astrid said, then she was silent, and Clare remembered that she had referred to a bereavement of her own. Everyone had their own reasons for coming here, she thought.

Lucy continued to confide in this trio of women, as if an impromptu sisterhood bonded them. 'Michael was married to her, you know,' she said. 'Although, he chose not to mention it, in there.'

'Goodness. Was it a complete shock to you that he was here?'

Astrid's question seemed rather nosy, Clare thought. She noticed how Jackie seemed to listen closely for Lucy's answer. Another voice replied, however.

'Not such a shock to me.' Pippa had appeared, moving quietly across the grass to stand near the group. 'He's been preoccupied about Victoria ever since she went missing. It's sick. And very weird that he's here, too.'

'You know Michael, too?' Astrid asked.

She really *was* nosy, Clare decided, but her curiosity was proving very useful. To lead the retreat well, Clare wanted to know what was behind the tension between Pippa and Michael.

'This is awkward, but I think you know who I am, Lucy?' There was a weary resignation in Pippa's tone.

'Of course I do.' Lucy was terse, and she angled her body away, as if rejecting any engagement with Pippa. 'You were shagging Michael and then he left Victoria for you. I hope you were pleased with yourself, breaking up a marriage and landing a prize git like him.'

'Prize git. Nice title,' Pippa murmured, looking out to sea. 'Could make a tattoo of that.'

Incredible, Clare thought. Victoria's sister, her husband *and* the woman he had left her for were all at the retreat. And they all hated each other. Great. But, however curious Clare might be to hear what else would be said, she couldn't stay and collude with this character assassination of another retreatant. Even if Michael was as terrible as Lucy and Pippa clearly thought, Clare's job was to support him, too. She drifted away with a quiet, 'Excuse me.'

She went up the wide stone steps to the upper lawn and came across Vincent, the moustached older man from Devizes, seated at a table. He was deep in discussion with a young waiter with an eye-catching cascade of black hair, who stood with a notepad, ready to take an order.

'Clare, can I buy you a drink? I know we've got some on the way later, but perhaps I could get something for you now?' Vincent offered, and with courteous efficiency added her request for a gin and tonic to his order.

Leaning back in his chair, Vincent smiled.

'I love this view. What an outlook! Quite a rum bunch

you've got here, haven't you? A "Convergence of the Twain", so to speak.'

Vincent obviously wanted to expand on his theme, and Clare was happy to oblige. 'How so?' she asked, wondering what he'd been discussing with the waiter.

'Well, in that poem, Hardy describes two massive things coming together – the *Titanic* and the iceberg – each formed entirely separately, the ship in Belfast and the iceberg in the depths of the cold sea, and yet a malevolent fate was drawing them inexorably towards one another, destined to collide. And here we all are, a disparate group of people, yet each of us drawn together at the Morva. Things won't be dull, that's for sure.'

'Interesting,' Clare said, while considering how best to respond to this unnerving suggestion of impending catastrophe. She opted for thoughtful head-nodding. Could it be sheer coincidence that people with connections to Victoria were here? It had struck her as odd when Lucy and Michael first appeared. Now, with Pippa too, it seemed as if something more sinister might be afoot. Clare recalled the phone call she had overheard earlier. Could that be related to whatever was going on here? The thought was not reassuring.

Her companion was content to continue: 'It's a powerful poem. We're shown the inevitability of that collision. It's fated.'

Clare stirred herself. 'Hardy sees it that way, but I think we have choices and agency, too,' she said. 'There were mistakes, oversights and other errors of judgement about the *Titanic* and her voyage, weren't there? Aren't tragic happenings often a mixture of circumstance and our human folly or shortcomings?'

'You're an optimist,' Vincent replied. 'You want to see the sunny side of things. But there's trouble ahead, Clare – I'm with Hardy on that.' He seemed to relish the idea.

Clare hoped he was wrong and looked out to sea.

CHAPTER 14

As Jackie watched the retreatants gather for dinner, she thought they were much as she had anticipated, each of them affluent and content to fritter away their money being fussed over at a fancy hotel. They seemed absorbed with their own affairs, and Jackie was pleased by that – it meant no one would take an interest in her and she could seek out information about Victoria.

She would begin with Victoria's ex, she decided, as she eased herself into a seat next to Michael, at a table slightly removed from the others. She had been a police officer long enough to suspect any partner's involvement when someone went missing, and was not to be beguiled by tears or other expressions of grief. She had been caught out by those in a previous case. Never again.

'How was your journey?' she asked, fixing a pleasant smile on her face. Her plan was to be an amiable, unthreatening companion, to lull him into a false sense of security and gain his confidence.

'Good, thanks.'

'It seems such a long drive to get here, but it's always worth it,' she commented, looking out at the scene framed by the large window. 'And what a spot this is.'

It was some moments before she continued, still keeping her eyes on the view, as if preoccupied by it.

'Cornwall is such a special place – I feel very fortunate to be here, I think we all do. How is it for you, being here?'

She dipped her spoon into the first course of gazpacho. She was enjoying herself – incognito investigation had its own satisfactions, and the gazpacho was tasty, too.

'I suppose it was strange for me to discover that Lucy is here,' he began, clinking his spoon against his soup bowl. 'You all heard what she said earlier – about how . . . well, about mine and Victoria's relationship. It was hard for me to hear her speak about it to the group, as if she's the only one grieving.'

'Right.' Jackie nodded, sympathetically. Just as Clare would do, she thought.

'We were married.' He picked up the bread roll resting on his side plate and tore it in two, forcefully. 'And happy. Then it was as if a kind of madness came over me. I was bewitched, you might say.'

Jackie nodded again, as if concurring that Michael had no choice in the matter, while hoping that no one else would join their table and stem this outpouring.

'We split up. It was messy. Lucy thinks I was unkind to Victoria, but I wasn't really myself, let's put it that way.' He gulped some water.

Jackie tilted her head, respectfully. This response was effective; Michael kept his voice low and continued his story. He seemed unaware of the livelier conversations of others in the dining room, and the noise of chatter and tableware afforded a degree of privacy.

Then Jackie realised that the older man, Vincent, also seemed interested in what Michael might be saying. He leaned back in his chair from the next table, as if to try to overhear snatches of their conversation. If Michael noticed, he didn't give any sign.

'I had no idea what I'd lost,' he continued. 'It was as if a spell had been broken, once I heard that Vicki was missing. A terrible awakening. Since then, I've been searching for her, and remembering all the time we had together.'

He drank from his glass of water again, then lifted his spoon and focused on his soup, as if doing so would help to keep his emotions in check.

'I thought that coming here might help, somehow. Give closure. She's gone. But this longing for her is only getting worse. Cornwall was special for her. I can see her now, on the beach.'

'I'm sorry,' Jackie said, but she felt little sympathy. She wanted more information. 'When did you last see her? Was it here, in Cornwall?'

Something about the question struck a nerve. 'I last saw her much too long ago. Vicki loved the sea – Cornwall, Northumberland, all over.' Michael's voice had lost its tone of wistful reminiscence and become defensive. He seemed eager to change the subject. 'Northumberland has incredible beaches.'

'So, how did you hear she was missing?' Jackie was not to be deflected so easily.

'The police were in touch.'

'That sounds awful. I'm sorry.'

'By then, she'd been gone for days, and I hadn't even been aware of it.'

'Were you at home?'

If Michael thought her rapid-fire questions were intrusive, he gave no indication, simply answering, 'By the time I was informed, yes.'

That was consistent with what Jackie had been told by the investigating officer, DCI Nick Faux, of the Devon and Cornwall police. Michael had been away from home on the night that Victoria had disappeared.

What Michael was omitting to mention, as he confided in Jackie, was that he and his then partner, Pippa, had been staying in a cottage on the Lizard Peninsula on that night, only a few miles from the hotel. Quite some coincidence – though, neither Jackie nor DCI Faux viewed it as such. Yet, Pippa had vouched for him, and there was no obvious motive for conflict between Michael and the wife he had left. Sometimes, coincidences do happen.

CHAPTER 15

Victoria

I saw them first. I bought a takeaway tea from the Watch House and took it up on to the Todden, where the seats overlook Cadgwith beach. From there, you can see the cottages stringing up the length of the valley and the fishing boats drawn up on to the shore. It's very picturesque.

Lucy had a hot chocolate. She kept away from the edge because she hates heights, but she was OK sitting on the bench. An old couple sat on another seat, with two small dogs on tartan leads – highland terriers – enjoying the view.

And there they were, Pippa and Michael, on the beach below us. He was all over her like a rash. Then, throwing pebbles into the water and eating ice cream. I must have only just missed the pair of them, if they'd bought cones at the Watch House.

Lucy suggested going and letting their tyres down or going to the pub and spiking their drinks. Both stupid ideas. I don't think there is any such thing as letting car tyres down, it's just something people say, and we'd no idea whether they'd been to the pub, let alone whether they had drinks there. She was just angry. She's annoyed with me, too, but I can't bankroll her forever.

She asked why they'd come here, and I kept quiet, but I know why. Michael loves Cornwall. He grew up in Enfield, which he always said was all right, but he came on a caravan holiday to Land's End when he was about ten. Cornwall's represented heaven to him ever since. He likes the surfing, too, so I would have thought he'd prefer the north coast, but maybe Pippa wanted to come this side.

Lucy seemed more bothered by their presence than I was. Sure, I'm not thrilled, but maybe this happening is a celestial sign that I'm on the right track, leaving them behind. My life is separate from theirs – my destiny, too. Sure, it hurt a bit, seeing them together, I'm not going to lie. But it's time to breathe and keep going.

CHAPTER 16

Dinner was a tense affair for Clare, as she tried to keep an eye on all the guests, mindful of the freshly revealed antagonism that existed between half of them. Vincent seemed to be in good spirits, going around chatting with the various participants. First, he loitered in the doorway, engaging Jeremy in conversation, which seemed to make the events manager ill at ease, shifting awkwardly on his feet and running his hands through his hair. Then, he questioned Pippa and Clare about themselves and their experiences of Cornwall, before asking Dan where his T-shirt had come from. The young man had changed for dinner and now wore one which said, *I'm not arguing, I'm just explaining why I'm right*. Clare laughed when Dan grinned and said that it had been a Christmas present from his mum.

Pippa ended up sitting next to Clare and they chatted about the local area.

'I think episodes of *Poldark* were shot locally,' Clare said, although she only had a vague idea about it. 'I think there was a fishing series set in Cadgwith, too – and a film made there, with Maggie Smith in it.'

'I don't know anything about that,' Pippa said, dismissively.

'Wasn't that movie about a mysterious man who was washed up on the beach?' Astrid asked. 'Identity unknown.'

'Mullion Harbour is still in use, just below the hotel here and along the coast – there's a path down,' Dan said, and Clare wondered if he had deliberately moved the topic of conversation away from people being washed up on shore. If so, she was grateful.

'The harbour had a Christmas tree made from a stack of lobster pots – there were photos of it online,' Clare added. 'I'd like to walk down there – thanks for the reminder, Dan.'

'I'm looking forward to our trip to Kynance Cove tomorrow,' he replied. 'Queen Victoria visited – but, then again, she went everywhere.'

At that bit of historical knowledge, Vincent chimed in, telling Astrid that Mary and Kate Hardy had studied in Salisbury. He really was a Hardy enthusiast, Clare thought.

'They were the poet's sisters, and both became teachers,' he continued. 'Their mother didn't want any of her children to marry, but Thomas disobeyed her.'

'Maybe some of his marital issues stemmed from that,' Astrid suggested, flicking her eyes towards Michael and then back again. As one, the group moved the conversation on to the merits of gazpacho soup and other Spanish cuisine. But their thoughts were elsewhere.

At that moment, Rachel arrived in the doorway, cradling a large basket of purple and blue flowers. She scanned the dining room, then smiled as she saw Clare and walked towards her. Clare still found it strange to see her in her receptionist's outfit, rather than in her riding-stable gear.

'These just arrived for you,' Rachel said. 'I can take them up to your room, if you like, but I thought you'd want to see them first.'

'Thanks very much, Rachel – that's lovely.' Clare took the flowers and pulled out the note, realising as she did so that the others were all looking with interest at this floral delivery and must have been conjecturing what it was about. Jackie had even twisted in her seat to watch.

We miss you, take care, can't wait to see you soon. All my love, David xxx

Clare felt a warmth in her chest as she read the message. She had smoothed over her disquiet at Jackie's presence, but her husband was no fool. He must have known from their conversation earlier that she was uneasy about that, as well as anxious about other unanticipated arrivals and the charged dynamics of the group. These flowers had been sent as a tangible reminder of his care. He, Anna and Tom would be with her soon, and, whatever challenges the retreat might involve, her family were a constant.

'Is it your wedding anniversary, Clare?' Astrid asked, ever curious.

'Maybe you have a secret admirer,' Pippa suggested, arching her eyebrows.

'Nothing so exciting.' Clare was slightly embarrassed by such a public display of affection, while simultaneously feeling rather pleased that Jackie was witnessing it. 'Just something from my husband, wishing us well.'

'No pressure,' Vincent commented. 'Though, of course, now we're all wondering whether that's true, or if you have something clandestine happening in the romance department.' It seemed that Vincent was not averse to a bit of pot-stirring. 'Maybe I should be more organised about my wife's birthday – it's coming up soon.' He stroked his moustache and sipped his wine.

Rachel took back the basket, praising David's thoughtfulness.

Vincent cocked his head, curiously. 'Have you looked after Clare here before, Rachel? Does she always get sent flowers?'

But, before Rachel could reply, they were all distracted by the sight of a new diner being ushered towards them by a waiter.

'I meant to say, too, here's your late arrival,' Rachel said. 'He had a problem with his flight or his car hire. Then, I think he wanted to go for a swim, after checking in.' She shrugged.

The man's wet hair gave credence to this. He looked athletic, dressed in casual sports gear, shorts and a running top, an expensive sports watch flashing on his wrist with every movement.

'I'm sorry to be so late for dinner,' he said, smiling at Clare. 'It's frustrating to be delayed, when I've been looking forward to the trip.'

Clare reassured him that it was no problem and that he was very welcome, adding that there would be plenty of time to meet everyone. Rachel left them to it, taking Clare's basket of flowers with her, although Clare kept the card, slipping it into her pocket.

'Thanks,' the man said, looking at the faces around the table. 'I'm Gareth. And I'm sorry to be joining you guys late.

I had to work today and then flew into Newquay, then there was an issue with my car rental. My fault, and it's all sorted now, so here I am.'

Fair enough, thought Clare. But why was Lucy looking at him so curiously?

CHAPTER 17

The next morning, Clare took her own car to Kynance Cove, forgoing the hotel minibus for the sake of a bit of independence. Independence that was short-lived, because, unexpectedly, Pippa asked if she could come along with her. Clare supposed Pippa wanted to avoid Lucy and felt it would be best for the two of them to have some space. After all, Lucy seemed to blame Pippa, as well as Michael, for Victoria's unhappiness and broken marriage.

The morning was sunny, and today Pippa was dressed in beachwear: a yellow T-shirt, pink shorts and sky-blue sandals. She seemed to switch identity with each new outfit, or costume. From silver-ringed businesswoman to seventies hippy, and now a youthful holidaymaker.

'How are things with you, today?' Clare asked, as she started the engine and pulled out of her parking space.

'I'm still sorting myself out, I guess, getting over the shock of who else is here.'

'Yes, of course.'

'I'd no idea that Michael would come,' Pippa continued, before they had even driven out through the stone gateposts which guarded the entrance to the hotel car park, 'and I'm still a bit shaken. He's not too happy to see me, either.'

'Sounds like it was quite a surprise.' Clare was simply relieved that there had been no further dramas that morning, and that yesterday evening's Epilogue had been uneventful.

She had used candles to change the atmosphere in the Leven Room, and the group was quiet, without conversation or conflict. Gareth had no idea about the earlier tensions, and Clare hoped it gave others a respite from them and a sense that the retreat could be helpful for every participant, whatever the complexities of their relationships. After they'd listened to some Celtic music and prayers, Clare had added a general blessing:

Deep peace of the running wave to you
Deep peace of the flowing air to you
Deep peace of the quiet earth to you
Deep peace of the shining stars to you
Deep peace of the Son of Peace to you.

Dan might have preferred a more scriptural choice, but it gave a gentle end to the day for everyone.

'I liked that prayer you said last night,' Pippa commented, as if reading her thoughts. 'About peace from the sea and the stars and everything.'

'That's good to know,' Clare said, as she manoeuvred the car past a group of walkers and their dogs, who stood pressed against the hedge on the narrow lane.

'I guess I came here to find some peace, after everything,' Pippa added.

'It sounds as if you've been dealing with a lot, and it sounds tough,' Clare prompted as she drove. She hoped that getting Pippa to talk about what had happened might help her.

'He dumped me. Michael did. I'm not used to that, I guess. But there's no competing with a dead woman. If she is dead.'

'Sounds like *Rebecca* – have you read it?' Clare moved the conversation to less personal territory.

'Is that the one with the dead wife and the creepy housekeeper? I think I saw the film when my mum was watching – she loves it. Lily James wore a great cloche hat.'

'They've made a musical of it, too.' They drove past the Old Inn in Mullion, and Clare remembered a delicious meal she and her family had enjoyed there one rainy day, sitting at a round table set in the inglenook fireplace.

'I don't feel much like singing. But I know what it is to have a partner obsessed with someone else. Michael chose me, but his feelings for Victoria were still strong. Then he became remote after she went missing – distanced. He'd go off on walks, moping. He got into revisiting places they'd spent time together, and he didn't want me tagging along. London parks they'd walked in, weekends in York and Edinburgh. They'd holidayed down here, too.'

'Were you here last summer?' Clare couldn't resist asking. She wasn't here to investigate Victoria's disappearance, but she still wanted to know what Pippa might say.

'Yes, I was,' Pippa said shortly.

They drove past the kite shop with its fluttering sign and the secondary school which served the students from across the peninsula. Clare was silent as she navigated sharp bends in the winding road, before trying to press her passenger further.

'How was it for you, being on that trip?'

'It's hard to say.' Pippa sighed and shifted in her seat. 'But we saw her, you know. Victoria. When we were staying in Cadgwith, which is a bit further down this road. It's a tiny place, and we were staying in a cottage, just up from the pub, with a blue front door.'

'I know the village,' Clare said, wishing that Jackie was with them in the car to hear this. Did the police already know about that sighting, or was this new information?

'We were on the beach, the one they launch the boats from, and there are a set of seats above the beach, sort of opposite, overlooking everything.'

'Yes, I know where you mean – the Todden, beside that yellow building.'

'Whatever it's called, I saw her there, sitting and watching us.'

'Victoria? What was that like?'

'I wasn't that surprised. It was as if I knew that part of the reason Michael wanted to come down here was to "accidentally" bump into her. He'd mentioned early on when we got together that they used to go to Cornwall together – and, just before we went on our trip, he was acting a bit different.' Pippa grimaced, then stared at the road, which had straightened out and now opened up before them.

Clare glanced at her, then turned her attention back to driving. 'It sounds difficult. I'm sorry – relationships are complicated,' she soothed. In the back of her mind, she wondered if perhaps it had been a genuine coincidence. Could Pippa be reading too much into what happened? 'Did Michael talk to her, that day?'

'He pretended not to notice her. That's when I knew something was up. He said nothing to me. He reacted, but then just picked up some piece of wood or a shell – as if she wasn't there, sitting and looking down on us.'

'Did you say you'd seen her?'

'No, and I'm not sure why. It just seemed easier to keep quiet. It was obvious he didn't want to talk about it. Maybe I was afraid he'd lie to me.' She smiled, wryly. 'As you say, relationships are complicated.'

'But do you think he met up with her?' Clare prompted.

'I don't know for sure whether they did meet,' Pippa said thoughtfully. 'Thanks for listening, Clare. Seeing Michael again here reminds me how uncomfortable I feel about the whole thing. I told the police we were together all the time, when they asked, but that's not necessarily true. Sometimes, I had to make phone calls, and the signal in the cottage was terrible. I'd have to walk further away from the village and along the coast path, just to make a call, and who knows what Michael got up to then.'

Clare wanted to know more, but a glance in the rear-view mirror stopped her short. A large, intimidating black car was closing in behind her and seemed eager to overtake. Clare didn't like it when other drivers came so close, but she was a slow driver. When she had fallen foul of the yellow traffic cameras in Tunbridge Wells and had to attend a 'speed awareness' course to avoid getting points on her licence, her son had asked with an ironic smile if that meant she might learn how to drive a bit faster. Cheeky monkey.

She braked to make a turn off the road and on to the track towards the National Trust car park at Kynance, bracing herself for a series of vicious speed bumps. It was possible to swerve round some of them, but not all. Ahead, the hotel minibus bounced alarmingly, as Jeremy approached a speed bump too quickly. Clare didn't envy his passengers.

Clare took another glance in the rear-view mirror. The car behind her had closed the distance between them and she could now make out that it was Michael behind the wheel, wearing dark sunglasses. She turned her attention away from him and back to the rutted track ahead.

What Pippa had told her was disturbing. Certainly, it painted Michael in a bad light. But, if she was now admitting that her alibi for Michael was unreliable, that suggested that she could have left their cottage undetected, too. Pippa obviously hadn't been happy about Michael being so fixed on Victoria – how deeply had she resented her, and might she have played a part in her disappearance?

That seemed too far-fetched, but Clare was troubled. There was something inconsistent about Pippa, and it wasn't just her clothing.

CHAPTER 18

Victoria

Now the retreat is full on, there's less time to write, and I don't want Lucy to spot me scribbling. There's a lot to process – future plans, past hurts, and everything that Lucy is dealing with, too. She's got herself into this mess, and she can't sponge off Dad or me anymore.

My head is spinning, but walking on these beaches helps – it was lovely to finally go to Kynance today; a shame it was raining, though. We had coffee in Lizard village afterwards, and then a swim in the hotel pool, which was refreshing, if chilly. If Lucy and I hadn't argued last night, it would have been a great day.

OK – plans.

On a basic level, I'd like to get the most from this retreat. Talk more frankly with Luce about some things, without losing my cool.

Use my new wetsuit. Maybe try a night swim, off Poldhu?

And maybe a rendezvous is the way to go. Get things

settled. Closure. Perhaps I will go ahead with a meetup, then.

This retreat is an opportunity to take time out before my new start – but I feel anxious.

CHAPTER 19

'Has anyone ever been here before?' Jackie asked, as the minibus pulled into the car park. As part of her plan to find out more about Victoria's disappearance, she'd decided to travel to Kynance with the others that morning. It hadn't been particularly fruitful or comfortable, and she watched enviously as Clare pulled in behind them in her red Suzuki, followed shortly afterwards by Michael in his sleek black car. The minibus had been cramped, and now Jackie wanted to stretch her legs.

'I have, yes,' Dan replied, as everyone slowly clambered out. He straightened his shirt as he stood upright. Today, it proclaimed, *I may be wrong, but it's highly unlikely*. Jackie thought her boss ought to have one just like it.

'I did the coast path from Mullion to Kynance with friends,' Dan continued, 'and we went on round the tip of the peninsula to Cadgwith. It was a long day's walking, but I hardly felt it, it was so beautiful.'

Looking out over the horizon, Jackie could see what he meant. The ocean below and beyond them sparkled in the bright sunshine. She breathed in the fresh air and thought how good it was to be away from the relentless demands of work, and to be somewhere as spectacular as this. No wonder people went on about Cornwall so much.

'For those who haven't been here before, there are two paths down to the beach,' Jeremy explained, as the group began sorting their bags and beach hats. 'One is a bit further, but less steep – and you can access it whether the tide is in or out. The other path is quicker, but it gets covered at high tide.'

'Oh, I heard about that,' Astrid said brightly. 'I wonder if people used it in the past, like in *Poldark*. The guy behind the bar was talking about it, last night. Smugglers used to store cargo in hiding places like the caves here, and secret rooms in houses and pubs.'

'What do you reckon, Jeremy?' Vincent said. 'Any smuggling still going on, around here?'

'Kynance beach is too busy for that kind of thing,' Dan interrupted. 'Nothing secret happening there.' He looked unhappy at the number of people from other vehicles already setting off for the cove ahead of them. 'In fact, I might not stay long – it's far too crowded. I think I'd rather carry on along the coast path, back to the hotel.'

'I'll join you, if that's OK?' volunteered Gareth. He bounced up and down on his heels, then made to do some stretches. Once again, he was dressed in expensive-looking running gear, this time in muted colours. His clothing was monogrammed, as was the small rucksack on his back. 'I could do with the exercise, and this coastline looks amazing.'

'I might not make it as far as you guys, but I'd like to see as much of the coast as possible, so maybe I'll come part way with you,' Astrid suggested. 'Is that OK, Jeremy?'

'Whatever you'd like,' Jeremy answered. 'I'll be down at the café and will head back up to the minibus at about eleven thirty. Whoever needs a lift back can meet me there, so we can return to the hotel with plenty of time to freshen up before lunch.'

As Jeremy finished speaking, the group began to disperse. Lucy, Gareth, Dan and Astrid made their way across the car park's grass and towards the descent first. With most of the group gone, Jackie spotted an opportunity to speak to Michael in private and deliberately arrived at the head of the path at the same time as him. But catching him alone was not to be, as Clare joined them and they set off down the steeper track together, Michael sandwiched between them.

'How was your night?' Jackie asked. 'I slept well; it must be the sea air.'

'Fine, thanks.' Clare was cheery. 'How about you, Michael? How are things?'

'OK.' Brevity was clearly the order of the day, as far as he was concerned.

Jackie longed to be in an interview room, so she could interrogate him properly. Instead, she made some comment about the stream beside the path and the flowering gorse bushes. Clare reciprocated with enthusiasm about the scent of heather and the shape of the sloping moorland on either side of them. This is good, Jackie thought. Ease into it with small talk, then get him to open up.

'Kynance is so beautiful, isn't it? I've never been here

before – have you, Michael?' she asked. She thought that he'd probably visited before with Victoria, and was interested to see if he'd tell them about it.

'Yes.' His reply was curt.

'Was that recently?' Clare said. 'I think the car park is bigger than the last time I was here, and the café has longer opening hours.'

'It's a popular spot,' Michael said. 'I've been here many times over the years, and with Pippa more recently. I can't believe she chose to join this retreat. I'm sorry, Clare, about the awkwardness between us yesterday. I'll try to steer clear of her to avoid causing any further disruption to the group.' He looked down at the ground as he spoke, sheepishly scratching his head.

He seemed contrite enough, Jackie thought, but she was still suspicious of him.

'Thank you, Michael, that's very considerate – and I hope this retreat can be helpful for you, too,' Clare said, her voice gentle, as they continued downwards. 'It's important that you use this time in whatever way works best for you. What brought you here?'

There was a pause, and Jackie snatched a sidelong look at Michael. His face was creased with worry, and he bit his lower lip.

'I've been struggling to process that Vic is . . . gone. And I wanted to be where she last was,' he eventually said.

Jackie wondered whether he spoke slowly because he was feeling overwhelmed with emotion, or so that he could choose his words carefully.

'And how do you feel about what may have happened to Victoria, Michael?' Clare asked.

That was a decent stab at moving the investigation on, Jackie thought. Or maybe Clare was just in caring-vicar mode.

'Angry? Sad? Guilty?' Michael laughed, but without humour.

'And why's that?' Clare asked.

'I think Victoria might have been more affected by our break-up than I realised. And if I'm right . . . then I may have to accept that Lucy's anger towards me is more justified than I'd like to admit.' Michael stopped walking and shook his head. Then he abruptly strode out ahead of the women, so they could no longer see his face.

'What do you mean, Michael?' Jackie called after his retreating back. She wanted to get more answers. As if reading her mind, Clare shook her head – *Don't overstep* – and they picked up their pace to catch up with him.

'This must all be so hard,' Clare said. 'But talking about these things might help. What do you think happened?'

'I don't know.' He stopped walking and turned to face them, his expression pained. 'Maybe someone attacked her, or perhaps she fell. But it's agony, because . . . because I'm afraid that perhaps she decided, after I left her, that she couldn't go on. That life was too difficult. She was always vulnerable to mood swings.'

'So, you think she may have deliberately ended her life?' Jackie clarified, scuffing at the ground with her foot, but keeping her eyes fixed on him.

'I don't know, and I'd rather not talk about it.' Michael bridled at her question.

Jackie grimaced. Clearly, she didn't have Clare's soft touch in getting Michael to open up.

'I think I'll jog on down ahead,' Michael said.

'Sure, take care,' Clare called, as he accelerated away, lurching over the uneven ground.

'Don't fall!' Jackie added as he stumbled, hoping she kept the bite from her voice. Clare might sympathise with this overly mournful man, but Jackie thought she detected both obsession and deviousness in him. His mention of Victoria's vulnerability to mood swings seemed calculated, and convenient.

'Shall we take a breather?' Jackie suggested as the two women came to a bench perched between outcrops of rock interspersed with sand. She wanted to discuss the conversation they'd just had – to see if Clare was as suspicious of Michael as she was – but, before she could begin, Vincent and Jeremy came upon them. Vincent seemed to be asking Jeremy about the cove and its history, and Jeremy was describing some archaeological features that were due further exploration.

Vincent lingered beside the women, but Jeremy merely waved a greeting without breaking his stride. He seemed content to carry on alone.

'Tell me, Clare – when did you learn about Victoria's disappearance last year?' Vincent said. 'I've been wondering how you felt about the retreat going ahead, and about having Michael and Lucy both here, in the circumstances?'

Jackie admired his directness. He was as frank as she wished she could be with the others on the retreat.

'It is such a sad situation,' Clare replied vaguely, and Jackie admired her subtlety. 'I had heard something about it, yes, and I feel so sorry for everyone impacted by Victoria going missing. I think it makes it very difficult, having such an unresolved situation.'

'I wonder what the police view is. Any thoughts about their take on things, Jackie? Jackie Casey, isn't it? What do you think?'

Jackie started as he turned to her. She was not going to show any disquiet and ignored the provocative gleam in his eye. He was stirring, and she wondered what he might know.

'I'm thinking it's time for ice cream,' she said evenly. 'I'm off to the café.' She headed down the path, following in Jeremy's wake. Both she and the hotel events manager were content to put some distance between themselves and Vincent's questioning. What was his game?

CHAPTER 20

Clare stepped gingerly over the rocks at the end of the pathway, relieved that she'd finally made it to the beach and glad not to be carrying the usual family paraphernalia of bags, picnic supplies and body boards. It was a nice change, and she was pleased not to have to persuade anyone to use sunscreen, either – the retreat participants were old enough to decide that for themselves.

The larger rocks before her sat humpbacked and squat on the sand, with people standing amongst them and admiring the aquamarine sea and the rush of waves flecked with white foam. Clare headed on, resisting the call of the café just above this section of cove. She made her way through a gap in the rocks on to the further beach, only accessible at low tide. There, she came upon Astrid, who had settled herself on a towel.

'Isn't this amazing,' the slight young woman said, smiling.

Clare was pleased to see that she was no longer sneezing; perhaps the sea breeze helped.

'I had no idea.' Astrid shuffled along to let Clare sit down next to her.

To their left, a father and son were building a sandcastle with an intricate moat system, and another group lay sprawled on the sand, either drowsing or reading, using their hats and a canvas windbreak to keep their books in shadow. Over the ridge behind them, a young child was calling out excitedly about a cave they had found, and another high-pitched voice answered them.

Hearing the children around her, Clare wished Anna and Tom were here, playing beach football with David, or scooping up sand to make a fortress of their own, with feathers and shells to decorate it. She was grateful for them and reminded herself not to take them for granted. Sure, it was far easier not to feel irritated when no one was badgering her to carry their stuff or to buy yet another snorkel. But today she'd even welcome that.

'Gareth and Dan have decided to walk the whole way back. I said I'd let you and Jeremy know,' Astrid said, squinting at the bulging waves which crashed down and then oozed across the sand towards them. 'I didn't go, though; I'd rather enjoy more time here.'

'This is a special place, isn't it?' Clare agreed, mesmerised by the motion of the water. 'I love it.'

'I find it consoling. It feels like there's a sense of something bigger than all of us, here.'

'Yes. It's certainly a place to think about things, or to be aware of them, maybe,' Clare said. She didn't want to intrude too much on Astrid's thoughts, and the two of them stared out at the sea in companionable silence.

'You know, I feel very sorry for Lucy,' Astrid said, suddenly.

'We got to talking on the way down, and it's so awful for her, to have her sister go missing. My dad died recently, and I miss him terribly, but at least I know what happened to him. It must be a nightmare for Lucy, having her sister disappear like that. I'm glad she came on this retreat; I hope it helps her.'

'Yes, it's so tough – and I'm very sorry to hear about your dad.' Clare nodded in support, as Astrid poked her finger in the sand and drew circles and spirals with it.

'Thank you, Clare. I know that I have to carry on without him.'

Astrid's stoicism reminded Clare of an elderly widower in her parish. 'This too shall pass,' was his oft-repeated motto. Clare had sat with him in his sparse kitchen on the day after his wife's death. On the wall had been a faded print of two harnessed shire horses pulling their heavy dray. His late wife's walking aids and other mobility equipment were stacked in a corner, awaiting collection. His sombre fortitude continued on later visits, as they drank tea and Clare listened to him repeat his motto and describe his memories.

A gull landed in front of her, then swivelled its head sharply this way and that, before launching itself skywards again.

'Clare, there's something I think I should mention,' Astrid said, eventually. 'Lucy and Gareth had quite a chat, coming down the track, and it seems that Gareth knew Victoria, too.'

'Wow. That's quite a surprise.' Clare could think of no other response to this. Could this really be another coincidence? She tried to absorb the news. Perhaps another seagull would land in front of them in a moment and announce that it had a special relationship with Victoria, too.

'They weren't keeping it quiet, so I thought you might like to know.'

'You're right – thank you.' Clare removed her beach shoes and scrunched her toes in the sand. 'What did they say?'

'From what I could tell, Lucy thought she recognised Gareth from a photo Victoria had shown her. He got a bit upset when she confronted him, though – I think he might have been seeing Victoria casually and felt awkward being asked about it.'

'Well,' Clare said, 'it's hard to know what to make of this.'

'Yes,' Astrid admitted. 'Exactly. Anyway, thanks for the chat, Clare. A chaplain was kind to my dad, too, when he was ill. It helped. I'm off to meet Lucy, now – I said I'd see her at the café. You're welcome to join us, if you'd like?' She got up and shook some sand from the back of her skirt. Clare stood too, to allow her to gather her towel. Astrid obviously wanted to be on the move, and maybe she regretted confiding in Clare about Lucy and Gareth. It was good to hear that a chaplain had supported her father when he was ill – perhaps when he'd been in hospital, or a hospice.

'Thanks, but I'll stay here for a bit,' Clare said, as she caught sight of Jackie walking across the beach towards her.

As soon as the DCI reached Clare, she threw herself down on to the sand, taking Astrid's place.

'I found enough signal by the café to google Vincent, Clare. I thought he was being pushy and invasive, asking all those questions. Guess why.'

Clare shrugged.

'Brace yourself – it turns out he's a journalist who specialises in stories about unsolved crimes and police failures.'

Clare groaned. What fresh hell was this?

CHAPTER 21

Clare looked out over the waves and rocks of Kynance Cove and took stock of the revelation that Vincent was a journalist – and not just any sort, but someone who dug up stories of unsolved crimes and explored them in sensationalised detail.

What a nightmare. Vincent may have been sent away on this retreat by his wife, but, given his stirring and questioning, Clare suspected that he had developed an interest in writing about the people here and their connections with Victoria. If he also worked out that Jackie had changed her name to go incognito on another police force's turf – and, even worse, that Clare and Jackie knew each other from a previous murder investigation – the whole retreat would be upended.

'He must be interested in writing about Victoria's case,' Jackie declared. Clearly, she was thinking along the same lines as Clare. 'And maybe about us all – he's always publishing those stories you see online. I can see it now: his exposé about how all these people who are somehow related to a missing woman have turned up at the same retreat a year after her disappearance, and the failure of the police to act.'

'Yes, and I suppose you could be in trouble for coming here, if Vincent starts looking into you,' she said carefully. 'Is there anything I can do to help?'

Jackie stiffened. 'No need, thanks,' she said, crisply.

Clare nodded. Obviously, offering help had been a step too far. Even though it seemed as if she had gained the trust of the DCI, their relationship was still fragile.

'I've learned a few things, too,' Clare said, to change the topic. As they sat on the sand, she updated the DCI on Astrid's report that Lucy had confronted Gareth about knowing Victoria. As Clare explained, the father and son continued to build their sandcastle nearby. One of the squat turrets tilted to one side as part of its undergirding of damp sand gave way. Hasty repairs were needed and sharp taps with a spade to fix the reinforcements in place.

'That's interesting,' Jackie said. 'DCI Faux mentioned that there had been a possible new man in Victoria's life, and his officers had interviewed him in their initial enquiries. They concluded that the relationship was very much in its infancy, though, and the man had a solid alibi, so wasn't regarded as a person of interest.'

'Hmm.' Clare was unconvinced, and, judging by the look on Jackie's face, the DCI felt the same way. But Clare didn't press further – she could sense Jackie was reluctant to question the conclusions which another DCI and his team had reached. Trespassing on another force's investigation wasn't something to be done lightly. Jackie had come here because of her friendship with Victoria, and, in doing so, had already strayed beyond her comfort zone. To undermine the work of another police service would be a step too far.

'I can't get this out of my head – it's too odd how there are so many people at the retreat this year who are connected to Victoria, isn't it?' Clare said.

'I agree.' A frown crossed Jackie's face. 'It's too unlikely that they all happen to be here because of unresolved questions about Victoria's disappearance or because of their grief. Lucy, Michael, Pippa – and now Gareth? I've never believed in coincidences, and, even if I did, I wouldn't like those odds.'

Clare closed her eyes and nodded in agreement. The retreat was compromised, and likely to fail, too. How had she ended up in this situation? She felt sorry for Dan and Astrid, coming to Cornwall in all innocence and being caught up in this drama.

'Once I realised about Vincent, I messaged the local DCI, Nick Faux, to let him know that I'm here,' Jackie continued, standing up. 'It's much better that he's aware, and there have been one or two things that it would be appropriate to mention to him, including Vincent's presence.'

'I see,' Clare said, standing too. The lapping waves were getting closer; it was time to leave.

'I'll go straight back to the car park,' Jackie said. 'There's likely to be a better signal up there, and I can reach Nick Faux directly and have a call with him before anyone else comes back to the minibus.'

Before Clare could reply, Jackie turned on her heel and began to make her way across the beach. Clare understood that having a journalist aware of Jackie's presence, and perhaps discovering her identity, changed things for the DCI. She needed to get her story across to her counterpart in the local police force quickly, and before anyone else outed her for trespassing on his jurisdiction and meddling in his case. Jackie would have some explaining to do.

Clare took a long look at the expanse of sea before trudging in Jackie's wake. It was a horrible thought that the retreatants could have their privacy invaded by Vincent, and Clare knew she needed to gather her strength and to be wise, as well as suspicious. It was possible that Vincent wouldn't do anything harmful, but she mustn't be naïve. At least Jackie had come clean with DCI Faux, now.

CHAPTER 22

As Clare clambered up the steps to the beach café, she could hear familiar voices in conversation. Sure enough, when she arrived, she found Lucy, Vincent and Astrid clustered at one of the outdoor tables, chatting with a tall man with a freckled face and shoulders, whose wetsuit was rolled down to his waist. Next to him sat Jeremy, whose eyes were glued to a puzzle on his phone.

From the café's raised position, a breathtaking panorama could be seen, with dark rocks rising from the sand and the aquamarine blues and greens of the sea made even more vibrant by the day's bright sunlight. The glistening waters were ever shifting – in contrast with the still, vivid green of the moorland grass, which stretched over the undulating land above the cliffs on either side of the cove.

Clare checked whether anyone wanted another drink before going into the café to order one for herself, mentioning that her husband loved the granny apple cake here, in case anyone wanted to try some. Astrid joined her and the two women stood together amongst the shelves of sun cream and the array of books about Cornish folklore, ghosts and recipes. On the wooden floor were plastic buckets of flip-flops and shrimping nets.

'Perhaps it's better not to say that I told you about Lucy and Gareth's conversation,' Astrid said. 'Perhaps it's a bit private.'

That ship had already sailed, Clare thought. She knew that Jackie was updating Nick Faux about that nugget of information, amongst other things, even as she and Astrid stood in the café queue. She sidestepped the issue and said something innocuous about focusing on making the most of being in such a place, and then attempted to divert Astrid's attention further by commenting with enthusiasm on the sketches of the cove which were for sale in the café.

As they returned to the group, Clare made an effort to keep the conversation general. It was difficult, with everything she had just learned on her mind. They discussed the importance of sun cream, even in May, and the unusual colouring of the aquamarine tones of the sea here, and the dark greens and reds of the serpentine rocks. Lucy asked how old the cliffs were, which caused the man in the wetsuit to make some quip about never guessing a lady's age.

Clare described how the children at her church had made a large card for a member of the congregation who was celebrating her hundredth birthday. The youngsters had emerged from their craft activity to present it and to sing to the elderly lady. It had been a fraught moment, as the serenading procession had walked towards the wrong woman, heading for a smartly dressed person who was some thirty years younger, and who would not have been amused by the children's mistake.

The actual centenarian noticed the frantic redirecting of the children and thought it was very funny.

Clare loved that sparky older lady, who often found amusement in people's reaction to her age. She smiled as she recalled another memory, of the day the centenarian had gone to her GP surgery with a minor ailment. It was the first time in years she'd had need to visit her doctor, who soon realised that her medical notes were nowhere to be found.

'They'd assumed I was dead, Vicar!' she chuckled, gleefully. 'They were so embarrassed!' Then, she leaned forward conspiratorially. 'There's no finishing me off, you know. One day, you'll just have to shoot me, Clare!'

While Clare savoured the memory, Vincent stroked his moustache and said that he sympathised with those children.

'Estimating ages is so difficult,' he said. 'How old do you think I am? Or even Jeremy?'

Before anyone could answer, Jeremy looked up from his phone. 'I'm twenty-one and not a day older,' he growled. He added that it would soon be time to head back, so if anyone wanted a paddle in the sea, or even a swim, now was their last chance.

Clare thought it was still some while before they needed to leave, and wondered whether the events coordinator, usually so gregarious, wanted to be left in peace with his sudoku or whatever it was, rather than be made the subject of conjecture. Vincent was not to be deterred by Jeremy's stand-offish behaviour, though. Despite the uncomfortable looks that crossed the faces of Lucy and Astrid, he continued to prod Jeremy on his age, before asking which part of the country he was from and whether he had always been in the hotel business, and enquiring how long the events manager had been based in Cornwall.

The grilling confirmed Clare's suspicion that Vincent was interested in writing a story, or making a podcast, about the retreat. She needed to be on her guard against the journalist, and it seemed that others did, too.

She took her chance to interrupt the flow of questions being directed at Jeremy, leaning forward and smiling in what she hoped was an engaging manner. 'I don't want to guess your age, Vincent – that seems too personal. But I'd love to know what you do?'

Jeremy glanced at her gratefully, perhaps acknowledging Clare's attempt to interrupt Vincent's interrogation of him.

Vincent looked at her too, and Clare saw the spark of mischief in his eye. He must find it fun, she surmised, to be a journalist undercover.

'I'm a writer,' he said, 'and I can tell you no more. I keep all my work confidential, as I imagine you do, too, Vicar?'

'Do you keep everything confidential, Clare?' Lucy joined in, looking at her seriously.

'That's the general rule, isn't it, but in certain circumstances there have to be exceptions,' Clare replied evasively. People had to be able to trust her to respect their privacy, and her parishioners sometimes had complicated lives. But she was uncomfortably aware that she had just told Jackie all about the conversation which Astrid had overheard.

'I've researched criminal trials where confidentiality was of supreme importance,' Vincent said, sounding sombre. 'Screens put up in the courtroom to protect the identity of witnesses, all that sort of thing. Separate entrances, extra security, the whole hog.'

'That sounds fascinating,' said Astrid, and now everyone else was listening intently, too. 'Tell us more.'

'In one case, the defendant interrupted a witness who was giving evidence from behind a white screen. Shouted out that he could see him. Of course he couldn't, it was just an attempt to intimidate, and the judge gave the man short shrift. It was obvious he was guilty as hell and he was just trying to frighten the bloke who was giving evidence for the prosecution. "We know who you are," that sort of thing.'

Vincent was a good storyteller, Clare thought. She found herself visualising the scene as he described it.

'How utterly horrible,' Lucy commented dramatically, picking up her sunglasses from the table and putting them on her face, as if to distract herself from such unpleasantness. Their large dark lenses gave her the appearance of a magnified insect.

'Yes, giving evidence against some of these guys is tough. And keeping away from them afterwards, too,' Vincent said.

'Well, let's enjoy being here and not in some stuffy courtroom.' Astrid was more upbeat. 'This place is amazing.' But, while she sounded cheerful, Clare noticed how she wiped her eyes, lips trembling. She seemed distressed, but it could also be the hay fever. Clare decided not to say anything, as Astrid seemed resolute on being discreet.

Jeremy put away his phone and stood up to leave, looking discomforted. Clare assumed he had wanted a bit of peace to concentrate on his sudoku and hadn't been pleased by the conversation. As Lucy asked Vincent to tell her more about the court cases he had seen, Clare followed Jeremy. She wasn't interested in hearing more about criminal convictions – the murder case with which she and Jackie had been involved during the previous summer still lay heavy in her consciousness.

Clare wanted resolution for everyone about what had happened to Victoria, but she knew it was unlikely to be achieved. She reminded herself that her job here was to provide as helpful a retreat as possible, and to accept that there would often be unfinished business for people – that was part of life. Jackie would investigate as much as was practicable and would liaise with her local counterparts. Clare told herself that her own priority must be supporting the retreat participants and facilitating useful sessions for them.

This didn't stop her asking herself where Pippa had wandered off to that morning. Had she met up with Michael, despite his apparent wish to avoid her? Clare was curious about that. She hoped that Dan and Gareth were enjoying one another's company on their scenic walk back to the Morva. She asked for blessing for them all, and for guidance as she led the retreat as best she could.

Clare didn't follow Jeremy on the more arduous route, but set off on the longer, less steep track back to the car park. She was content to have time to herself and to walk at her own pace. The banks held a colourful variety of wildflowers: purple loosestrife, delicately laced cow parsley, clumps of heather and the yellow flowering gorse. The sound of waves receded, replaced by the trickling of the stream and the varied notes of birdsong. She paused by a cattle grid to listen.

Then came the noise of an engine. Heading towards her up the slope was a wide-tyred quad bike driven by the tousled-haired young man who had served her and Astrid in the café. It towed a trailer with black bin bags and a pile of empty cardboard boxes stowed in it.

Clare stood beside the track, watching as he approached, glad of the opportunity to catch her breath before continuing the climb. To her delight, the driver slowed and offered her a lift. Her day had just improved. A hurried prayer of thanks was in order as she clambered aboard and held on tight, and they roared off and upwards. A prayer that she didn't fall off and break a limb seemed like a good idea, too.

CHAPTER 23

Back at the Morva, Clare discovered that Rachel was on duty at reception and was eager to chat. She quickly told Clare that Gareth and Dan had returned in high spirits not long ago and had headed straight to the dining room to get something to eat.

'Do they seem to be getting on OK?' Clare asked, and was relieved to hear that things seemed convivial. Fostering positive relationships between them all would make the retreat a better experience for everyone. 'I don't know if you heard, but several people close to Victoria have shown up this year, and it's made the start of the retreat difficult, to say the least.'

Rachel was happy to add her views on the group dynamics. She'd already overheard Nadiya, her turquoise-haired colleague, and Jeremy discussing the tensions between Michael and Lucy.

'Jeremy was worried sick about how the retreat would go, and he wasn't sure whether or not he should bring it up with Gail, our hotel manager.

'I first met Lucy last year, of course,' she added, raising her eyebrows as she leaned across the reception desk and lowered her voice: 'She's a funny one. But sisters can be complicated. It takes all sorts.'

'In what way?' Clare said, surprised.

'Well, I wasn't the only one to hear the two of them arguing, and Nadiya had to clear up a right mess in their room, too.'

But, before Rachel could continue, the minibus passengers began to arrive back in reception; at the same time, a harassed father holding a wailing child approached the desk asking for something to soothe a wasp sting. Rachel turned her attention to them, allowing Jeremy the opportunity to pull Clare aside.

'Clare, I wanted to let you know that I've reminded the group that there's no specific time scheduled for their lunch today. The buffet is laid out in the dining room, and some guests plan to take their meal a little later than others. Michael, for example, let me know that he might not return until the afternoon. I left him down at Kynance; he has his car there.'

Jeremy was doing his best to help things run smoothly, and Clare thanked him. She wanted to say something more about appreciating his help in difficult circumstances, but he was called away before they could talk further; Rachel had a room-change issue which needed his attention.

Clare went first to drop her things off in her room, before making her way to the pool area on the west side of the hotel, keen to test the water temperature before committing herself to a swim.

As she approached the walled enclosure, she could see a man lying prone, floating in the water. He lay still, with his arms outstretched, unmoving. Clare was horrified. Was he drowning?

She stumbled as she began to run across the grass, ready to wrench open the gate and launch herself into the water. As she opened her mouth to shout for help, the figure suddenly moved, using his arms to steer his position, before raising his head and laughing.

'How long was that?' he asked, flicking his head to clear the hair from across his eyes and sending a spray of water arching away from him.

It was Gareth, Clare realised. Now that she was closer, and no longer worried about having a dead body on her hands, she registered that he wasn't alone. Dan and Pippa were sitting on sunloungers beside the pool.

'Hello, Clare!' Gareth called from the water, as she reached the gate and opened it, breathing heavily. 'We're cooling off after our hike. It's chilly when you first get in, then it's great.'

'I've only just got out,' Dan added, 'but I'm persuading Pippa to have a dip. It's so refreshing. Is there time, before lunch finishes?'

'Yes, absolutely,' she replied. In as measured a voice as she could manage, Clare reminded them about the flexible schedule for the rest of the day. The afternoon session in the Leven Room would begin at two thirty, for those who'd like to attend.

Just as Clare finished speaking, another figure leapt into the water with a splash, which made Pippa shrink back. It was Vincent, now surfacing with water dripping from his hair and moustache alike, and challenging Gareth to a race.

Dan promptly jumped back in to join them, giving Clare the opportunity to sit beside Pippa and to enquire about how the rest of her morning had been.

Pippa looked different, once again. She'd shed her shorts and T-shirt, and now sported a flowing maxi dress with split sides, which revealed her designer Greek sandals with long laces that criss-crossed up her legs to her knees. She had clipped her hair up into a classic bun, but left tendrils falling loosely around her face, not quite covering her gold hooped earrings. She could have stepped out from a mural in Knossos or Pompeii. Pippa made reinvention an art form, Clare thought, from batik-clad hippy to a Grecian handmaiden to whom John Keats might have dedicated an ode. The woman was a chameleon.

Dan, Gareth and Vincent were playful in splashing and racing one another and calling out to Pippa to referee or be their timekeeper. Pippa's beauty in this latest outfit did not seem to have escaped their notice, and she looked pleased at the attention. In fact, she was the happiest that Clare had ever seen her.

The walled pool area was a suntrap, protected from any sea breezes. It was great to see people relaxed and enjoying themselves, Clare thought. She closed her eyes, thankful for the moment, lifting her face to savour the warmth of the sunshine. Perhaps things might be OK, after all.

CHAPTER 24

Victoria

I'm so glad I spoke to Lucy again. It's much better to be open and I wish I'd known about how bad things had got sooner. She usually has things so sorted – perfect home, white carpet and coordinating cushions, smooth-running life, loyal (if boring) husband. Turns out there's trouble in paradise and I shouldn't have judged her so quickly.

Things are clearer for me now, and I can see my road ahead. Some ends to be tied up here, and then onward into my brave new world. I'll take a memento with me. Driftwood from Cadgwith and a stone from Kynance, maybe?

Enough introspection, although journaling is helpful. I get in touch with my feelings and priorities.

I will do the meetup, and then I will move on.

CHAPTER 25

The Leven Room was hot and stuffy in the mid afternoon, so Clare opened the door to the garden. She was pleased that everyone had chosen to attend the session, even Michael, who'd returned from the morning expedition later than everyone else, looking refreshed and recounting his adventures exploring the cove and its caves.

Jeremy was not part of this gathering, and Clare was slightly relieved not to have any of his long-winded interventions. To open the session, she spoke about the Celtic world view of the interweaving of spiritual life and daily activity, and the tradition of having prayers to accompany the most ordinary of tasks.

'A prayer for use during a morning workout would be good,' suggested Gareth.

'Jesus shared in every aspect of human experience, in work and in friendships,' Dan interrupted, cutting off Gareth's train of thought. 'I try to remember that and to pray throughout the day and in everything that I'm doing – when I'm commuting, when I first open up my emails and when it's time to head home, too.'

Vincent rolled his eyes, muttering under his breath that he hoped Dan prayed for safety, if he closed his eyes while driving.

Jackie responded with good humour on the younger man's behalf: 'My grandmother always prayed about her driving, and for any vehicles that might be in the vicinity,' she remarked.

Lucy, Michael and Pippa each held back from contributing to the discussion, seemingly content to simply listen. They had seated themselves carefully distanced from each other, as if by mutual agreement. As Michael browsed a collection of poetry and Pippa examined pictures of Celtic designs from the Book of Kells, it felt as if some of the group's tensions had eased. Clare was relieved – she wanted them all to stay for the duration of the retreat and to be glad of having done so, whatever its challenges might be.

Encouraged by Astrid, Clare agreed to teach them a Celtic walking prayer which she knew and loved. She explained the idea that reciting it, step by step, was one way of remembering that the sacred or spiritual side of life was entwined with everyday activity:

> '*Father above me,*
> *Son beside me,*
> *Spirit within me,*
> *The Three all around me.*'

'That's great, Clare,' Gareth said. 'It's in the rhythm of walking, so you can repeat it, stride for stride.'

Clare thought he was perhaps familiar with similar Celtic ideas, being from Welsh heritage. Though he would probably jog to this prayer, rather than walk. Gareth was in sports gear again – a dark-green tracksuit this afternoon, still accessorised by that oversized watch.

'It's a circle prayer, too,' Dan commented, somewhat pompously. 'A prayer for protection from evil, like St Patrick's breastplate. Ah, here's another good one,' he said, looking up from the illustrated book which Jackie had just been reading. 'For you, Lucy, and for anyone taking a journey, or on the journey of life.'

Clare thought irreverently of the clichés surrounding the *Strictly* 'journey' undertaken by celebrities, but maybe she was just finding Dan a tad irritating. There was plenty of joy in *Strictly*. Maybe she could compose a prayer to use during the dancing of a salsa, or the spraying of fake tan.

It was time to finish their session, and Dan did so by reciting the benediction he'd found. He read it well:

> '*God be with thee in every pass,*
> *Jesus be with thee on every hill,*
> *Spirit be with thee on every stream,*
> *Headland and ridge and lawn;*
>
> '*Each sea and land, each moor and meadow,*
> *Each lying down, each rising up,*
> *In the trough of the waves, on the crest of the billows,*
> *Each step of the journey thou goest.*'

Listening to his mellifluous voice, Clare found it easy to echo that request for blessing on them all. That sometimes proved more difficult when having to actually interact with each of them, with their differences and difficulties, but Clare gave heartfelt thanks for the fragile peace between them, at that moment, anyway.

After their Celtic spirituality session, the retreat group moved as one to the bar area, with its huge window allowing them to enjoy the late-afternoon sunlight, now playing over the water. Pippa moved on past the bar, towards her own room, saying that she wanted to change for dinner. Clare wondered about the dimensions of her suitcase. It must be at least twice the size of Clare and David's big Narnian wardrobe, if it contained her whole range of outfits.

Jeremy and the young waiter took drinks orders, Jeremy checking with Clare that the session had gone well.

Clare felt emboldened to put a significant question to Vincent, in front of everyone: 'Your court-room experience sounded fascinating – especially the one you told some of us about, at Kynance café. In your work, you must have all sorts of interesting experiences and stories. Can you tell us anything else, or are your sources for your writing confidential?' she asked.

'I suspect that Clare may be wanting to out me as a journalist.' Vincent smiled, but without any glint of humour in his eyes. 'So, your question about not disclosing information about my sources is somewhat ironic, in the circumstances.'

'But you have responsibilities, surely,' Astrid interjected, before Clare could reply. 'And if you make a mistake, if you publish something untrue, how do you live with the consequences of that? What about the impact on people's lives, when you write about them?'

Clare was struck by Astrid's vehemence, and the way the young woman had clenched her fists as she spoke. For someone so physically slight, she could be surprisingly intimidating.

'I use Tripadvisor reviews and they're usually reliable, but not always,' Gareth added. 'The views from our walk today were incredible, just as they said they would be.'

Clare wondered whether the young man had any awareness of the group dynamics now bubbling to the surface, with Astrid's strange forcefulness and widened eyes.

Others were also oblivious to Vincent's evident displeasure at Astrid's challenge, and the anxious expression now visible on Lucy's face. Michael was impassive, but he sat on one of the rattan sofas with a quality of stillness which Clare found unnerving. He seemed alert to the potential implications of Vincent's profession, even though Dan blithely pursued the topic of Tripadvisor ratings.

'I'll post a great review of this place, even though the pool is a bit chilly.'

Ignoring him, Lucy looked at Vincent steadily, and asked, 'Will you be writing a story about us and our retreat, as a journalist, Vincent?' As she spoke, Michael seemed to become even more still, if that were possible, and the rest of the group seemed to be awakening to the implications of Lucy's question. Gareth was now frowning slightly.

'Surely not,' Dan said. 'That would be a travesty. We trust one another in this group, don't we? We support one another.'

Lucy still had her gaze fixed on Vincent.

'If you write about crime, like those court cases you describe, are you planning a piece about Victoria and what may have happened to her? I would like to know. You've been asking plenty of questions, that's for sure.'

'I came here on a retreat, not looking for work, Lucy. But you must admit, we're quite a collection of people, gathered here,' Vincent replied. 'There's always scope for many different stories to be told, and not necessarily the ones you might expect. But I'll not be drawn any further than that. Not everyone's as candid as you are, Dan.'

'What does that mean?' Dan looked perplexed and was willing to challenge Vincent's air of world-weary condescension. Clare was glad of that.

'I think it means it is almost time for dinner.' Jeremy moved seamlessly centre stage. 'And there are some specials to mention, which the chef has prepared from today's catch.'

As the events manager discussed offerings of lobster and other seafood delights, Jackie moved towards Clare from her seat at the perimeter of the group, murmuring that she had some things to check out and would give dinner a miss. Clare had assumed the DCI would remain in situ, as people seemed likely to open up further about their misgivings at Vincent's information-gathering, but perhaps Jackie wanted to avoid coming under any awkward scrutiny herself, if Vincent decided to question why she was there, or to make any further hint about her surname. Surely, he didn't know about Jackie's friendship with Victoria, even if he was aware that she was police.

'I'll be back for the Epilogue,' she added, then left Clare

listening to Dan's interrogation of Jeremy about the deployment of lobster pots.

'I'm off, too; I need to make some calls before dinner,' Gareth said, and, at this, the group in general began to disperse, as if everyone wanted to distance themselves from Vincent, now that his interest in them had been exposed, and to escape his self-satisfaction about it, too. Clare was relieved that people were aware of the risk his profession might pose, even if the group was more divided as a result.

There was a tap on her shoulder. Rachel had finished her shift on reception and was standing beside Clare's chair, a bag in one hand and a set of car keys in the other.

'Can we have a word about ponies for Saturday?' she asked.

'Sure!' Clare smiled.

'I wanted to ask about how tall Tom is, now.' Rachel's words were innocuous enough, but she was standing with her back to the others and flaring her eyes at Clare, while also indicating the urgency of the situation with a twitch of her head towards the door.

Clare tried to look unconcerned, thanking Rachel and saying that she would like to talk about the other family joining them for half-term this year. She stood up as she started to describe their riding capabilities, following Rachel from the room. For good measure, she added that their friend Cassian was allergic to horses and had endured an acutely uncomfortable experience of trotting on Icelandic ponies during a previous holiday, and wanted to avoid any repetition of that agony.

She chatted on while following Rachel, who walked

straight through reception and the heavy front door and on towards a far section of the car park, where staff vehicles were parked behind the big wheelie bins, beside a rear entrance to the spa building. Clare's own car was nearer the main hotel, and, as she passed it, she noticed that Jackie's BMW was no longer there.

'What is it?' she asked, once they were alone.

Rachel was trembling, leaning her hand on the bonnet of a car to steady herself.

'There's something I need to show you,' Rachel replied. 'One of the housekeeping team found something in the lost-property hamper, and Nadiya told her to bring it to me.'

'What is it?' said Clare. What could they have found that had left Rachel so distraught and coming to Clare for help?

'Look, Clare.' Rachel extracted a rainproof jacket from her bag. 'It was Victoria's. From last year. And it has her journal inside it.'

CHAPTER 26

Lord, help me, Clare thought. Victoria's journal.

'Are you sure?'

Rachel nodded, holding it out towards Clare. 'Take a look.'

Clare did so gingerly, taking the journal from the pocket of the rain mac it was bundled up with. The soft cover had a design of birds flying over a seascape, silhouetted in front of a setting sun. She held the book by its edges, worried about leaving fingerprints, but too curious to hold back. Only the first few pages had been written on.

As she scanned the initial entry, the significance of the find was brought home to her. Victoria had written this here, at the Morva. This journal was fresh evidence that revealed her state of mind and might shed light on how and why she had disappeared. The importance of the discovery made Clare catch her breath as she flipped through the pages.

'She wanted a child,' Rachel said. 'Have you got to that bit?'

'Yes.' Clare's eyes filled with tears, and she looked up at Rachel, who nodded in solidarity. Victoria's hopes and plans leapt off the page, and Clare was now certain that Victoria hadn't chosen to disappear. She had made plans for the future – with joy and optimism.

'The police need to see this,' she said, wishing that Jackie hadn't chosen that evening to go for a walkabout. 'Where did you say the lost property is kept?'

'In that big hamper, next to the sofa in reception, under the mirror.' Rachel had obviously prepared her answer. 'It was right at the bottom, under everything else, so it could have been there for a while. But not for longer than a few weeks, at the most – we clear the lost property every couple of months or so.'

'But why didn't anyone find it last year?' Clare asked. She was baffled – how could this crucial piece of evidence only be turning up now?

Clare's head spun as she called Jackie's number and tried to work out what needed to be done. When no one answered, she rang her husband, David, instead. Sometimes, it was useful to be married to a senior civil servant in the Home Office, who could liaise with police forces across the country. Instead of calling the police herself and trying to explain to a nameless operator exactly what was going on, she could get a message delivered directly to DCI Faux, without delay.

'Hi! How's the handsome Heathcliff?' her husband asked, cheerfully. His tone changed as soon as Clare explained she needed the local DCI, Nick Faux, to call her urgently. Conscious of Rachel's presence, Clare told David briefly about the journal and only hinted at some of the group dynamics that continued to brew. In her mind's eye, she could see David listening with new focus, analysing her words and what might lie beneath them.

'Is Jackie with you?' he asked.

'I'm sure Jackie can look after herself,' she answered sharply, then told herself that he was concerned for the safety of them both, and that this wasn't the time for petty jealousies.

'Of course. Well, I'll get this Nick Faux to call you,' he said, placatingly, as if reading her mind. 'Take care with everything. Anna and Tom send their love. We're playing *Settlers*,' he said.

'And I'm winning!' Tom called, from the background.

'You wish. See you soon, Mum,' Anna chimed in.

Clare knew that David's reference to Jackie would not have escaped her daughter's notice. Anna's antennae had an uncanny knack of identifying the DCI's presence as a source of discomfort to her mother.

'Yes, great. Fight on – and I'll beat the lot of you, next time.' Clare was all cheeriness for her children, and she suspected that David was putting it on a bit, too. 'See you soon – lots of love!'

How she wanted to be at home with them, dog at her feet, mug of tea beside her and a board game in progress.

Clare braced herself for what might lie ahead as she put her phone away. The journal was a significant clue that could reveal what had happened last year. But its discovery also posed questions. Where exactly had it been all this time? And how and why had it resurfaced now?

Clare had prayed for answers about Victoria's disappearance, and it seemed as if some aspects of what happened might come to light. Hopefully, there would be resolution for Victoria's family and friends, or perhaps more trouble lay in store.

CHAPTER 27

Phone call over, Clare stuffed the diary and the jacket back in the bag Rachel had given her and made her way back to her room. As she passed through reception, she spotted the innocuous-looking hamper next to the sofa. There was no one about, so she lifted its wicker lid. It creaked as she did so. A jumble of coats and hats lay inside, along with a cracked yellow spade and a couple of paperbacks – an assortment of holiday detritus. She didn't want to delve too deeply, so dropped the lid, which creaked again as it fell.

'Have you lost something?' Jeremy was standing beside the reception desk, looking concerned. 'Can I help at all?'

Clare jumped at his voice. How could she have missed him when he was wearing another ludicrously loud shirt? Zigzags, this time.

'No, but thanks, Jeremy. I was just admiring this wicker trunk. It's such a good size – I'd love to get one like it.'

Since when did I become so adept at lying? Clare thought. She should go on *Traitors*. She'd love a chance to wear Claudia Winkleman's red gloves.

Thankfully, before Jeremy could ask any more questions, he

was interrupted by Dan, who wandered out from the lounge with a drink in his hand.

'I wanted to ask you exactly how local tonight's lobsters might be, Jeremy,' he began, much to Clare's relief. 'Vincent's been telling me all sorts of tales of life on the water in these parts. I hadn't realised how often he'd stayed here before.'

Clare left them to discuss fishing and hurried off towards the staircase up to her room. Astrid was coming down, and Clare took the opportunity to say that she probably wouldn't make dinner.

'Something bad has come up at home,' Clare improvised. She couldn't face going to eat with the group and seeing Lucy, not now she had this clue in her hands that might shed light on Victoria's disappearance.

'I'm sorry.' Astrid tipped her head sympathetically, halting her descent. Her hay fever was in evidence again; she held a hanky in her hand, tightly.

'Yes, poor Anna – my daughter has had a horrible day at school. She has a ghastly science teacher who terrorises them all. There's been a mix-up about some experiments to be written up, and things got nasty. You know how mean youngsters can be. I need to talk with Anna again and work out what's best to do about it.'

Sorry Anna, but this story was the best I could manage, she thought, heading on past Astrid's commiserations and finally reaching the sanctuary of her room. With no prospect of a meal, she seized the packet of cookies on the hospitality tray, grateful for the hotel's luxuries as she awaited the call from DCI Faux. She had texted Jackie frantically, but there was still no response from her. The basket of flowers from David kept her company, although the purple tulips drooped a little in the warm room.

Clare munched her way through the entire supply of biscuits and paced the room. She had read every journal entry, at least twice over. Every time she reached the places where Victoria described the feeling of being watched, a chill crept over her. Victoria had questioned herself – suggested she was being neurotic, even – but that feeling had reoccurred. And now she was gone. It was evidence that someone had been out to get her.

Victoria's most private thoughts and hopes would now be known, everything would be laid bare as part of the police investigation. It was horrible.

Clare had Rachel's number to give to Nick Faux, and she was grateful that the friendship formed with her over years of meeting at the riding stables meant that the receptionist had trusted her with the journal. The hotel staff must have their own network of relationships and insights. For whatever reason, Nadiya had insisted the journal was brought to Rachel, and that had meant it came to Clare. Clare supposed she would have trusted Rachel with it, too, rather than the verbose events manager.

Clare made a mug of peppermint tea and then perched on the dressing-table stool, looking out over the sea and watching as gulls circled and a distant ship appeared on the horizon. She was disconcerted by the tensions Victoria wrote about between her and her sister. Lucy had indicated that she and Victoria were the best of friends, but it seemed like they had been arguing in the run-up to Victoria's disappearance, and Rachel had also commented on that. Clare couldn't imagine Lucy doing anything to hurt her sister, but was there some dispute between them that had led to Victoria going missing?

When Clare's phone eventually rang, the caller ID was unknown.

'Detective Chief Inspector Faux, here. I've been asked to ring this number.' The voice on the other end of the line was curt, and Clare wondered how his evening had been interrupted and whether he had eaten yet.

'Thank you. I'm Clare Brakespear, staying at the Morva Hotel.'

'Yes?'

She thought that the DCI might lead the conversation, but it was clearly up to her to make the running, here.

'I understand you're leading the enquiry into a missing person, Victoria Armstrong? And DCI Jackie Carter has updated you about the retreat currently being held here, at the Morva again, and who is attending?'

A pause. 'DCI Jackie Carter?'

'Yes, she's out at the moment and I've come across something that urgently needs to be shared, regarding Victoria's disappearance,' Clare said.

'DCI Jackie Carter is at the Morva Hotel?'

What was wrong with the man? Jackie had been in touch with him herself, so why the note of surprise?

Clare stood up and moved towards the window, trying to make sense of this.

'Yes,' she said, as there was no avoiding that admission.

Was he completely unaware? 'Not in any official capacity, of course,' she added, lamely.

'I see. And I understand that you have some connection with the Home Office? That's highly unusual.' The Cornish DCI did not sound at all happy to have been contacted by an external authority about his investigation.

Awkwardly, Clare explained how her husband worked for the Home Office and how she had asked him to make contact.

'I see. And why did you want to speak to me?'

Finally, Clare thought. She sat down and succinctly explained the discovery of Victoria's journal. She winced when admitting that she had held the book to read it, but felt more confident in her actions when explaining that she had the contact details of the staff involved in finding it, and that, as yet, none of the retreat participants knew about it.

'Right,' he said. 'Thank you. Obviously, this may be of significance. I'm calling you from Helston – I happen to be in the area this evening and can be with you in twenty minutes to collect this jacket and its contents. My team can work on it and ascertain its authenticity. How much longer is this retreat continuing?'

As she updated him, Clare was surprised at his request that she simply continue with the Epilogue that evening as expected. Surely this discovery warranted more urgent investigation?

But then DCI Faux continued: 'If DCI Carter returns before this Epilogue, please do not tell her about the discovery either, or of my involvement. I would much prefer to interview her myself about this.'

Interview? Surely it would be a discussion between colleagues who were both committed to finding Victoria. Then it dawned on her. The Cornish DCI had no idea about this retreat, nor Jackie's presence on his patch, because Jackie had lied when she told Clare about making contact with him, earlier that day. Clare had assumed that Jackie was telling the truth, and now Clare had landed her right in it. She wasn't looking forward to seeing Jackie again, after this.

CHAPTER 28

Jackie wanted to get away from Vincent. He had locked eyes with her at the bar before dinner and his amused expression made her uneasy. Now that Jackie knew he was a muckraking journalist, the way he had provoked her at Kynance made sense. He obviously knew her real name wasn't Jackie Casey and that she was at the Morva for a reason.

Jackie surmised that he had an informant on the local force; there would be a record of that interview about her friendship with Victoria, and those messages sent before the disappearance. A tale of police incompetence and failure could be spun all too easily from that revelation. Vincent had enjoyed hinting about there being unexpected stories to be shared, stemming from their gathering.

As she drove away from the hotel, Jackie found herself looking out towards the horizon and mutely asking the sky and sea for help on her quest. She wondered whether Clare would count that as prayer.

No matter, Jackie's priority was to get the job done. She wanted to pursue a hunch of her own, which had been dismissed by Nick Faux as having no relevance to the case.

Her first stop was a scruffy village pub, and she parked discreetly, away from its illumined frontage. A brief conversation with the young barman inside, and a lightening of her wallet, provided her with the necessary lowdown, and she continued on her way to another bar, this time in Helston, the nearest town.

This bar was crowded but dingy, and smelled of beer and cooking fat. The clientele was mixed – from youngsters sitting around tables, chatting, to a more raucous gaggle who were playing darts, with shouted encouragement and some loud goading from the opposing team. Most people looked to be locals, but Jackie thought she spotted holidaymakers, too, in Breton striped tops and newly pressed jeans. Two grey-haired couples chatted over their drinks and plates of scampi and fries.

When one of the younger darts players from the home team headed for the loo, she followed him.

'Just a word,' she called brightly, catching up with him in the wood-panelled corridor. She pulled some cash from her pocket. 'Just between ourselves. I'm doing some private research.'

He was hesitant, looking suspiciously at her and flicking a glance back towards the door to the bar.

'No trouble for anyone here,' she said, quickly. 'I'd just be grateful for a number to call, or a place to be, to pick up some stuff.'

'Are you police, or what?' he said, eyeing the cash.

'No, just looking to help a friend.'

'Nothing doing – I'm only here for the game.' He scowled

at her, plainly regretting not getting his hands on the money, but obviously determined not to be involved, and pushed his way into the gents.

Jackie returned to the bar and nursed a second drink, as unobtrusively as possible. The young man didn't glance at her as he returned to his darts team, nor did he seem to be telling them about her enquiry.

One man lolling at a corner table caught her attention. He was joined by a heavyset individual in a sweat-stained baseball cap, who Jackie would bet had been familiar with prison life at some point in his past. Perhaps several times. There was an air of menace about him as he scanned the room appraisingly, and Jackie busied herself with her phone. She was wary of being spotted as police, nor did she want to interfere with any local surveillance operation. It was obvious what kind of deals happened in the car park or toilets here, and it was time to remove herself.

As Jackie finished the last of her drink, she thought she might as well return to the hotel and attend the evening Epilogue. On her way back, she could also take a look at some of the more remote car parks and coves of the peninsula. She had her theories about what might go on there. The area had a trading history that went back centuries, with local gangs who evaded or fought the revenue officers. The cargo might differ these days, but it was essentially the same game, whether using lanterns on cliff paths or smartwatches to illuminate landing points and to organise the drop-off and collection of illicit goods or people.

Victoria hadn't been a user, as far as Jackie was aware, but people often kept secrets from friends, especially if they were police officers. If Victoria had stumbled across the criminal network here, she could have been roped into something dangerous. Jackie had suggested this to DCI Faux when he interviewed her the previous year, and had been dissatisfied by his quick dismissal of her theories. Now, Jackie was on the hunt, whether DCI Faux liked it or not.

CHAPTER 29

'Good evening, and welcome to our Wednesday Epilogue,' Clare began, scanning the faces of the assembled group. Jackie was not amongst them, nor was Vincent.

DCI Nick Faux had arrived earlier and collected the journal from Clare. He was older than she'd expected, with greying hair, and was wearing a crumpled navy jacket over an ancient pair of jeans.

'Sorry you didn't make dinner,' Astrid said. 'Is everything OK for your daughter, Clare?'

'Teachers can be mean, can't they?' Dan added. 'And other students, too. Group work can be awful.'

'I was never good at science,' Gareth commented. 'I could never remember any of the periodic table, and my career's been just fine without it.' He tapped his expensive watch, and Clare presumed he meant to indicate that he was well able to afford it, whatever his scientific qualifications, or lack of them, might be.

The hastily manufactured story of Anna's unpleasant school day had obviously been repeated, grown legs and run. Clare was ashamed of her duplicity. Instead of joining further discussion of fictitious science coursework issues, she reassured Astrid that the kitchen had made her a cheese sandwich, and she asked after their lobster.

'We had a great dinner – it was delicious,' Dan enthused. 'And we heard lots of interesting tales. Vincent is quite the raconteur.'

'He's not here.' Astrid looked round the room, noting the two empty chairs in the circle. 'That's odd; he said he'd see us later. He was very specific about it, saying he'd catch up with everyone at the Epilogue.'

'Jackie's not here, either.' Pippa placed her hand, with her palm downwards, on the vacant seat beside her. 'It's a lovely evening – maybe they've gone for a walk. I thought I'd go down to the beach after this; it's still light enough to see.' Pippa seemed increasingly relaxed as the retreat continued, and tonight's clothing reflected this. She now sported a pair of jeans, with a pink T-shirt and open-toed sandals. Clare liked the shade of her scarlet nail varnish.

'Yes, Vincent said he'd be at the Epilogue. And Jackie was supposed to be here, too, I thought.' Lucy's voice held a note of concern.

Clare hadn't realised that Jackie's quiet words to her before leaving had been overheard, but perhaps Jackie had mentioned her expedition to others in the group, too.

'It *is* a beautiful evening; perhaps they've changed their plans.' Clare sought to reassure Lucy, all too aware that freshly troubled waters lay ahead, given the discovery of her sister's journal.

The worried look didn't leave Lucy's face, though, and

Clare imagined that the disappearance of her sister a year ago had made her sensitive to people not showing up as promised. When a person you loved went missing, it was probably all too easy to believe that anyone else might disappear as well, Clare realised.

'The clear sky means we'll get wonderful starlight later,' Clare said, speaking more loudly now, addressing the room. Was she really wittering on about stars, while Jackie, if she had returned, was probably being contacted and reprimanded by Nick Faux? But Clare had a job to do, so she continued.

'Shall we listen to some music, and give ourselves time to reflect on the day? Perhaps thinking of things that have been helpful or enjoyable, as well as holding in our awareness the things that have been challenging or painful for us.'

Thankfully, that caught everyone's attention, and Dan piped up to say that he had tried using the walking prayer after the afternoon session and had been reminded that Jesus described himself as 'the way, the truth and the life'.

'Yes, that's so interesting.' Clare wanted to head off the mini sermon which she sensed Dan was about to begin. 'Members of the earliest Christian communities called their faith "the Way".'

'That links with my thoughts about being on a journey through all this,' Lucy said. 'People describe grief as a journey, too.'

'One that never ends,' Astrid replied.

Clare was pleased to see her opening up more; she thought it would be good for her. Some positive things were still happening during this retreat.

Astrid continued: 'I've got plenty of mileage left in mine, and I'm missing my dad. I've got plenty of anger, too.'

'I think we have all sorts of reactions to loss,' Clare suggested. 'Anger and volatility, extreme weariness or unusual energy – I think we're all different in how we respond.'

'I'm sorry to hear that, Astrid.' Dan spoke with confidence. 'A friend shared this with me – maybe you'll like it.' He took some paper from his pocket and read, 'Do not hurry as you walk with grief; it does not help the journey. Walk slowly, pausing often. Do not hurry as you walk with grief.'

Astrid looked round at them all. 'Maybe that's something we can do here – give ourselves some time.' She bit her lip, as if to stop herself saying more.

Astrid's comment seemed to lull the room into thoughtful silence, and after a moment Clare got up to put some music on. She turned the speaker on low to play Margaret Rizza's 'Celtic Blessing', to tie in with Dan's words.

As the melody continued, the door from the terrace opened and Jackie came in discreetly. She sat carefully beside Pippa and closed her eyes. Clare wondered whether she had received her texts explaining about the journal and making contact with DCI Faux. Then Jackie flicked open her eyes and looked straight at her with unmistakable fury. Ouch. If looks could kill, DCI Faux would be extra busy tonight.

As the music came to an end, Clare bade the group members goodbye and goodnight, but the detective continued to sit brooding and hunched in her seat.

Michael also lingered a while, sitting still and in silence. Clare wondered if he was planning to outwait Jackie, but eventually he stood, moving slowly and stiffly, and with a gruff, 'See you in the morning, Clare,' he left, and closed the door to the garden behind him.

Clare took her time shuffling her papers into a tidy pile before closing the door to the foyer.

'DCI Nick Faux got in touch,' Jackie finally announced, in a low voice. 'He said he wants to come around later to talk; he'll find us in here.'

'You've heard from him?' Clare asked, realising as she did so that the question was redundant. 'And you got my messages, about the journal? I tried to call you first, but you weren't around.' She stopped speaking when she saw Jackie draw a hand across her face, as if she were tired and barely holding herself together.

'What did she say?' Jackie asked fiercely. The look of exhaustion on her face had been replaced with one of intense concentration. Clare realised it was concern for her friend that was uppermost in the detective's mind, not any concern for professional niceties or protocol. Jackie cared about Victoria, and about what had happened to her.

'I'm not sure how candid to be,' Clare said. She didn't know how much she could say. Were the contents of the diary privileged information? It was private, certainly. The stuff about wanting a child, the suggestions of a disagreement with Lucy, the hinted plans to meet and resolve things with an unnamed person – how much could Clare tell Jackie? And Clare suspected that it had been the sense of being watched that had caused Victoria to reach out to Jackie for advice.

'Please, Clare.'

There was no resisting that heartfelt request. So, Clare told her as much as she could remember about what Victoria had written. She trusted in Jackie's commitment to do her best for her friend.

It was another twenty minutes before Nick Faux made his way cautiously from his car and round to the sea-facing side of the building, and then carefully down the grass slope to the door leading to the Leven Room, where Clare and Jackie sat, speaking in hushed tones. He walked in quickly, closing the door to the darkening sky behind him.

'This is a highly irregular situation,' he began, addressing the women as if they were ill-behaved teenagers with whom he was tasked with making the best of things. 'I've sought advice from my superiors.'

Clare tried to imagine these discussions, wondering how much trouble Jackie would be in, and whether David's boss would object to his use of the Home Office's access to the local police force.

'Ms Armstrong's diary apparently being discovered at this juncture is an extraordinary development,' DCI Faux went on. 'I want to get as clear a picture as possible from you this evening, before getting a full team here early tomorrow to pursue the investigation further. What exactly has been going on?'

CHAPTER 30

The next morning, Clare was in no hurry to go down to breakfast to rejoin Jackie and the group. The day ahead would be difficult. She took her time over the set Thursday-morning prayers and emerged from her room at nine.

As she made her way down to the dining room, she was surprised to see that a swathe of the hallway and reception area had been taped off. When she spotted a police officer crouching beside the lost-property hamper, now surrounded by plastic sheeting, she realised it was because of Victoria's journal. To divert people from the cordoned area, someone had erected a blackboard bearing a chalked message giving apologies and directions for guests to use other entrances to the hotel.

Clare was distracted by this police activity and, before she reached the dining room, was waylaid by Lucy at the door to the women's loos.

'Any news of Vincent?' Lucy asked, without preamble. 'At least the police are taking this disappearance seriously. Was it you who reported him missing, Clare? No one has seen him since dinner yesterday.'

Before Clare had composed a suitable reply, Lucy barrelled on, having made her own assumptions about the reasons for the police presence.

'Thank God you're here. I only wish you'd been part of last year's operation. Perhaps, with your input, we'd have got more action. Vincent told me what your husband does. He'd googled you – that's what journalists do.'

'Sorry, what?' Clare was struggling to keep up.

'Yes, before he disappeared, or had some mishap.'

'There are other possibilities,' Clare said, mildly, thinking that a late arrival for breakfast was no reason to panic. But things were different for Lucy, who had a taste for drama.

'Are you talking about Vincent?' Dan joined them, coming out from the dining room. 'Lucy told me about her concerns, Clare. I'm praying for his safe return.'

Why was handsome Dan's mention of prayer irritating? Clare thought. She was, after all, praying for them all herself. At least he'd toned down his T-shirt. This one merely had Donald Duck on it.

'I haven't reported Vincent as missing, Lucy,' Clare said firmly, keen to nip these anxieties in the bud. It *was* odd that Vincent hadn't shown up since last night, but, on this sort of retreat, Clare wanted people to feel free to skip sessions, and to pace themselves in whatever way they chose. 'Vincent only missed last night's Epilogue; I'm sure there's no cause for concern. The police must be here on other business,' she offered.

'I've knocked on his door and there's no reply, and Astrid tried last night, too. She wanted to talk to him.' Lucy was not to be persuaded; Clare supposed that her memories of a guest going missing were too raw. 'And if *he's* not the reason, then why are the police here? What aren't we being told, Clare?'

At that moment, Clare was relieved to see Jackie approaching along the corridor, dressed casually in jeans and a shirt, maintaining her identity as another, rather anonymous, retreatant. Though displeased that Jackie had come to the retreat undercover in the first place, DCI Nick Faux had agreed that this was the best way forward – for Jackie to retain her low profile in the group. He granted permission as if it were a beneficent gift, but Clare suspected that Jackie would have remained in situ anyway, with or without his agreement. She respected her more for it.

'What's going on?' Jackie asked, looking at Lucy. The DCI was all mystified concern.

'The police are here,' Dan explained, 'and Lucy's anxious about Vincent's whereabouts.'

'I think Clare got them here.' Lucy was on a mission and was not to be deflected from her insistence that the journalist was missing and that it was Clare who had involved the police. 'Her husband is connected in high places,' she announced with a flourish, as if proud of this vicarious sphere of influence.

'Wow.' Jackie widened her eyes at this, and Clare's stomach clenched. Did Jackie think that Clare had bandied David's name about in this pompous way?

'I think I'll just grab some breakfast; it's a lovely morning,' Jackie continued, clearly wanting to avoid further conversation. 'See you at the first session, and let's hope that Clare's husband and the cops have found Vincent safe and sound by then.' She gave a little beam at Clare, before moving off. Ouch.

Dan and Lucy seemed to consider themselves dismissed, and trooped away along the corridor, towards the lounge, while Clare followed Jackie into the dining room. It was almost deserted. The early breakfasters had departed, and there was a lull before the late risers appeared.

Nadiya was replenishing the bowls of chopped fruit which sat on the buffet table, beside the baskets of croissants and cinnamon swirls. When she saw Clare, she paused.

'Good morning.' Clare smiled. 'How are you, Nadiya?'

'You know my name?' the turquoise-haired woman replied. Her accent sounded Eastern European, Clare thought – maybe Polish, or perhaps Ukrainian.

'Of course,' Clare said, noticing that, although Jackie had drifted further away from them, she still remained within earshot. Clare had told her the night before that it was Nadiya who had ensured the journal reached Rachel's hands, and she suspected Jackie wanted to stay close in case anything else might come out in conversation. 'Thank you for everything,' Clare said.

'I do nothing,' Nadiya said, her brow furrowed.

'You've brought out a lovely breakfast.' Clare smiled again. 'Not to be missed.' She began to help herself to a bowl of sliced melon. Clare could tell Jackie was listening in by the way she affected to stare with fascination out of the dining room's large bay window, towards the sunlit lawn and sea.

'The sad sister is worried about the old man in your group, I think?' Nadiya almost whispered.

'Yes, indeed. From Room 17?' Clare had remembered Vincent's room number, from Jeremy's list.

'It is not my business to say about hotel guests, but . . . the old man does not always stay in his room,' Nadiya said. She looked like she wanted to say more, but when she caught sight of Jeremy walking past the dining room, she scurried off to the kitchen.

Clare's mind was reeling. She was unsure what to make of Nadiya's disclosure, and, judging from the look on Jackie's face, she didn't know what to make of it, either. If Vincent wasn't staying in his room while at the Morva, where was he sleeping?

Wanting to sit with her thoughts, Clare headed towards a small table tucked into an alcove beside a window and next to a large fire extinguisher. The waiter found her there and took her order for a breakfast omelette with a cappuccino. She wanted some decent food to start the day.

As she waited for her dish to arrive, more diners trickled into the room, amongst them Astrid, as well as an older couple whom Clare had gathered were celebrating their ruby wedding anniversary, and a younger family who had clearly already been outside, their child trailing deposits of sand from a wet spade which she dragged across the floor.

'Do you mind if I join you?' Astrid asked. 'It would be helpful to have a private word.'

Though dressed in a tightly belted green and white checked frock, Astrid looked less neat than usual. Her hair was unkempt, as if she had run her hands through it multiple times, and her eyes darted anxiously around the room.

'Of course,' Clare agreed. 'Why not help yourself to fruit and cereal? This melon is gorgeous.' She spoke warmly, wanting to tend to Astrid, who was clearly agitated.

Astrid ignored the suggestion, simply seating herself opposite Clare and drawing her chair in close to the table.

'If Vincent is missing, as some people are saying, there's something you should know, Clare. About my family's connection with him. The police will discover it soon enough, anyway.'

'The police aren't necessarily concerned about Vincent,' Clare soothed, thinking how bizarre it was that Lucy and now Astrid seemed so fixated on the journalist's supposed disappearance.

'It's about my dad,' Astrid said, chewing a fingernail, then running her index finger to and fro across her lips.

'Your dad?' Clare was perplexed.

'Yes. Do you remember the chaplain I told you about, who helped when my father died? He was a prison chaplain, Clare. My dad was in prison.'

'Right.' Clare attempted to look unsurprised and thought she almost succeeded. 'And Vincent knew him? Your dad, I mean.' Vincent didn't seem the type to be buddies with a prison chaplain, but then prison chaplains cared for everyone, and journalists had connections everywhere.

'When he was talking about trials with screens up, to shield witnesses, that's when I knew.'

'I'm sorry – was your dad involved in one? A trial like that?' Clare was trying to piece this together.

The waiter arrived and placed the omelette and its salad

garnish in front of her, politely asking if there was anything else that she or Astrid wanted. Once he'd left them, Astrid leaned forward, across the table.

'Exactly. But my dad was innocent, Clare, and he died in jail anyway.' The young woman looked stricken at the memory. 'It was horrific, what Dad went through. He was always chained up or being watched by a prison officer, even for medical stuff and at the end. I know he was innocent, whatever my mum or others believed.'

'I'm so sorry,' Clare repeated. 'That sounds horrendous.' No wonder Astrid had taken some time out from work and come here to rest and recharge following her bereavement.

'And guess who wrote the piece that put Dad in prison?' Astrid asked. Clare knew better than to interrupt her with a reply. 'It was Vincent. His article about malpractice at Dad's investment bank was complete nonsense – he used gossip and hearsay to make something out of nothing. That pot-stirring led to a long fraud trial, and some creep testified against my dad, while safe behind a screen. As if my dad and his co-defendants were a threat.'

'How awful for you,' Clare sympathised again.

'I'm worried, Clare. If anything really has happened to Vincent, the police might suspect me – once they discover the link with my dad. I can't trust them to get it right – Dad was put behind bars for nothing. What should I do?' Astrid resumed biting at her fingernail, then snatched up a spoon from the table and began twisting it in her hands.

Clare's omelette lay cooling on its plate. She cut into its yellow fatness, taking time to think about how to reply.

'This sounds so difficult,' she murmured, and then delayed her response further by chewing her first mouthful. Then she realised that she could alleviate Astrid's anxieties in one stroke. 'But, as I've said to everyone else, Vincent has only missed one session and it's highly unlikely that he's gone missing. The police are probably working on something else entirely.'

'Like Lucy's sister, again?' Astrid leaned back in her chair and sighed, looking relieved as she considered that possibility. She was no longer twisting the spoon in her hand; now, she tapped her palm with it instead.

'Perhaps, yes.' Clare compromised by half-agreeing and nodding, while also trying to look pensive. She noticed that Jackie got up to leave the dining room, without even glancing in their direction. It would soon be time for Clare to go down to the Leven Room, too, to prepare for the morning session.

Then, she saw Rachel rush past Jackie in the doorway and come straight across to Clare and Astrid's table. Her curly hair bounced as she moved, and she caught her breath before blurting out, 'Clare, they've found a body.'

CHAPTER 31

'My brother works for the council, and the bin-lorry people saw the police cars heading for the cove below the hotel,' Rachel said.

'The cove,' Clare parroted. She sat, stunned.

Astrid's hand had flown to her mouth.

'Now, Gail, our manager, has had a call from that policeman, Nick Faux,' Rachel continued. 'I took it and put him through to her, in her office.'

'But that might mean anything.' Clare was trying to compute all this. 'It's not definitely something as bad as that.'

Astrid was more canny. 'Did you hear more?' she asked.

'It took a moment to put the call through, and her door was open.' Rachel's face bore no trace of embarrassment, and Clare realised that anyone would have delayed coming off the line or would have managed some other way of listening to the call, as presumably Rachel had done. 'It's definitely a body, found on the beach.'

'What did he say about it?' Astrid asked.

'Nothing else,' Rachel said regretfully, as if apologising

that the hotel's private information service had proved unsatisfactory.

'Presumably that will all be kept confidential,' Clare said. She wondered whether she would catch David if she rang him now, or whether he would already be in a morning meeting. She would message him instead, she decided. She wanted him to know this news, even though its implications were unclear. Could this body belong to Vincent, or even Victoria? Or someone else entirely. Perhaps this could even be a false alarm, a dead seal or some waterlogged cargo washed up to shore, which someone had mistaken for a corpse.

Don't be absurd, Clare, she told herself. If the police say it's a body, it's a body. And think about the morning's session. She looked at her watch: twenty minutes to go. She must take care of the group, whatever happened.

Surely, if it was Victoria's remains down there, they would have told Lucy. But, after a year in the water, no identification would be possible, except by dental records or by some process of DNA testing, maybe. Clare was hazy about all that.

'Is everything here carrying on as normal?' she asked Rachel, trying to focus on what needed to be done, given the serious turn of events. 'Or as normal as possible? The beach will be cordoned off, I suppose.'

Before Rachel could reply, Jeremy appeared, seeking Clare out. Rachel hurried away, muttering something about attending to a request for another guest. She seemed anxious to leave before the events manager instructed her to do so or asked why she was in the dining room with Clare.

'We've had to close the main hotel entrance to guests,' he

announced. 'You may have already seen the blackboard re-directing people.'

Was this all that he had to say? It seemed that Jeremy was unaware of the gruesome discovery on the beach below the hotel. Or he was avoiding any mention of it.

'You may find that more guests use the door near the Leven Room,' he continued. 'I do apologise for any disruption this might cause.' He hitched up his trousers as he spoke. 'But these maintenance issues do crop up in a building of this age and size. So, if you could remind guests of the alternative doors to use, Clare, that would be most helpful. Thank you.'

And, with that, he was gone, before Clare or Astrid could ask him anything about what was going on down by the beach.

He passed Gareth, who entered the dining room looking red-faced from exertion, and with damp hair. The athletic young man came over to wish Clare and Astrid good morning and apologised that he might be delayed for the start of the session. He still needed to get breakfast, he explained, as he'd been for a run and lost track of time.

'That's no problem,' Clare said. 'What route did you take?' The question was innocent enough, but Clare thought that Gareth might notice how intent she and Astrid were to hear his answer.

'I went a bit further than I intended, but it was great. I started down the track to the cove, but got turned back,' he said. 'So, I came back up, went past the hotel and on the other way, out to the headland, then dropped down to the harbour and back uphill along the road. I met Dan at the harbour – he'd breakfasted early. It really is a lovely morning.'

'Who turned you back?' Astrid asked. Her face was ashen and Clare knew that the body on the beach was still on her mind.

'That was the odd thing,' Gareth said. 'It was a police officer in full rig blocking the way, and there are two police cars in the hotel car park, too.'

His brow creased as he caught the concerned look on the faces of the two women, and he wiped his hand across his forehead as if to brush away an unpleasant thought.

'You don't think this has something to do with Vincent not being around, do you?' he asked, and then his face drained of colour. As the flush of his earlier exertion disappeared, he also swayed slightly. He gripped the back of Astrid's chair for support.

Clare got up and quickly pulled a chair from an adjoining table towards him. Gareth sat on it, heavily.

'Or is it something to do with Victoria?' he whispered, as Clare helped him to lower his head, to stop him passing out. He groaned. 'Lucy's right, isn't she? Victoria is dead and that bastard Michael did it.'

CHAPTER 32

'What makes you say that?' Clare said. She hadn't realised that Gareth harboured such misgivings about Michael or gave credence to Lucy's views.

'Because, even after he left her, she was never truly free.' Gareth sighed. 'I met her not long before she disappeared and . . . I think Michael hurt her a lot by leaving but never quite letting go, if that makes sense.'

'Do you think they were still in touch?' Clare asked. She wondered, if they had been, how that would have made Pippa feel.

'I don't know,' he admitted. 'Lucy and I talked about all this the other day,' he said. Then, looking at Astrid, he continued, 'You probably heard us, when we were walking down to Kynance.'

Astrid nodded, and he continued to explain.

'Lucy recognised me from a photo with Vic and wanted to know what I was doing here. And what I thought of Michael.'

'What did you say?' Clare asked.

'That Michael was a control freak,' he said simply. 'Although I only knew Vic for a little while, she told me that about him.

We got friendly quickly – it can happen. I think Vicki was ready to move into the future, and that was what coming here was about, too.'

Clare thought how right he was, and how his words resonated with Victoria's journal. It made it even sadder somehow, that Victoria had not been able to have a future with this man, who already seemed to understand quite a lot about her, or with anyone else. Her future had been stolen.

Gareth seemed to want to explain himself further.

'I knew Vic had holidayed here, and I wanted to see where she'd been – although, looking back, we knew each other for such a short time. Perhaps I never knew her that well.'

'Who knows anyone, really?' Astrid was abrupt. 'Thomas Hardy mourned some kind of fantasy about his wife, not a real woman.' Then, she leaned more sympathetically towards Gareth and put her hand on his arm. 'I'm sorry. Of course you knew Victoria. This morning must be a real shock.'

'Yes, things are very difficult,' Clare added. 'Would you like to stay here a while, Gareth, and eat some breakfast?'

Gareth nodded and, as if out of thin air, a young waiter approached, ready to take his order. As Clare and Gareth sat together, Astrid went to collect some cereal, returning quickly to place one bowl of chopped fruit and another of Weetabix in front of Gareth.

Rachel returned to the dining room, carrying a clipboard and looking more composed. Her hair was tied back and she had donned a jacket with the hotel logo embroidered on its breast pocket. She might have been welcoming passengers on to a cruise liner, Clare thought. How different she looked from the horsewoman in jeans and wellies escorting rides from the local stables, allowing Tom to canter across a field and watching Anna rocket off on a high-spirited mount.

'Clare, sorry to interrupt,' she said. 'Just to let you know, Melanie has arrived, and I've taken her down to the Leven Room – the way through reception is still closed off.'

'Melanie?' Clare was confused, then appalled. 'Yes – sorry, Rachel – of course. She's taking the morning session with me, isn't she? It had slipped my mind.'

Can't think why, with journals being discovered, DCI Faux prowling about, guests at each other's throats and a body on the beach. If Clare wasn't so overwhelmed, she would laugh.

'I'll come straight down.' Clare stood quickly and her napkin fell from her lap to the floor.

Astrid and Gareth looked at her quizzically.

'Who's Melanie?' asked Astrid.

'Melanie will be hosting our breathing and relaxation session this morning,' Clare explained. 'She ran the retreat last year and it's great to have her back, if only just for one session.'

'Sounds like good timing,' Astrid said, and Gareth concurred with a nod, his mouth full of breakfast.

Clare thought she needed more than an extra dose of breathing to handle the day. She left them together, hoping that Astrid might join Gareth in eating something. Clare prayed for them and for the whole group as she followed Rachel along the corridor towards the staircase down to the meeting room, as well as praying for whoever might be on that beach. Selfishly, she hoped that unfortunate person had nothing to do with the retreat participants.

As they walked, Clare asked Rachel whether everyone had now made it down to breakfast, and tried to stop herself becoming agitated at the news that neither Pippa nor Vincent had yet done so. On the staircase, she was hugely relieved to meet Pippa hurrying up towards them. She was breathless, and her clothing looked slightly damp, as if she had been outside on an excursion. Her more stylish outfits had been replaced by simple black trousers and a black, long-sleeved shirt. She looked almost funereal.

'Morning, Clare!' Pippa said brightly, belying her sombre clothing and smiling vaguely at Rachel, as if unsure of the receptionist's name. 'How are you today?'

Saying that she felt relieved that Pippa wasn't dead didn't seem like the best response, so Clare mumbled something about how she was fine, thanks.

'I'll be down to rejoin everyone in just a minute,' Pippa continued. 'It's so nice that we're having breathwork to start the day! I just met Melanie and introduced myself.'

'Great!' Clare responded cheerfully as they passed one another, mindful of the need to greet Melanie herself. Now, it was only Vincent who was missing – and, according to Nadiya, he had been absent from his room on a previous night, so Clare told herself there was no undue cause for alarm.

But there was a body on the beach. And Clare felt sick at the thought of it.

CHAPTER 33

As she followed Rachel into the Leven Room, Clare was disconcerted to find that the circle of chairs was no more. Instead, blue yoga mats had been laid out in rows across the floor, and a woman in a startling shade of lime-green Lycra sat cross-legged in the midst of them. She had a cloud of snowy white hair, bronzed skin and large earrings shaped like the tree of life.

Rachel made the introductions. Melanie stood up in one fluid motion and clasped Clare's hand between both of her own.

'Thank you so much, Clare, for carrying this retreat. I'm sorry not to have been able to do more, this year.'

'It's been a pleasure,' Clare lied, then added, more truthfully, 'I love being here, and it's good to be with Rachel, too.'

Melanie was perceptive and didn't mess about. 'You're being upbeat, Clare. Last year was traumatic enough for me, and Rachel has told me some of what you've been coping with here.' Her words found their way beneath any veneer, and her unusually pale grey eyes looked intently into Clare's own.

'Yes, it's certainly been full of surprises,' Clare said, being as diplomatic as possible, aware that others would soon be joining them and could be within earshot.

Sure enough, the door from outside opened and Michael walked in.

'This is Melanie – she'll be leading us this morning,' Clare said.

'Hi, Melanie. Good to meet you.' Then Michael wrong-footed Clare by asking, 'Did you meet Victoria here, last year?'

His manner was terse to the point of rudeness, but Melanie didn't seem to mind, simply explaining that, yes, she'd had the pleasure of doing so, and that she was grateful to Clare for taking the bulk of the sessions this year. She added that she'd been told by a friend what a great job Clare did leading 'Quiet Days' in Kent, and other retreats.

Clare found the fulsomeness of this praise a bit much, but she coped with it. At her ordination beneath the dome of St Paul's Cathedral, the preacher had told the ordinands that, once they wore those clerical collars, some people would see them as the Archangel Gabriel, while others would regard them as the Breath of Satan. Reassuringly, he reminded them that they were neither, but they would have to manage views of both extremes.

However weird people's opinions of her might be, Clare understood that she could just be Clare, known by God. She could be Clare, who found Dan irritating at times, as she did in that very moment as he walked into the room, sniffing disparagingly at the mats and eyeing Melanie with suspicion. She knew she needed to make more of an effort with her attitude towards him. As she tried to be more generous, she noticed how he turned and welcomed Gareth pleasantly.

Gareth was still looking dishevelled and ill at ease. Astrid followed behind him and seemed content to relinquish her support role when Dan approached, leaving him to engage Gareth in conversation.

Rachel excused herself just as Jackie arrived. Clare suspected the DCI had timed her entrance to minimise the possibility of anything more than casual greetings before the session began. Not long after, Lucy walked in, coming from the foyer area at the foot of the stairs. She kept her head lowered, and Clare noticed that she and Pippa seemed to have established some degree of a truce. When Pippa settled on a mat adjacent to Lucy's, there were no greetings, but no evident animosity or friction either.

No one mentioned Vincent's absence, as if Melanie's presence allowed them to ignore anything which might disturb the peaceful ambiance of the room. As the session began, Clare made her escape discreetly, leaving everyone in Melanie's capable hands. She wanted to take the time to learn whatever she could about the police activity down at the beach, and to ascertain what DCI Faux and his team were doing with regard to Victoria's journal. Would they discover who had placed it in the lost-property hamper?

Clare also longed to speak to David. She hurried upstairs, eager to reach her room and to phone him in private. As she reached the corridor, she was forestalled by a bleep from her phone, signalling that a message from him had just arrived:

Hi! Change of plan. Have pulled Anna and Tom from school and we're heading down today, not leaving you with Heathcliff any longer, nor with the possibility of bodies turning up at the Morva. Sorry not to ask, was afraid you'd say no. Have spoken to reception – they can put a couple of fold-up beds in your room for Anna and Tom, and I get to share your bed – cosy. They're even offering dog treats for Mia. Love you. Take care.

He was right, she would have said no. She didn't want Anna or Tom anywhere near bodies on a beach, however enthusiastic they might be for a longer Cornwall stay, with more sandcastle building and horse riding – not to mention cream teas. But David would be here and they would care for the children together – and the dog.

The thought of Mia snuffling around the retreatants as they relaxed on their blue mats with Melanie was a disturbing one, but less worrying than the thoughts Clare had of what might be happening down on the beach this morning. And where exactly was Vincent? The longer he was gone, the more Clare began to worry that Lucy was right and he had gone missing. Maybe she could track Nadiya down and ask if she knew anything more about where he might be. Clare shook her head to clear away her anxiety – hopefully, the journalist was off somewhere writing a story that had nothing to do with the retreat this year.

She would go to her room; she needed the loo and she would get things ready before her gang arrived. Clare smiled. The news that her family would be with her before the day's end put a spring in her step. Even the prospect of David seeing his ex, DCI Jackie Carter, didn't dampen her spirits. Clare's family were coming, and she would be hugging them soon.

CHAPTER 34

Where was Clare sloping off to? Earlier, Jackie had seen her locked in intense conversation with Astrid, in the dining room. There was a restlessness in the group, despite Melanie's soothing voice explaining the merits of relaxing muscle groups and visualising scenes of contentment and calm. Lying on her back, with her knees raised and loosely bent, as instructed, Jackie felt far from any meditative state. The police team was working on the area where the journal had been found, but that didn't explain the degree of police activity she'd seen outside, with officers walking across the lawn in front of the hotel and presumably heading down the track to the cove.

Sunlight was pouring into the room and Lucy asked if the blinds could be lowered on some of the windows. While Melanie adjusted them, Jackie rolled on to her side and quietly asked Astrid, lying on the adjacent mat, what she thought was happening, and where Clare had gone.

Jackie was not used to playing catch-up when it came to a police enquiry. She thought Astrid might have something to say about the journal discovery, but was not expecting much more.

'They found something on the beach,' Astrid whispered,

then jerked her head towards Lucy and put her finger to her lips meaningfully.

Jackie wanted to ask a follow-up, but Astrid had closed her eyes. The conversation was over, as far as she was concerned, and she was probably right to be wary of disturbing Lucy.

Melanie and Dan were still discussing the precise degree of shadow needed in order to minimise glare while still allowing the morning sun to brighten the room, and the blinds were being raised and lowered accordingly.

Jackie slid her feet back into the shoes she had left neatly beside her mat and left, as inconspicuously as she could. She went out through the French doors in the foyer beyond the Leven Room and on to the lower terrace, hastening across the lawn and down the track to the beach. The sun was warm on her face. Seeing a uniformed officer standing on guard in the middle of the track, she punched some numbers into her phone and held it to her ear. Simultaneously, she found her police ID to show him, aiming to look as businesslike as possible, despite her relaxed clothing.

'DCI Carter here, please hold,' she said into her mobile as she walked. 'I'm on my way to meet him now.' She spoke crisply, even though no call had been made.

The community officer looked at her respectfully as she waved her ID towards him, hardly breaking stride as she approached.

'Morning,' she said. 'I'm joining DCI Faux. Is he still at the scene? He asked me to meet him down there.' It was a punt, using Nick Faux's name, but she was confident that he would be involved. Best to keep the momentum up.

Sure enough, the officer wanted to be helpful. 'Yes, but I don't think anyone else is supposed to go down. But, if he's expecting you, I think that will be OK. Let me just check.'

Before the obliging young man could do so, he was interrupted by the arrival of said DCI Faux, who came up the track from the beach, stopped beside him and regarded Jackie with raised eyebrows.

'Sir, DCI Carter was about to join you,' the uniformed officer said, suddenly seeming nervous in his presence, and obviously unsure why.

'So I see,' his superior replied. 'Perhaps we can have a conversation here instead, DCI Carter.'

'Thank you.' She was deferential, hoping that he would overlook her attempt to bluff her way on to the scene.

As one, the two senior officers moved off together. Jackie retraced her steps back towards the hotel, and Nick Faux kept pace with her, pausing once they were out of earshot of the community officer.

'What brings you here, this morning?' he asked, impassively.

'I gather a body's been found,' Jackie bluffed. Judging by the flash of Nick Faux's eyes in response to her words, she was on to something. She pressed on: 'Given the activity, I wondered if it might be Victoria. It's too odd, her journal suddenly reappearing now – it feels like a set-up.'

'There are several things which seem very odd to me,' Nick Faux said, apparently choosing his words with care, and looking at Jackie appraisingly as he did so.

Jackie looked down at the ground, examining the tufts of grass which bordered the path. There were tiny flowers amongst them, and a butterfly flew up and then settled again, a little further away, behind where Nick Faux stood. He was waiting to hear what else she had to say.

'Victoria was a friend of mine, you know that. Is there a possibility that you have found her?' Better to be honest, open. Nick Faux might be police, Jackie thought, but he was human, too. Surely he would understand why she was so interested in finding out what had happened to her friend? She had to ask, even if Nick Faux declined to tell her anything.

'It would be inappropriate to comment in any way, as you know,' he said, repressively.

Jackie narrowed her eyes at him and swallowed away any reaction, determined to show no emotion, despite her feeling of dismay. 'OK, I get it.' She shrugged. 'I would play it the same way.' Better to be conciliatory.

Perhaps it was her acquiescence that prompted the DCI to continue: 'We've not found the remains of a female,' he said, 'and I cannot confirm or deny that we have found any remains at all, at this stage of an investigation. I don't need to explain the protocols of a murder enquiry to you, of course.'

'Thank you.' She knew that he'd been generous in telling her as much as he had.

'I'd ask you to draw no further conclusions from what I've said, nor to repeat my comment that we've not found the remains of a female. In fact, I would prefer to continue on the basis that this conversation never took place.' He looked out towards the sea, as if mesmerised by the view.

'I understand. Is there any assistance I can offer?'

'At this point, no. But any information you might have

regarding the hotel's guests and staff may become relevant, and accurate timings of their whereabouts and activities over the last day or two, as well. You'll want to make some notes, while your recollections are still fresh.'

Was Nick Faux asking for her input in a murder enquiry? Jackie was surprised. He had been abrasive when they met the previous evening. Justifiably so, given Jackie's unauthorised involvement in his missing person's case. She had been candid with him about her trip to the pubs and bars of the area, and her scouting of possible handover points, but he had given no credence to the theory that Victoria might have stumbled across some drug-running activity. Jackie supposed he was wary of outsiders making clichéd assumptions about his patch and what happened there.

'One hotel guest, a journalist named Vincent Hyde, hasn't been seen since yesterday evening, I understand,' Jackie said. 'Some of the hotel guests are concerned about him. He said he would see them at last night's Epilogue, but didn't attend. He's on the retreat'.

'I see. Had you much contact with him?'

Jackie faltered at this. Should she reveal that she had been worried Vincent would write about the retreat and reveal that she had been trespassing on a case?

Jackie thought she'd better not appear to withhold any relevant information. Even if she risked giving the impression she had reason to dislike Vincent, that was better than the investigation team discovering she had actively concealed that fact. Clare would no doubt see it as her duty to tell them, anyway – and perhaps it was Jackie's duty to do likewise.

'Not much,' she said honestly. 'But he was a journalist who did in-depth features about unsolved crimes and their impact. He said his wife had booked him on this retreat, but he was asking a lot of questions. I worried that he would write something about the retreat – and include me in it – and turn Victoria's disappearance into a salacious story.'

Jackie found herself slipping into the past tense as she spoke. She couldn't help herself – now she knew there really *was* a body on the beach, and it wasn't Victoria, she assumed it was Vincent. If Nick Faux noticed, he didn't comment on it, nor did he correct her.

'I see,' he said, and continued up the path.

Before they reached the gate to the hotel garden, they met a trio of his officers heading down towards them. Evidently, it was time for Jackie to remove herself. Nick Faux thanked her, somewhat cursorily, as she did so, and didn't introduce her to his team.

She would go and make as detailed a timeline as she could remember of everyone's whereabouts over the previous two days, and note any interactions she had observed between Vincent and others. She also needed to contact her boss; she had some explaining to do about the use to which she had put her holiday entitlement. He might sympathise with her concern for her missing friend, but intruding on another force's patch and getting involved in their case was reprehensible, with no exceptions. She had been skating on thin ice, and now it was well and truly cracked.

As she closed the gate to the hotel garden behind her, Jackie planned a careful route back to the upper terrace. She would enter the building at that level, avoiding any contact with the group members who were, she presumed, continuing to breathe under Melanie's tutelage in the Leven Room. As she reached the glass doors into the large lounge and bar, though, Clare came into view. She rose quickly from a rattan seat as Jackie approached. It looked as if the vicar had been waiting and watching for her.

'Jackie,' Clare said, 'I'm sorry, but there have been some developments. Can we sit for a moment?'

Sympathy from Clare was the last thing Jackie wanted. She'd probably suggest they pray or breathe.

'OK.' Jackie's voice sounded as testy as she felt; she really didn't need this. But she was curious to know what Clare had been up to. She sat, and Clare wasted no time.

'Astrid talked about her family and Vincent earlier, and I think you should know about it. Also, one of the hotel team told me about a call DCI Faux made to the hotel manager. I think you may already know what that might have been about?'

Jackie had to hand it to the vicar – she wasn't slow on the uptake. But no way would Jackie tell her what DCI Faux had implied about their discovery. Jackie was a police officer, and there had to be loyalty amongst colleagues.

'Tell me about it,' she said, all signs of irritation gone and her face now masked with professional impassivity. They might not be a team, but there was no need for Clare to know that. Jackie would keep her cards close to her chest. She had her own position, and future career, to consider.

CHAPTER 35

Clare saw that Jackie had her detective face on – inscrutable yet alert. The DCI made no meaningful comment as Clare unpacked everything she'd learned since they last spoke, from Astrid's resentment of Vincent to the report of an unnamed body on the beach.

The DCI was unforthcoming about her own activities. Clare thought she'd probably left the Leven Room to go down to the beach, but she was wary of asking her directly about it. She posed some more general questions, instead.

'What do you make of things? Lucy's very anxious about Vincent going missing. Do you think he might have had an accident, down at the cove?'

'It's possible,' Jackie said slowly, and added nothing more.

Clare ploughed on: 'Supposing something has happened to Vincent, it could be connected to Victoria's disappearance. He's an investigative journalist, and he's been asking questions. He could be a threat to someone who harmed her.'

'It's possible,' Jackie repeated. 'But, as you learned from Astrid, other people may have reason to resent or fear his work. And, increasingly, journalists are at risk for simply doing their job.'

'Vincent didn't handle big international stories – he hadn't riled Putin, or another monster, or not as far as we know. But maybe he'd recognised someone, or agreed to meet a source? He skipped yesterday evening's session; he could have been following up some kind of lead.' Clare was counting the possibilities on her fingers, letting her imagination run wild.

Nadiya came into the spacious room and began wiping the tables closest to the big curving window. It gave a magnificent view of the sun shining brightly on to the sparkling sea. Clare noticed how she looked up nervously as Jeremy approached and began to descend the wooden steps from the bar area down to their level.

'Hello, Clare – I've been meaning to find you.' Jeremy sounded unusually formal, and his shirt was more muted, too: navy, with a pale blue stripe. 'I heard about your family arriving today. Arrangements are all in place and extra beds have been made up in your room.'

'Thank you, that's great.' Clare avoided catching Jackie's eye. There had been no need for her to tell Jackie anything about David arriving early – it was no concern of hers – but Clare still felt awkward about not having done so. Wanting to change the topic of conversation, she asked Jeremy about plans for the day and whether he would still be available with the minibus for the afternoon excursion to Cadgwith and Trelissick, as scheduled.

'No reason why not,' he answered more cheerily.

Clare thought darkly about the body on the beach, but held her tongue to avoid dampening his enthusiasm.

'After the buffet lunch, I'll be ready to chauffeur whoever would like to come,' he said.

'That's good. I'm going back down to the Leven Room, so I'll remind everyone about it and let them know about today's beach closure. Thanks, Jeremy.'

'I'll take my own car, if I go,' Jackie said.

Clare suspected the DCI wanted to be on hand for any further developments at the Morva, or to be able to return quickly, just as Clare did.

'No sign of Vincent yet, Jeremy?' Clare asked hopefully.

'Not that I'm aware,' Jeremy replied evenly. He flicked a glance up towards Nadiya, who was now sweeping the floor of the bar area above them with an old-fashioned broom.

'How odd,' Clare said. 'I've been meaning to ask . . . I remember, on our first evening, Vincent was talking to you in the dining room for quite a while; I wondered if you knew him at all?'

'Hardly – we have so many guests, here,' Jeremy answered. He clasped his hands together and twisted them. He seemed anxious, Clare thought. She was sure Jackie would notice his unease, too.

'I thought Vincent knew you, too,' Jackie chimed in.

'Well, I think Vincent was fond of Cornwall and he had visited us several times before,' Jeremy now said airily. 'I think he asked about the history of the hotel, how it has been developed and so forth.'

'Does he have friends in the area?' Clare asked. 'He must do, to want to come back so many times.'

'I've no idea. Possibly.'

At that moment, the sound of glass crashing came down from above.

'So sorry!' Nadiya called. 'I dropped a tray – so sorry to disturb.'

'No problem. Let me help you sort it, Nadiya.' Jeremy bustled off, without replying to Jackie or even bidding Clare farewell.

Was his concern primarily to help with the clear-up, or was this a convenient way to avoid any further conversation about his contact with the journalist? At the Kynance café, Vincent had asked about Jeremy's age and other particulars. Clare had thought it was intrusive then. Now, she believed that Vincent might well have known, or hinted that he knew, something about Jeremy, and it seemed that Jackie was exploring that possibility, too.

There was no time to confer with Jackie about it, even if she'd wanted to. No time to discuss whether Nadiya's timely intervention had been deliberate, either. Clare needed to get back to the group downstairs before they dispersed. She hoped that Melanie's breathwork had provided some deep relaxation and refreshment. They were going to need it.

CHAPTER 36

Rachel was waiting outside the Leven Room, still wearing her jacket with its hotel logo. As Clare joined her, they were both aware of the murmur of Melanie's soothing voice beyond the closed door. It seemed that the session was likely to overrun.

Rachel smiled conspiratorially, and, in those snatched moments together, she seemed more like the riding-stable friend of old than the formal Morva Hotel representative.

'How are you doing?' she whispered. 'It's madness, here. I'm glad your gang are coming today.'

News must travel fast amongst the hotel team, Clare thought.

'I'm OK, can't wait to see them, but this is grim. What do you think about the discovery? Is it who I think it is?' Clare wasn't sure why she avoided using Vincent's name.

'We'll know soon enough; they've taken Gail down to identify him. The boss.'

'Had she met him?' Clare herself still hadn't set eyes on the elusive hotel manager, so wondered how it was that Vincent would have known her.

'They go back a long way, I think.' Rachel raised her

eyebrows at Clare, as if to imply a deeper meaning. 'Gail worked in London before here. They were mates.'

Clare suddenly wondered about Vincent's whereabouts on those nights he hadn't slept in his own bed. Vincent was married, she thought, but had he been coming here to visit Gail? Perhaps he and Gail might have had a closer relationship than she'd imagined.

'Jeremy sent me down here,' Rachel continued, 'in case he couldn't find you. But, as you're here, you can tell everyone about the beach being closed off – I don't need to.'

'Sure.' Clare nodded, trying to think what else she could ask Rachel while she had the chance. 'Are Nadiya and Jeremy close?' She was still wondering about that conveniently timed breakage.

'I don't know.' Rachel looked at the floor, her demeanour evasive.

Clare aimed for easier territory: 'I guess everyone here just gets on with one another as best as possible. You mentioned that there was something funny about Lucy on that first day, didn't you? Having someone else go missing must be horrible for her. It's awful.'

'Horrible,' Rachel echoed. 'But . . . well, I'm sorry for her, but she's not our favourite guest at the hotel, let's just say.'

'What do you mean?' Clare said, hoping that Melanie would keep the session going long enough to allow Rachel to spill the beans.

'Last year, Lucy racked up a huge bill.' Rachel bit her lip.

Clare guessed she wasn't supposed to be sharing confidential information like this, but the receptionist continued, lowering her voice.

'She stayed on, because of her sister going missing, so she ended up with a mega bill. There were emails about it, lots of them. At first, management was pretty understanding. It was a real tragedy, you know? But they could only go so long without the money before it became a problem. And then, he paid her bill – Michael, that is,' Rachel finished.

Before Clare could voice her surprise, the door to the Leven Room opened and Lucy herself emerged.

'Clare, what's happened?' she asked, looking anxiously from Clare to Rachel and back again. 'Has Vincent been found?'

'I think everything's fine, Lucy,' Clare lied, deciding she really must get out of this habit of offering false reassurance. 'I just need to let the whole group know a couple of things. I hope you all enjoyed the breathwork – I'm sorry to have missed it.'

She entered the room, Lucy following in her wake. Gareth still lay supine on his mat, and Astrid sat cross-legged beside him. Dan was helping Melanie to roll up the other mats and stack them in the far corner of the room. There was no sign of Michael or Pippa. Had they left early? Perhaps they'd gone out through the door to the garden.

'Hi, everyone,' Clare said. 'I hope you've had a lovely session. Just to remind you, Jeremy is taking the minibus to Cadgwith after our buffet lunch, and then on to see the gardens at Trelissick this afternoon – and I thoroughly recommend both.' Clare sounded like a tour guide on a coach excursion. She'd be pointing out the best views to photograph or promoting an exclusive retail experience next.

'I've been asked to mention that we need to use alternative exits and not go through the hotel reception today, please,' she added. 'And, just for today, we've been asked not to go down to the cove below the hotel – but, of course, there is the coastal walk in the other direction, and the path down to the harbour, which you can explore that way.'

Perhaps if I keep talking, I won't need to explain why, Clare thought.

'I think you went down there this morning, Dan? And Gareth?' She looked over to Dan, usually so reliably upbeat, but it was Lucy who spoke, gesticulating at her phone.

'They're saying that a body has been discovered, Clare. Is that true?'

She looked aghast, and Gareth sat up abruptly, as if sprung from a jack-in-the-box. Astrid placed her hand on his arm.

'I'm not sure exactly what the situation is,' Clare responded, and that much was true. 'I'm very sorry not to have more to tell you.'

'It's not your fault, Clare, but this is horrific, all the same.' Lucy was surprisingly calm, standing stock still and holding her phone out for others to see.

Melanie approached her and put a gentle arm around her shoulders. Lucy now leaned towards her, turning her face away from Clare and burying it into Melanie's embrace.

'That's terrible,' Dan said, still stooping over the pile of mats, which he'd been straightening. 'Is there anything we can do?'

'Perhaps us all getting out of the way and off to Trelissick Garden this afternoon would be best,' Gareth suggested.

Clare fervently agreed with him and hoped the others would follow suit.

'I want to get away from here.' Astrid sounded close to tears. 'This is awful.'

Gareth placed his hand on top of hers, which still rested on his arm. 'We can take care of one another,' he said. 'It will all be OK.'

I guess it depends on your definition of 'OK', Clare thought.

'Thanks, everyone,' she said. 'I think we have to take things step by step, and care for one another, as you say. This is shocking news, if it's true. I am very sorry about this. We've got an hour or so to ourselves before lunch is served, and I'm around if anyone would like a chat, although I'm sorry not to have any more information for you.'

'I'd like to catch a word with you, if that's OK,' Melanie said, while smoothing Lucy's hair with her hand, 'when you're free.'

'I think I'll head up to my room.' Lucy raised her head and sighed. Exhaustion was etched on her face, and she seemed to have aged, even during the last few moments. 'I think some time alone would be best. This could mean bad news. I'll need to contact my family.'

Clare's heart ached for her. What a nightmare, to have to relive some of the pain, still unresolved, from a year ago.

'You'll need to tell Michael, or someone will,' Lucy added, and Clare thought it was generous that she had thought of him. But maybe they were closer than she realised – according to Rachel, he had settled her bill last year, after all.

'And Jackie, and Pippa,' Dan added. 'I can go and look for them, if you like.' He looked shaken, but resolute about doing what he could to help.

Astrid had crouched down, half curling herself into a ball, as if hugging herself for comfort. Gareth stayed beside her.

Clare was grateful for the mutual care within the group. She stood quietly, observing each of them and trying to work out how best to manage the situation and to offer support.

It had seemed odd, the archdeacon being so enthusiastic at the prospect of Clare taking a luxurious retreat in another diocese, and encouraging her to do so. Maybe he had a hotline to the Almighty and Clare was supposed to be here as events unfolded, even if she felt she had little to offer.

She needed to build bridges with Jackie. Together, they might be useful. They had to move beyond rivalries or resentments and work constructively with one another. The sooner things were resolved about whatever or whoever was on the beach, the better. Clare wished that could happen before her family arrived.

Why had David decided to bring the children here? She'd see if he could take them directly to their self-catering place instead; perhaps it hadn't been booked by anyone else this week. The Morva Hotel held too many tensions and uncertainties – and the possibility of violence, too. She wanted Anna and Tom kept well away. She'd like to leave herself, but her place was here, with the group. Clare would do whatever must be done.

CHAPTER 37

After the group scattered, Melanie poured fresh glasses of water, handed one to Clare and then drank deeply from the other herself.

'That's better,' she gasped, and drank again.

'Thanks for this morning,' Clare said. 'It made all the difference, you being here.'

'Shall we go outside?' Melanie suggested. 'I feel like some air would be good.'

She led the way, gathering up her large bag and holding the door to the garden open, then heading purposefully round the side of the hotel and up towards the spa building, on the far side of the car park.

'We can be more private here,' she said, and led Clare on past the spa and down some slate steps to a small, sheltered terrace, where half a dozen sturdy chairs were grouped around a wooden table. The spot was a suntrap; Clare could feel the heat from the slate tiles warming the air surrounding them.

'How are you coping?' Melanie asked, and Clare was grateful that she was taking the initiative in their conversation.

'Could be better.' She smiled, wryly. 'But you know about troubled events here, all too well.'

'That's why I didn't want to take any responsibility this year.' Melanie placed her hefty bag on the table and sat down beside it. 'I made more of my scheduling issues than was strictly the case, simply to minimise my involvement. I was grateful to you for stepping up to facilitate.'

'That's OK,' Clare said, thinking that it wasn't. Her children were about to arrive in this mess, thanks to Melanie, and others. 'Thanks for supporting Lucy just now.'

'Her grief is complicated, of course, with no closure about what happened to Victoria – and I imagine she's unhappy about how things were between them.'

'In what way?'

'I felt there were some sisterly tensions, shall we say – something of an argument, perhaps – but there's nothing so unusual about that. I wanted to talk to you about something else, if I may. The thing is, I feel uncomfortable about certain aspects of this place.' Melanie indicated the seat opposite as she spoke, and Clare sat down, wanting to know more, and felt comforted by the warmth of the wooden chair.

Melanie squinted slightly and brushed her hand across her face. 'Jeremy is a bit much, isn't he, and Gail keeps herself very much to herself. The reception team keep the show on the road, here, really.'

'Right,' Clare agreed. She'd never seen Gail, so that analysis rang true.

'I think some staff here may have a sideline operation in

place, and I wanted to alert you to that.' Melanie extracted some sunglasses from her bag and put them on.

'Right,' Clare repeated, while still having no clue what Melanie might be suggesting.

'Just a thought, and I wouldn't want to be quoted on this, Clare, but it could have a bearing on things.' The sunglasses added a sense of mystery to this conversation.

'A sideline of what sort, Melanie?' Clare needed more than this vague hint.

'Supply and demand, let's put it that way.'

'OK. Are we talking fishing trips? Raves? Horse riding and kayaking?'

'Not raves, Clare, but you're closest with that.' Melanie smiled gently as she realised how lost Clare was. 'We have as big an issue with drugs here as anywhere does, and I think some of your group may have been taking advantage of what's on offer,' she said frankly.

'What?' Clare was amazed; Melanie had spent ninety minutes breathing with them and had reached that conclusion. 'Who?'

'The young woman who left before you came back in – she seemed likely to have used something this morning, I thought. But I'm not sure, Clare. Don't get me wrong.'

'Pippa.'

'The one wearing black, and her breathing was faster than it should be. Her eyes didn't look great, either. She needed quite a bit of water, and took herself off, after Michael did.'

'I see,' Clare said. She nodded and licked her lips, not sure what to do with this information. 'Well, thank you for telling me. And having you here today was a wonderful help to Lucy,' she repeated.

'I wish I could have done more. I still feel very sad about Victoria myself. That was another reason I opted out of leading this year.'

'What was she like?' Clare had a stronger idea about Victoria's personality since reading her journal, and wanted to know Melanie's impression of her, too.

'Alive,' Melanie said, speaking with certainty. 'Victoria was very much alive, I'd say, and eager for life. That's part of the sadness for me – that a woman like that could just disappear. She was vibrant, ready for new things.'

'Yes, I've had that sense about her, too,' Clare said, being careful not to mention the journal.

She spread her hands out on the table, watching the shadows they formed. Glancing to the side, she could see the wisps of plants emerging from between the slates which surrounded them; several had delicate purple flowers.

'What did you think of the police investigation?' she asked, squinting at Melanie, the sun in her eyes.

'I guess it was thorough enough. I was interviewed, of course, but there wasn't a lot to say.' Melanie shrugged dismissively.

'Did Victoria seem close to any other retreat participants? Apart from Lucy.'

'Not particularly. Oddly, it's members of this year's group that seem to have been more connected with her.'

'Yes.' Clare sat, thinking there was nothing helpful to say. What were the odds that all these people in Victoria's life would be brought here, to the retreat? She felt increasingly certain that someone had engineered their attendance, or at least encouraged it.

'I should be going.' Melanie reached for her bag.

'Before you do –' Clare had to be direct, and needed to summon her courage to pursue this – 'is there anything else you can tell me about the sideline, here? Are there particular individuals who you think might be involved?'

Melanie pursed her lips. 'I can't say, Clare. People often have multiple jobs and contacts, connections with local bars and all the rest of it. I keep well out of it all; I don't want to be involved.'

'Sure, but could Victoria have got herself into something dangerous? Inadvertently?'

'I think that's incredibly unlikely. Much more probable that she had some kind of accident, some kind of bizarre mishap. The sea is dangerous, Clare, and the cliff walks around here, too.'

'You sound like my husband.'

At that, Melanie laughed. 'Well, I must be on my way; I have a regular class in Helston starting soon.'

'I hope it goes well,' Clare said automatically, as Melanie left. 'Thanks for the chat.'

Melanie looked relieved to be going, and Clare didn't blame her.

CHAPTER 38

Clare regretted not having her sunglasses with her, as the strength of the day's glare was forceful, even if its heat was welcome. She closed her eyes and basked in it for a while. She knew she mustn't linger for long, but even a few minutes refreshed her.

As she walked round to the front of the spa, she met Pippa, still in dark clothes and wearing wraparound shades, heading across the car park towards her.

Encountering her so unexpectedly, Clare just greeted her with a startled, 'Hi, Pippa,' before asking how she was doing, and how her day was going. It was certainly inappropriate to enquire whether Pippa had dosed herself with any illegal substances recently.

'It's all a bit strange, today,' Pippa said, reasonably enough.

'Yes, perhaps you have already heard that we've been asked not to go to the cove, but we can still walk the coast path in the other direction – that's no problem,' Clare explained, not wanting to say more.

'Dan just told me, thanks – but I thought I'd try the indoor pool today, and I'm going to have a sauna, too.' Pippa patted the beach bag which hung over her shoulder, and from which a rolled-up towel protruded. Perhaps she had another change of outfit in there, too. Her dark hair looked sleek: she had tied it into a ponytail, and it glistened as if slightly oiled. Presumably Dan had also told her about the police activity and discovery, but Pippa showed no sign of this.

'Did you go down to the beach earlier?' Clare asked. 'I thought perhaps you'd been that way this morning.'

'Why?' Pippa's voice was sharp. Then she paused, as if remembering her encounter with Clare and Rachel on the stairs, when Clare was hurrying down to meet Melanie. 'Oh, yes, I met you when I came back inside, and you're right, I did have a stroll that way, and also along in the other direction; it's a lovely day.'

'I don't suppose you've seen Vincent at all? I know Lucy is concerned that he's not been around since yesterday.' Clare thought she would push a bit.

'No. Why should I have done?' Pippa's testiness returned. 'Lucy seems rather overdramatic to me, to be honest. I'm sorry, Clare; I just want to relax; unless you need something from me, I'd like to get going.'

'Sure – I didn't mean to hold you up,' Clare said, chastened.

Perhaps Pippa was being too dismissive, she thought, but it was understandable, given the tension between the two women. Lucy was no fan of Pippa, that was for sure. And, if Clare considered things from Pippa's point of view, Michael had broken up with her as a result of Victoria going missing, so his maudlin fixation on her memory must be irksome, at the very least.

'Jeremy is heading to Cadgwith and then on to Trelissick with the minibus, this afternoon,' Clare said, hoping to smooth things a bit. 'The gardens there are lovely, and there's a second-hand bookshop, craft gallery and café, too.' Perhaps she'd be able to apply for tourism-guide accreditation after this, Clare thought. She wanted to keep the conversation going, but on more neutral territory. But Pippa bristled even further, pursing her lips. Why was she so short-fused today? Perhaps Melanie was right and she had taken something.

'I'm not very interested in Trelissick, Clare, and I'd prefer to avoid additional time with Michael, too. You're aware that there is history between us, and I'm moving on from that, now.'

Clare presumed that Pippa had no idea she was echoing the sentiments which Victoria had expressed in her journal.

'Well, having space to be refreshed and to move forward is part of what this retreat is about – so, good for you, Pippa,' she said, hoping that this complex woman would somehow still find it a helpful time.

Clare continued on round to the side of the hotel building, ready to go back inside through the garden doors. As she neared the tables and chairs on the terrace, her phone pinged. She had a missed call and a voicemail. She tapped 121 to access the message and listened to her children's voices excitedly telling her that their dad was giving them two days extra holiday, and that they were already past Stonehenge on the A303 and would be stopping for lunch soon.

'I think I forgot my wash bag, but Dad says it's no problem,' Tom declared. 'Dad forgot to bring a poo bag when we stopped to walk Mia. I guarded the poo while Anna held Mia, and Dad went and got a poo bag from the car.'

Clare smiled at the thought of Tom standing over a pile of dog crap, protectively.

She heard Anna's voice: 'Tom, give me the phone.' Some indistinct sounds ensued, then Anna's voice continued, more clearly: 'Dad says the cottage is free, so we can stay there instead of with you tonight and tomorrow, but Tom and I want to have hotel breakfast, please, Mum. And to see you, as well.' This enthusiasm to be with her was quickly added, and Clare suspected a prompt from David to that effect. 'Do they have vegetarian sausages? Tom wants hash browns. We had a crazy early breakfast this morning, and there was a big fox crossing the High Street when we left.'

'We're listening to *The Hunger Games*,' Tom called from the background. 'Dad says the book is better, and so does Anna, but I like the film.'

'That's because you haven't read it,' Anna retorted, and an all too familiar dispute about the merits of films versus books began between the siblings.

Clare heard David intervene again, multitasking as he drove.

'Dad says to say goodbye, now,' Anna said resignedly. 'See you later! Love you!'

'Mia says, "See you soon!"' called Tom, although Clare was sure that their golden retriever would be slumped in a drowsy heap in the boot of the car, dozing as the miles sped by.

As the message clicked to an end, Clare realised that several other hotel guests were making use of the outside seating area.

She was unsurprised to see Astrid and Gareth next to one another. Dan was with them, and he invited to Clare to join them. There was no sign of Michael, and Clare wondered if anyone had updated him about the beach prohibition since the morning's session. It would be better if he was told directly, rather than stumbling across a police cordon of some kind. She must look for him.

But then Michael himself emerged from inside the lounge, carrying a tray of drinks that looked pleasantly cool, with beads of condensation forming on the tall glasses.

'Clare, can I get you a drink?' he asked, pausing beside her. 'And you don't have to tell me anything – Dan updated me.'

'OK, thanks, Michael.' It was clear that he did not want sympathy, nor comment. 'I'll maybe get myself a Diet Coke; you go ahead.' She passed him and went into the lounge and up the wooden steps to the bar.

As she waited there, the young barman darted back to his place, coming from the main hotel corridor and looking flustered. Along the corridor came Rachel, no longer jacketed, but with her shirtsleeves rolled up and walking quickly. Behind her was a tall woman with a helmet of chestnut-brown hair; the woman's face was averted, and she held up one of her hands as if to shield herself from view. Her jacket was similar in style to the one Rachel had worn earlier. Could this be Gail, the manager, who had been asked to identify the body on the beach?

As the young barman went in search of ice for Clare's Diet Coke, Jackie arrived.

'Can we talk, Clare? I think it is him, on the beach,' she said, under her breath.

At the same time, Clare's phone pinged again. Another missed call – from David again – then a message. He must have stopped driving.

Hope you're OK. Ring when you can xx

Something was happening.

CHAPTER 39

'We can talk in the loo – it's this way.' Clare abandoned her drink on the bar and led Jackie off down the corridor to the Ladies. As she had hoped, the cubicles were unoccupied, giving them the privacy they needed to speak. There were even a couple of chairs in the small lobby area, beside the full-length mirror, opposite the elegant hand basins.

'Tell me.' Clare was not in the mood for prevarication. Her family would be arriving later, and she wanted everything to be resolved, without delay. How this odd partnership with the DCI had developed, Clare didn't quite know, but only by working together would they uncover the truth about what happened to Victoria.

'OK, steady on.' Despite having pulled Clare aside at the bar, Jackie seemed in no rush to show her hand.

Clare would have to go first; she often found that Jackie opened up more readily when she shared her findings. 'I'm not sure what to make of this,' she began, 'but I've learned that drugs are an issue in this area, and here at the Morva.'

Jackie simply nodded perfunctorily, as if that much was obvious. 'Anything else?' she asked crisply.

Clare was nonplussed, but pushed on: 'According to hotel records, Lucy's bill last year was paid by Michael, which doesn't make sense. Rachel told me that.'

Jackie frowned, then turned to one of the sinks and began to wash her hands, perhaps wanting to seem less suspicious if anyone joined them. She shook off the excess water and reached for one of the small towels left neatly folded in a wicker basket between the two sinks.

'Victoria wrote something in her journal about Lucy having financial issues, and that she wouldn't be able to bankroll her. So, I'm not surprised that she couldn't pay the bill here – that adds up,' Clare continued. 'But Michael stepping in – with the way the two of them are now – it just doesn't make sense.'

'Definitely not.' Jackie shook her head. 'That's useful to know – thanks, Clare.'

'You had something to say about the body on the beach?' Clare prompted. It was only fair that the DCI shared her findings too, she felt, now that Clare had divulged hers.

'Yes,' Jackie said. 'From what I understand, the hotel manager has confirmed that the body on the beach is Vincent.'

Silence fell as both women processed Jackie's statement.

'Gail,' Clare said finally. 'The hotel manager's name is Gail. I just saw her in the corridor, back there. She seemed upset. Rachel said she and Vincent have known each other for a long time. I think . . . I think Vincent may have been having an affair with her.'

Given what Nadiya had told Clare, this seemed like a fair conclusion to reach, but Jackie looked surprised to hear it.

'It's so horrible that he's dead,' Clare continued. 'Did he . . .

have some kind of accident, or a heart attack? What have you been told?'

Jackie dropped the hand towel into the large bin left out for that purpose. She was matter of fact: 'Nothing official. Nick Faux is here with his team – they'll get the results of the post-mortem to certify cause of death. In the meantime, Vincent's family must be informed. They'll be going ahead with all that, now.'

'It's his wife's birthday soon. How awful. He said he'd send her some flowers, after I got some from David, that first evening here.' Clare hoped this unnamed woman wouldn't have to know about her husband's overnight absence, or absences, from his room. But perhaps she already did. Things weren't always straightforward in a marriage.

The reality of this woman's loss sat heavily with them. Then Jackie continued, 'Of course, the reasons for Vincent's death, if it was foul play, could involve others beyond the group here.'

'Will we all be interviewed? Like last time?' Clare's memories of the Greenwood case were not happy ones. She washed her hands too, in part to give herself something to do, and splashed some water on her face.

'Perhaps.' Jackie smiled ruefully. 'I think Nick Faux may have suspicions about me, and perhaps he's right to keep all options open.'

'About you?' Clare couldn't keep the shock from her voice, turning to look at Jackie directly.

'I wasn't around yesterday evening, when Vincent went missing. And he had been asking about me, just as much as he'd been asking about everyone else. And Nick Faux is definitely uneasy about me coming here incognito. I think my interest in Victoria's case strikes him as excessive – so, unsurprisingly, he may question the reasons for it.'

'You're just being a good friend, surely? Keeping your professional life private hardly makes you a murder suspect.' Clare was surprised to find that it felt natural to defend Jackie. Somehow, on this retreat, things had shifted between them. Whatever residual animosity lay between the two women over David, Clare wanted to help her.

'Hmm, I'm not sure Nick Faux will see it that way,' Jackie said. 'What made you mention drugs, Clare?' She changed the topic abruptly and Clare could tell she didn't want to talk about her own problems any further.

'Something Melanie implied, but she didn't want to get involved with any specific accusations. She suggested that some staff here could be part of a local set-up.'

'More than likely – someone could well be a supplier, or with connections, at least. Or involved more deeply. Jeremy has links with London, too, I think? He's evasive about his past,' Jackie commented.

'Vincent grilled him at the café at Kynance, which didn't go down too well,' Clare added.

'Jeremy was here last year,' Jackie said, 'but there's no particular link established between him and Victoria.'

'Could she have stumbled across some info about his involvement with drugs, though? That might have been why she contacted you.'

'Potentially. But lots of things are possible. What if Vincent discovered Michael had done something to Victoria last year? And Michael had to get rid of him to stop him saying anything?'

'But Michael was at the Epilogue last night. He couldn't have done anything to Vincent.'

'He could have met with him later. We don't know when exactly Vincent was hurt.'

Their conversation was cut off when the door opened. It was Nadiya, carrying a pile of fresh hand towels. She looked hesitant at the sight of Jackie and Clare, and apologised for disturbing them.

'No problem, Nadiya,' Clare said, quick to reassure her. 'Are you OK? Did you cut yourself on any of that broken glass, earlier?'

'It's all fine, now.' Nadiya waved her left hand at them, and Clare noticed the white tape wrapped securely around one finger.

'It's nice that Jeremy helped you. Good to see a boss being useful.' Jackie smiled, and Clare thought she was deliberately building a sense of female solidarity. 'Is this an OK place to work, Nadiya?'

'Yes, I have a good job here. I like Rachel and Jeremy,' Nadiya said, placing the new towels in a tidy pile and straightening them.

'Yes, Rachel is brilliant, isn't she?' Clare smiled at her warmly. 'I probably shouldn't pry, but . . . what you told me about Vincent, the other day. About him not sleeping in his room. I wanted to ask, did that have something to do with Gail?'

'Gail is our manager. Her friendships are not my business.'

Nadiya pursed her lips, and her reluctance to say any more made Clare think she was on the right track.

So, Vincent and Gail *had* been an item.

'I must go; everyone is busy today,' Nadiya said, looking at them reproachfully.

'Of course.' Clare was quick to agree. But she managed one last question. 'Is Gail upset?'

Nadiya eyed her sadly, and Clare was ashamed of her clumsiness.

'I think you know that. There is nothing for me to say.'

CHAPTER 40

A strange calm descended over the assembled retreatants during the buffet lunch. With no updates from either the police or management about what was happening at the hotel or down by the beach, conversations were muted, and Clare could see that no one had much appetite – particularly Lucy, who left most of her meal untouched. They were all in limbo, and a listlessness pervaded the atmosphere.

It was a relief when Jeremy announced it was time to head to Cadgwith and Trelissick. People seemed to perk up as they discussed their plans for the afternoon. Both Lucy and Jackie elected to stay at the Morva, while Michael wanted to give Cadgwith a miss and head straight for the spectacular gardens at Trelissick. The rest wanted to follow the schedule as planned.

As everyone made their way out of the dining room, Clare was surprised when Dan sidled up and asked if he could travel with her, saying that he would appreciate time to discuss some things with her in more depth. She was happy to comply with this request, but had assumed that Dan, like Gareth, would prefer to be in Astrid's company. She had seen that Gareth had made a point of sitting with Astrid at lunch, and he was ushering her towards the minibus now, as the group went to join Jeremy there.

Today, Dan wore a slogan-free, green and brown patterned T-shirt, which brought out the colour of his eyes, making him look even more attractive, if that were possible. He seemed endearingly unaware of that fact, but Clare saw the appreciative glance which Pippa directed towards him as they crossed the car park together.

Clare did not linger to watch the bus depart, and, as soon as they were underway in her red car, Dan began asking her what she thought the likely outcome would be of the police presence at the cove beneath the Morva, adding that he was praying for a speedy resolution. He seemed relieved to unburden himself, and Clare was pleased he felt able to do so.

'Do you think they have found Lucy's sister? Or her remains? And what can have happened to Vincent?' he asked.

He was asking important questions, but she had no satisfactory answers for him; everything Jackie had told her was in confidence.

'Thank you for your care for everyone,' Dan commented. 'This must be very difficult, leading us through this. Is there anything I can do to help?'

Clare expressed her gratitude for the way he had supported Gareth that morning.

'Yes, Gareth's hard to understand,' Dan said. 'Astrid told me that he'd known Lucy's sister, Victoria – but now he seems quite fixed on Astrid. Sorry, perhaps I shouldn't say that.'

'Say whatever you want, Dan – it can be good to talk.'

Clare wondered what he thought of the group and wanted to encourage him to tell her. It might help him to feel useful, too.

'Gossip about others is unhelpful, and unchristian,' Dan corrected her.

Clare realised that he expected her to look chastened, rather than patronised. She compromised, asking instead if he had any suggestions about how best she might support everyone. She was sure he would enjoy advising her.

The humility in his reply was unexpected. 'I think you're better than me at doing that, Clare,' he said. 'I think, when we first met, I underestimated you. I'm sorry.' He spoke with a disarming candour.

'Really?' She was surprised at his admission. 'Not a problem, Dan. And how has this time been for you? I wondered what brought you here.'

'It's hard to know how to put this, but I think you'll understand. I've always been sure of my beliefs, ever since uni. My father has been in poor health, and his faith has grown strong. My mother's, too. I've always gone to good churches, with clear teaching.' He answered with a measured consideration.

'Right. I'm sorry to hear about your dad's health problem.'

'Thanks.' Dan brushed off this expression of concern. 'I go to two churches, actually. The one near my work is different in style, more reflective. They have a midweek Holy Communion, and sometimes I just go and sit in the church at lunchtimes, too. I like the quiet. I don't agree with that church's theology, though – they're very liberal on social issues.' He frowned, disapprovingly.

'I guess different churches have a different emphasis about some things.'

'Yes, but there is clear scriptural teaching for us to follow.'

'I think we can understand or interpret texts differently, and perhaps come to fresh conclusions about some issues, over time,' Clare said carefully.

Dan was engaging more deeply with his faith than she had realised. Even considering another church's departure from the certainties of his previous churches' teaching was probably unsettling for this devout young man. She wanted to give him time to talk.

'I came away partly to explore some new possibilities, but it's difficult not having such definite scriptural exposition.'

So, Dan was feeling vulnerable without such authoritative teaching along familiar lines, and with more opportunity for his own reflection. No wonder he had been critical on that first day, when he'd complained that Clare's selection of retreat materials hadn't been sufficiently biblical.

'Where's your parish, Clare? And do you like being a vicar? I'm curious about that life.'

So, that was it. Dan was wrestling with the idea of becoming a minister and what that might entail. She wondered how often he had the opportunity to discuss it, and knew she must tread gently with him.

'Our church is in Kent,' she said. 'I love my job – it's the best job in the world – but, of course, it drives me crazy sometimes, too.'

'I don't think I'm pastoral enough to be a vicar. I can be tactless.'

Clare wanted to reassure him. He was probably hard on himself, as well as being judgemental of others, sometimes.

'There are different types of vicars: some are more pastoral than others; some are hopeless at all the tech stuff, but theologically astute; some are very organised, others a bit haphazard. There's no one size fits all. I think it's important not to count yourself out, Dan. If you're wondering about it, it can be good to explore the possibility and not prejudge the conclusion.'

'You're taking this seriously.' He patted his leg, as if to bolster himself.

'It's important to listen. It doesn't mean you are going to be grabbed hold of and have a clerical collar jammed round your neck. The discernment process about whether it's right for someone to be trained for ordination is slow and careful, as it needs to be.'

'You're different from a lot of vicars I've met.'

Clare suspected that many of those had been of a type, and very sure of themselves, but knew that she was biased.

'Well, God calls many different sorts of people to serve as priests – and that variety is helpful, I think. We're stronger in the Church when we embrace diversity and work together.'

Dan drew back, discomforted. He stared out of the passenger window, even though it only faced a tall hedgerow, his head turned away from her. Of course he would be uncomfortable with such wishy-washy inclusive thinking. The word 'diversity' had become an alarm bell for some, rather than cause for celebration.

But Clare continued, focused on helping him: 'I suppose what matters is being open to possibilities and asking God for help. Coming away on such a different kind of retreat shows an openness to trying new things – so, good for you. Trying something different can stop us controlling everything so tightly, and perhaps make more space for God to surprise us, maybe?'

'I'm not sure.'

'Well, your care for Gareth, in such unexpected circumstances, suggests that you're more pastoral than you might think. And you've noticed his attentiveness to Astrid.'

'I think he's a bit full on, to be honest.'

'That's interesting. And I don't want to push you towards exploring ordination, Dan – I hardly know you. But sometimes people count themselves out or judge themselves too harshly, so I want to encourage people to be open to the possibilities, and to explore that with others. You might want to mention this to your vicar, and, in time, to your diocesan team, too – they're very experienced. And it really is different for everyone. There isn't an indentikit version of priesthood, or ministry. All sorts of people become clergy.'

'My job's well paid,' Dan suddenly said. 'My family are proud of me.'

'Well, I only became a vicar for the clothes and the money.' Clare smiled. 'Seriously, you're wise to be aware of all that – the income drop is no joke. My husband earns well – if he didn't, we'd be sunk. No Cornish holidays, or not so many, and no trips to Italy, that's for sure. We've got a summer holiday booked there, later this year.'

'I like to travel,' Dan confided. 'I guess options would be limited, on a vicar's pay.'

'Very much so. But who needs to travel abroad, with places like this to visit?' Clare asked, as they turned off the main road to follow the narrow lane towards the fishing village.

They passed a few houses on the way down. One had two slanting roofs, like butterfly wings, with a balcony jutting out from an upper floor. A gull strutted along its railings.

'I wonder if Michael is already at Trelissick?' she mused. 'It's beautiful there. I didn't see him leave ahead of us, but he drives much faster than me.'

'He'd set off before we went out to the car,' Dan said, and again his awareness surprised her. 'I think he may have health issues, Clare,' he added, thoughtfully. 'Sometimes, he seems to be in pain while walking, but that's just an impression I got. I wonder if that's why he travels separately, so that he can walk at his own pace when we're visiting somewhere.'

'Interesting,' Clare said, then teased him: 'You're definitely more pastorally aware than you might realise, young man.' Now, it was her turn to patronise. 'Or should I call you Poirot?'

At least she hadn't called him Heathcliff.

CHAPTER 41

Once they arrived in Cadgwith, Dan split off from Clare to join Pippa and Astrid in exploring the Crow's Nest Gallery. Left to her own devices, Clare crossed the road and walked on to the shingle beach, stepping over the metal winch chains which were used to drag fishing boats up from the sea. There, she found Gareth, looking at his phone despondently. Its shiny case was monogrammed, like his clothes.

He shook it at her in mock frustration. 'No signal,' he said. 'How anyone copes with this is beyond me.'

'Yes, it's annoying. I've been trying to call my husband, too,' Clare replied. 'How are you doing, Gareth? I know things are difficult today.' She thought about his earlier outburst about Michael, at breakfast.

'Yes, I'm sorry about earlier. I don't know what came over me.' He looked sheepish at the memory. 'It was good Astrid was around; she's got a very calming presence. This is a friendly group, by and large.'

'I've not really asked what brought you to join us.'

'Same as Lucy – and Pippa, too, I think. Details came by email, and I remembered that Vicki had been here; it was in the news when she went missing. It seemed like a lovely spot.'

Clare stood beside him as waves with ripples of foam swung gently towards them, then retreated again. 'That's interesting; I wonder why you guys were contacted.'

'Me, too. It just seemed like a coincidence, but when Pippa told me about getting her email, I wondered; and then Lucy told me that she'd also got a similar email.'

It was odd that someone had tracked Gareth down to send him the retreat material, but Clare didn't want to pursue that now.

'It's so sad about her disappearance. And, today, Lucy's concerned about Vincent, which is understandable.' She was fishing for information and hoped it wasn't too obvious.

'He seems nice enough, but I didn't get much time with him.'

'He was curious about everyone, I think; he asked Jeremy and others about themselves.'

'Well, he wasn't very interested in me. I suppose he did ask a few questions, down at the pool; it was a bit much, to be honest. But then he got into a conversation with Dan; they were talking about the coastal path.'

'Yes, you two made good time, yesterday – that was impressive.'

'I like to keep fit. I travel quite a bit with work, so I get to run in different places, and I try to stay somewhere with decent gym equipment, if I can.'

There was a crunch of stones behind them and Dan arrived, saying that he'd left Pippa and Astrid admiring the gallery's wares. The two men were at ease with each other and soon started to compete about how far they could each throw stones from the shore. Gareth began stacking some into a pile to have a stock of suitable missiles readily available, and that became a competition too, as Dan began building his own tower and attempted to make his taller.

They were absorbed in the game, and Clare left them to it. She made her way from the beach to the footpath that threaded up from the harbourside and between the assortment of cottages, towards the tiny blue-painted chapel, which had become the parish church. This little tin chapel was dedicated to St Peter and was very much a fishing community's place of worship. As Clare entered, she noticed a painting of the risen Jesus welcoming fishermen to him through stormy waters, hung to the right of the simple altar table. To the left, Jesus was depicted above the waters of Lake Galilee, showing His disciples where to cast their nets.

Both paintings were dedicated to villagers lost at sea. The peril faced by everyone whose livelihoods came from the fishing fleet was very evident here. This sanctuary of peace held memories of anxious prayer and deep grief. It was no place for bland assumptions about life, or death.

The church was well cared for. The four rows of bright blue benches were freshly painted, likewise the white windowsills. The wooden floor was clean and smelled of polish. Sitting on one of the benches, Clare could look out over cottage roofs and see the sea glistening at the base of the valley. The sound of the stream rushing down to reach the ocean was constant, along with intermittent birdsong and the more distant cry of gulls.

At the back of the chapel were a range of second-hand books for perusal and purchase. A visitors' book lay open for recorded comments, and Clare saw that Pippa and Astrid had both written in it. They must have called in before heading off with Dan, Clare thought. Astrid had expressed delight at the beauty and calm of the chapel; Pippa had simply signed her name.

Against the back wall was a locked cupboard with a few vases perched on the top of it, and shelves opposite held some neatly stacked hymn books and Bibles ready for use. A tiny table and two miniature chairs were tucked beneath, left ready for any children to seat themselves in comfort. All was left in careful order, with a simple hospitality.

Clare told herself not to rush or hurry, but to take the opportunity to sit, rest and pray. She thought of the fishing community and the holidaymakers who came here, of her family and of their friends who would join them for the half-term break. She prayed for each member of the retreat group and for the hotel staff, for Nick Faux and his team, for those involved in investigating any drugs ring and for all those caught up in it. She prayed for Vincent and his family, for all who mourned for Victoria, and for some resolution about whatever had happened to her.

Then, she simply sat, made newly aware of divine mercy and reminded of God's presence with all people in their suffering.

She heard the murmur of conversation and footsteps as a group of walkers headed down the path; they carried on past the little church without stopping to come in. Someone reprimanded a dog, which was apparently pulling on its lead and needed to be brought to heel.

About five minutes later, an older couple opened the door and exchanged greetings with Clare. The woman told her that, the last time they had visited the village, it had been during a downpour, commenting that, although it had brightened up later in the day, the weather had been fierce.

'When it rains here, it rains,' she said, decidedly. She asked her husband what month they had made that trip through the violent squall and intermittent cloudbursts, saying she would turn back the pages and find their entry in the visitors' book. She did so, while her husband leafed through a cookbook amongst the second-hand volumes for sale.

'Here we are!' she exclaimed, indicating it to him, and she laughed as she told Clare that the paper was crinkled, no doubt due to all the rainwater she and others had dripped on it that day.

Clare smiled, not mentioning that the pages of her pastoral-services book containing the liturgy for churchyard burials were similarly mottled, soaked by rainwater whenever she'd said the prayers of committal as a coffin was lowered into a grave on a wet day. That was too much information for this pair of friendly holidaymakers.

After they'd left her in solitude again, Clare took their place beside the visitors' book. Why hadn't it occurred to her to check and see if any familiar names had signed it, a year before?

She turned back the pages and, sure enough, there were

messages and signatures left by Lucy and Victoria.

Victoria's message was poignant: *A lovely place. Thank you.*

The sisters had written on the first lines of a new page, and there were no signatures left by anyone else known to Clare below their entries.

But, on the last line of the previous page, someone had written: *Please pray for me. M.*

Of course, that could be anyone. A Mary, a Melissa, a Madeleine. Or possibly a Martin, a Matthew, or perhaps even a Michael?

It was a tenuous link, but suggestive, nonetheless. Victoria had written in her journal about seeing him and Pippa in this village the same day that she and her sister had visited, so it was plausible that this entry in the visitors' book had been made by her ex. Had Victoria noticed it, and its appeal for prayer? What was the reason for that? Clare might not recognise the handwriting, but surely Victoria would have, if this was indeed written by Michael.

Michael had deliberately avoided coming to Cadgwith today, saying that he would go directly to Trelissick Gardens. Did this village hold distressing memories for him?

Clare heard the familiar voices of the retreat group approaching up the path, so she hurriedly closed the book and resumed her seat. She could hear Astrid commenting on the chapel as she passed, and Dan answering her. He voiced his concern about getting to Trelissick with enough time to see everything, and Clare could hear Gareth and Pippa reassuring him as they continued past the chapel on their way back to the car park.

As she sat, Clare decided she would make some amendments to that evening's Epilogue, finding some paper in her bag to write an outline and fetching a Bible from the back of the chapel to look for a suitable psalm to read. Dan had been disappointed that Hardy's poetry and other texts formed much of the content of earlier sessions, so he at least would be pleased to have more scripture included tonight. A psalm of lament seemed appropriate, given the day's tragic discovery on the beach beneath the Morva, and the continuing mystery of Victoria's disappearance, too.

Clare took time and care over her choice: *Come quickly to me, O God. You are my help and my deliverer, O Lord, do not delay.*

There had been quietness on the path beside the chapel for some while and she didn't hear the next visitor's approach. She turned at the sudden click of the handle as the door opened. There was Michael, who looked as surprised to see her as she was to see him. He had told everyone he was going straight to Trelissick, so why was he here at Cadgwith?

CHAPTER 42

Jackie was determined to make the most of the time available to prove herself a useful colleague to Nick Faux. Having skipped the afternoon's outing, she had sent him an efficient timeline of events, notes on her knowledge of each member of the retreat group and the hotel staff, and what she had learned about drugs in the area. She held nothing back. She and Clare had amassed a considerable amount of information which she knew he would find useful. If he trusted them, of course.

He clearly had some misgivings about her, and she could understand that.

Jackie sat in the hotel lounge as she waited for his response. She was sipping an Americano when she spotted Lucy drawing near. It must be an anxious wait for her, Jackie surmised, as Lucy stood looking out to sea with her hands on her hips, arching her back slightly as she surveyed the view.

'You gave the expedition a miss too, then,' Jackie said conversationally, conscious that she had no right to interview Victoria's sister, however much she might wish to do so. And that she would likely need to offer some information in order to receive anything back.

The seats nearby were unoccupied, so there was no risk of being overheard. Jackie stood. It was better to be at eye level for this.

'Lucy, there are some things I'd like to mention to you.'

'Things,' Lucy repeated dully, looking rather uninterested and still gazing out at the vista in front of them.

'At one time, I lived in Stockwell, on Clapham Road.'

Now, Lucy reacted. She recognised the address and immediately turned away from the window, giving Jackie her full attention.

'I lived opposite the Ryman's shop, next door to your sister.'

'You knew her?' Lucy gasped and took a step forward.

'Yes.'

'Why didn't you say? Why are you here?' Lucy's eyes flared wide with indignation.

Her intensity was understandable and Jackie answered as succinctly as she could. They both sat as she explained her friendship with Victoria, and her reluctance to say anything to Lucy or anyone else about it. However, Jackie said nothing about Victoria contacting her, nor did she mention her work as a police officer. There were limits to this disclosure.

'I had no idea that you would be here, this year – that came as a shock, and that Michael was here, too.'

'That makes two of us,' Lucy said. 'And I find his mopey wistfulness about Victoria nauseating, after the way he treated her.'

'Were you in contact with him much?' Jackie was curious about that hotel-bill payment and wished she had the authority to investigate it fully. That would be up to Nick Faux, but she could try to fish a bit.

'No – he tried to make contact after she disappeared, but I wasn't interested.' Lucy looked down and rubbed her shoe along the wooden floor. There were marks from when others had done likewise, and darker lines from occasions when furniture had been dragged across it.

'It's strange. That Michael came here, I mean.' Jackie left the comment hanging, hoping that Lucy would say more.

'It's horrible having the police here, just like last time.' Lucy looked directly at her again. 'They tell us nothing. Their cars were here this morning, and then they went to the beach, but no one knows anything about what they're doing. Or they won't say. I asked Jeremy before they left, and the manager. Have you met her?'

'No. What did she say?'

'Well, here she is.' Lucy looked up as a smartly dressed woman with gleaming chestnut hair came down the steps from the bar area and headed towards them.

'Hello, Lucy,' Gail said, nodding politely at Jackie, too. 'I wondered how you were doing, and if I can get you anything? I know Jeremy has been looking after you, but he's not here this afternoon.' Gail was clearly sensitive to the emotional pressures Lucy was under, and Jackie waited to see whether the hotel manager would divulge anything about what she had been shown on the beach.

Lucy ignored the offers of drinks or anything else and asked directly what Gail knew about the police presence, and if there was any news about Vincent's whereabouts. Her voice trembled as she spoke. 'I'm so worried about him; his disappearance is just like what happened to Victoria, and no one seemed to take that seriously.'

'Did you know Vincent at all?' Jackie asked Gail quickly, managing to take the hotel manager by surprise.

'Yes, I did, a little, as it happens – just slightly,' she said, blinking as she answered. Her discomfort was obvious.

'I didn't know that – how come you two knew each other?' Lucy frowned.

'Vincent and I happen to have friends in common, in London.' Gail was more assured in her answer now, and Jackie was certain that things were being skated over. 'His work as a journalist brings him into contact with so many people, and he's always enjoyed coming to stay here.'

Jackie wanted to ask more, but their discussion was cut off by the arrival of an overexcited golden retriever, which bounded down the stairs towards them, noisily trailing a purple lead that bumped down the steps and snaked quickly across the floor behind it. The dog was followed by a boy giving chase, which the animal seemed to regard as an enjoyable game, darting away from him and accelerating past Lucy and Jackie and along the glass wall. A girl appeared at the top of the stairs, calling 'Mia!' and instructing her brother to go one way to catch the dog, while she went the other.

Jackie knew exactly who these children were and prepared herself to meet their father David again, too – her ex. She'd known him years ago, before he'd married Clare.

The girl descended the stairs and successfully grabbed the dog, while her brother, Tom, came to an abrupt halt beside

Lucy and Jackie, almost skidding into Gail, the hotel manager, as he did so.

'Sorry,' he said, then looked at Jackie in astonishment. 'Detective Jackie!' he exclaimed. 'I didn't know you were here, with Mum.'

Lucy and Gail stared at him in shock, and then both women turned to Jackie as one, awaiting her explanation.

Her cover was blown, and her friendship with Clare would be revealed, now, too.

'Hello, Tom,' she said. 'Is this your dog?'

CHAPTER 43

Michael stood in the doorway of the Cadgwith chapel and stared at Clare.

'I thought you'd gone off to Trelissick,' he said, 'with the others.'

'Hello, Michael.' She stood to greet him. 'No, I've stayed on here. It's lovely, isn't it?'

'Yes,' he agreed, then added, 'The pub is good, too; they sing sea shanties there on some nights. Fridays, I think.'

Clare sat down on the blue-painted pew again, and, as she had hoped, Michael came and settled himself next to her. The coincidence of them meeting like this felt as if it was meant to be, and she waited to see what might happen next.

'Were the others in here?' Michael asked.

'Some of them, I think,' Clare said. She made no reference to the visitors' book. That could wait.

Michael remained still in the quietness alongside her, and there was an unexpected ease between them.

'You described somewhere as being a "thin" place – was that Kynance?' he asked, eventually.

'Yes, it's definitely a place where things connect, isn't it? It has a sense of the numinous. Like here.' She stroked the blue bench next to her, where it stretched on towards the window. Its painted surface was glossy and smooth to the touch.

Silence settled again within the chapel, while the sound of rushing water and birdsong continued outside.

Michael spoke, placing his hands on his knees: 'I'm not religious, but I feel closer to God here, or whatever you call the universal force, or our maker – Him upstairs, anyway.'

'Yes. It's a place in which I find it easier to pray.' Clare wanted to ask why he'd requested prayers in the visitors' book a year before, but she still held back.

'It makes you think about what matters, and what you want to be left behind after you've gone,' Michael said. 'Like that "Afterwards" poem, when Hardy thinks about what people will say about him, after he's dead. About him noticing beautiful things. Being attentive.'

'Yes. I guess it's probably a useful thing to reflect on, what our life is about.'

'Illness can do that,' Michael continued, and Clare remembered Dan's remark that Michael had sometimes seemed to be in pain, and to be disguising that fact.

'Have you had some health issues?' she asked, quietly. He didn't have to answer her, she was only enquiring, she told herself.

'Not so much now; things are stable,' he confided, after a pause.

'That sounds good.'

'It was one reason for finishing things with Pippa, but I

couldn't explain everything.' He hesitated. 'She was upset, and angry. Still is.'

'Right.'

'Things will get worse again. Even if things are stable for a while.'

'That sounds very challenging.' Clare kept her eyes on the altar table in front of them, and on the vase of purple and yellow wildflowers which someone had placed on the shelf behind it. Michael must be suffering from a degenerative condition; Dan had been perceptive to notice the signs.

'Did Victoria know about it?' It was a risk, asking this – but it would explain that note of sympathy for Michael in Victoria's journal.

'In the early days, I hardly believed it myself; it was hard to talk about it. But I did tell her something, yes. I would have explained more, but never had the chance.'

Michael swallowed, and she realised that he was trying not to weep as he sat beside her, apparently so calm and controlled.

She told herself not to be fooled by him. Most women who were murdered were killed by someone they knew, and if Victoria had been harmed, it was most likely to have been at Michael's hands. She must at least keep an open mind. Not believe everything he told her. But she sympathised. He was very convincing, and she didn't want to be guilty of misandry, but nor did she want to be naïve about misogyny or abuse.

'I messed up, very badly, and there's no possibility of making amends. I think my illness is a kind of payback, for all the hurt I've caused.'

'What makes you say that? Illness comes to most of us,

eventually, whoever we are.' She mustn't get sidetracked by the theology of suffering. She wanted to know whether Michael tried to meet with Victoria, a year ago. She decided to be more open. 'Michael, did you hope to meet with Victoria, last year? It's just that I noticed something in the visitors' book here, which made me wonder,' she added, in hasty justification. She couldn't say anything about the journal.

'I'm sorry, I can't tell you anything more, Clare.' Michael sat up straighter and set his jaw more firmly. 'It's better that I don't. I did let her know something, and we would have met. But she never came. I've not told anyone even this much. It's better to keep right out of it, all of it.'

He stood and walked towards the back of the church. There was a stiffness in his movement – Dan was right.

'Thanks for listening, and I'm sorry to burden you,' he said. 'Goodness knows what the police have found back at the Morva, or where Vincent has got to.'

There was no point trying to delay him or asking for more information. Clare let him go and continued to sit, mulling over their unexpected encounter. Certainly, what he'd told her was consistent with Victoria's journal. But Clare still believed he should be treated as a suspect. He may seem genuine, and his awareness of his own mortality may be authentic, but Clare had been mistaken about the perpetrators of crime before. It could easily happen again.

CHAPTER 44

The weather changed as Clare drove from Cadgwith back to the hotel. Splatters of rain hit the windscreen and heavy banks of dark grey cloud loomed overhead, moving across the sky. The peninsula was exposed to sudden shifts like this, and Clare hoped that the wind would clear the skies again before evening came. The car in front of her dawdled slowly along. It was unusual for her to find a driver even more cautious than herself, she thought impatiently. Perhaps these holidaymakers were unnerved by the narrow, winding lanes and the sudden onset of rain.

The downpour increased in ferocity as she reached the Morva, so she scurried quickly from the hotel car park and arrived rather breathlessly in reception, shaking the rain from herself as she moved on into the large lounge. The main hotel entrance had reopened, it seemed. Clare deduced that the examination of the lost-property hamper had been completed.

There was a scuffle and rush of movement towards her, accompanied by joyful barks of welcome. It was Mia, her paws skittering across the wooden floor as she bounded up the steps to greet Clare. Anna gave chase and then flung her arms around her mother, while the dog jigged about them both excitedly.

As she hugged her daughter, Clare looked down into the lounge area to see her husband and son smiling up at her, the table in front of them laid out with the remnants of a cream tea. With them sat Jackie, sipping her own hot drink, looking settled and comfortable beside David.

'Wow, this is a surprise!' Clare tried to sound delighted, but neither David nor Anna looked fooled.

Anna said, 'Mum, Jackie was here when we arrived – Mia landed on her and two other people; Tom let go of her lead.'

David stood, saying that he thought she'd like a cream tea too, and that he would request a pot of Earl Grey for her.

Nice try, Clare thought, but her husband had some ground to make up. How come he was cosying up to an ex-girlfriend, and with the children here, too?

'Great – thanks,' she said, hurrying to hug Tom, too, and to kiss him hello.

'We saw Rachel,' he announced. 'I can ride Nugget on Saturday, and Anna will have a new pony. Hers will probably be faster than Nugget, but I don't mind.'

'They were desperate to see you, so I brought them here –' her husband's tone was apologetic – 'but we can stay at the cottage tonight.'

'Please can we be with you, Mum?' Tom's look was beseeching, but Clare suspected his enthusiasm was as much to do with having a hotel breakfast in the morning as about remaining in her company.

David busied himself by moving an additional chair over

to their table for Clare, and Jackie manoeuvred her seat to make more room.

'How was your afternoon?' the DCI asked.

'Eventful,' Clare murmured, not wanting to say more in front of the children.

'Tom told everyone that Jackie was a police officer,' Anna informed her.

'Jackie said it didn't matter,' Tom added defensively, 'although the lady did seem a bit shocked.'

'They both were,' said Anna.

'Right. And who is "everyone"?' Clare kept her tone level, taking off her damp jacket and hanging it over the back of her chair.

Jackie's face was similarly impassive. 'Lucy and Gail.'

'Wow. OK.' Clare was not going to apologise for her son's mistake, but she didn't envy Jackie having to deal with its fallout. She brushed her rainswept hair back from her face with her hands.

'I'm sorry to surprise you like this,' David said.

As far as Clare was concerned, he had a lot of apologising to do. What had he been thinking, showing up here unannounced? No way was she going to berate him in front of Jackie, though.

'It's great to see you all,' she breezed, 'but I am sort of at work, you know. I'll need to be ready for the group when they all get back from their afternoon trip. I hope they escape the rain.'

'Can we go down to the beach?' Tom asked. 'Mia's been so good, and she hasn't been in the sea yet.'

'Maybe take her to Poldhu,' Clare said quickly, while Jackie watched.

David looked worried. 'It's raining, Tom,' he said, dubiously.

'Mia doesn't care,' Tom answered, as if that was all that mattered. 'And Poldhu has a café.'

'Are you OK, Mum?' Anna asked. 'Rachel says you've been brilliant with everyone. What does she mean?'

'Well, there's a lot going on,' she improvised.

'There always is.' Tom nodded, sagely. 'Mum, Jackie's been telling us about how she arrests someone, and what she's allowed to do if they resist.'

Jackie looked uneasy at this description of their conversation, but Clare only remarked that no doubt it was very useful to know, and she'd expect a demonstration later.

'Why don't you guys all take Mia down to Poldhu now? The weather will brighten soon, and you've had your tea, and I can catch up with Jackie before the others get back,' she suggested. 'I can drive over to the cottage later and see how settled in you all are, before it's time for bed. Maybe you can have a late night – it is half-term, after all.' And David could manage that, she thought, wet beach walk and all.

'It's not really half-term yet –' Tom was always one for accuracy – 'but we're starting ours early, thanks to Dad.'

'Come on, Tom – Mum needs us to go, now,' Anna intervened, and Clare felt a pang at her daughter's intuitive understanding that their presence was making her uneasy. She was certainly anxious to avoid any mention of Nick Faux or his team's investigations in front of the children, and very grateful that Rachel and Jackie had avoided any unwelcome revelations on that score. So far, anyway.

Mia had already scrambled up and was wagging her tail at the mention of a beach excursion. The children shared more hugs with their mother and said polite goodbyes to Jackie before heading to the door with their eager dog. David waited only briefly to apologise again to both women, and to kiss Clare farewell and nod a hurried goodbye to Jackie. It was obvious that he wanted to chaperone his children and prevent any more unfortunate conversations occurring before they were safely off the premises. They had already blown Jackie's cover, as far as Lucy and Gail were concerned, and presumably they would now tell others that she was a police officer, and that Clare was well aware of that fact.

It was uncomfortable, to say the least.

CHAPTER 45

'I'm sorry that Tom outed you,' Clare ventured. Initially, she had resolved not to apologise, but she couldn't keep to it. It must have been so awkward, and the implications were serious.

'It is what it is – too late to worry about that, now.' Jackie's response was somewhat minimalist, but she wasn't one for demonstrating much emotion.

Clare wondered what she had been like as a girlfriend, all those years ago. Self-contained? Mysterious? Clare had never even tried to achieve the 'woman of mystery' vibe herself, and David seemed happy enough that his wife wore her heart on her sleeve, even when she tried to be poker-faced.

'How did Lucy take it? And Gail?' she asked, staring out through the picture window as the remaining rain clouds blew across the horizon, and the distant waves increased in size.

'Gail was low key – perhaps she wasn't surprised. It was less straightforward with Lucy.'

'I can imagine.'

'I'd already explained that I knew Victoria, and that we were neighbours.'

Clare was surprised at that. Jackie had seemed determined to keep her friendship with Victoria quiet. 'Did that help, when Tom told her you were police?'

'Possibly. But in some ways it made it trickier – she thought I'd come clean with her, but then realised I'd still been holding things back.'

Their conversation paused as Nadiya cleared the table of the debris from the cream tea, which Clare's family had consumed with enthusiasm, and she asked whether Clare still wanted to have one herself, now that they had left. Clare was hungry and welcomed the idea. With everything so unpredictable, she didn't want to risk missing dinner again, as she had done the previous night. Someone might want to talk with her, or she might be needed by her family before it was time for the Epilogue. Jackie asked for an Americano – decaf, this time. That was very Jackie, to be measured about such things, and not to overeat, either. Clare decided she'd put plenty of cream on her scones when they arrived.

'Your dog is very energetic,' Jackie said, disapprovingly.

Were they really going to fall out over Mia? Clare resolved to keep a sense of perspective and not to be overly defensive about her golden retriever. She herself might complain about Mia's liveliness, but she was never happy if others criticised their boisterous dog.

She shifted in her chair and managed a calm reply: 'Yes, she's full on, especially after a long car journey. A beach walk will sort her out.'

'Good that you suggested going to Poldhu, not here – David looked dumbstruck at that request.'

Why did Jackie presume to comment on David? Don't be petty, Clare, she told herself. Ignore it. But there was some asperity in her voice when she replied, 'Let's focus on the next steps. Will Nick Faux come back here, do you think?'

'Yes, but how soon, I just don't know. I've sent him all the information we've got so far.'

'Right.' Clare nodded, aware that she hadn't told Jackie about Melanie's suspicions of Pippa's drug use, nor Michael's admission of some contact with Victoria last year, or of some plan to meet.

Nadiya reappeared, carrying a tray laden with drinks over to a group of young people who were seated on the far side of the room. Her turquoise hair looked very much at home with the purple locks of one of the young women amongst them and the cerise pink of another. Clare thought Nadiya's shade of turquoise was now a bit darker; perhaps she had coloured it again.

Beyond the young people, the heavy clouds parted, revealing shafts of brilliant sunshine, and a half rainbow appeared, arching down between the clouds to the sea. The group exclaimed at the sight, and it made Clare smile, too.

Jackie didn't seem to notice; she was perusing her phone. 'Nick Faux just confirmed he's got my report.' She looked up as Nadiya approached them again.

'I heard you are police?' Nadiya said, tentatively, clutching the empty tray.

Clare marvelled at how fast this news had travelled. Presumably, Gail had told her.

'Yes, that's right. But I didn't come here to work,' Jackie said, not entirely truthfully.

'Jeremy is not a bad man. I tell you this,' Nadiya said in a rush, her accent more pronounced. One of her fingers was still encased in white tape.

'What do you mean by that?' Jackie was quick to follow up, but Nadiya was already retreating, pausing only to look over her shoulder.

'Not a bad man. It is important to say that.' And she left, presumably to fetch Clare's cream tea. Or so Clare hoped. The heavy rainfall might have resulted in the retreat participants departing early from Trelissick, and she wanted something to eat before facing them.

Just as she thought of their return, there was Jeremy, running his hands through rain-sodden hair and hurrying down the stairs, intent on joining them. There was no sign of any of the others; perhaps they had gone straight to their rooms to dry themselves off, if they had been caught in the cloudburst.

'Jeremy, you're soaked,' she said. 'It came on so suddenly. Did you all get drenched?'

'It's no matter.' Jeremy hitched up his trousers and smoothed down his damp hair again. 'Most people were in the tea-room when it started. I just got a bit wet going to get the minibus, before we drove back.' He hardly paused before asking, 'Everything OK with you both? Have you seen Lucy at all, this afternoon?'

'She seemed OK earlier,' Jackie said, blandly. She made no mention of Lucy's shock at the news of her friendship with Victoria, nor about her identity as a police officer being revealed. But it became clear that Jeremy had already been informed of both these things – perhaps by Nadiya or Gail.

'I understand that you are with us on retreat, Jackie, with no professional responsibilities, but I'm aware that you bring particular expertise to us, at this juncture.'

Clare wondered if he would bow to the DCI in supplication, and he did bob down with an awkward knee-bending manoeuvre as he spoke.

He then turned to Clare and said, less fulsomely, 'I gather that you and Jackie have cooperated together on previous matters, Clare.'

She nodded, mutely. Then added, 'Very tangentially, Jeremy. And it was a surprise to me to discover that Jackie was here.'

'I see.' Clearly, he did not – and he made no attempt to disguise his scepticism.

'Please, let me know if there's any assistance which I, or my team, can provide, Jackie. Or should I address you as DCI Carter, perhaps?'

So, Jeremy, or someone at the Morva, had also googled Jackie and discovered her real name. Clare was impressed by the detective's poise – she looked entirely unruffled by this.

'Jackie is fine, Jeremy, thank you. As you say, I'm not here on a work assignment, and the retreat has been excellent.'

Clare thought that was pushing it, but Jeremy seemed pleased.

Nadiya approached again, carrying a tray laden with a

teapot and teacup, a plate of scones and two little bowls, one overflowing with clotted cream and the other with jam.

Jeremy stood by and watched as the tray was unloaded, and Nadiya didn't even glance at him. Instead, she turned and made her way over to the young people's table, where she began clearing away some empty glasses.

'Jeremy, are you wet through, or can you sit with us for a moment?' Clare asked, slightly surprising herself with the question.

Cautiously, Jeremy sat, balancing himself on the front edge of the chair, as if wary of what she might say next.

It was Jackie who spoke: 'Jeremy, I wonder if I could clarify something with you?' She was straightforward. Forceful, even. 'Why are some members of the team here so protective of you? I'm curious. Is there something you would prefer remained unknown about you, that probably has no relevance to the current police enquiry?'

'I have no idea what you mean,' he blustered, with widened eyes, and Clare knew that Jackie was on to something. 'I simply want to offer you both any assistance with the remainder of the retreat, at what is a difficult time for everyone.' He ran his fingers through his hair again, then leaned forward and straightened the salt and pepper pots and the small vase of flowers which were on the table beside Clare's substantial tea.

Jackie continued, 'Of course, in any enquiry, my colleagues have to discriminate between what information has relevance and what is entirely unrelated. I'm wondering whether there is anything which you might be able to clarify, to prevent any unnecessary confusion or delay to the investigative process?'

She might not be on duty, but the detective was not giving up.

But Jeremy was no pushover, either. He stood and apologised for not being able to be of more help, professing ignorance of anything which might relate to issues which concerned the police with regard to the hotel or any of their guests.

'After the tragic disappearance of Victoria, last year, of course we want to render DCI Faux and his team every assistance. My hope is that concerns raised today will prove to be groundless, and that any guests currently off-site will soon return, right as rain.' With that, he hitched his trousers once more, and Clare thought it was high time someone advised him to buy clothing that fitted him better or to get himself a belt.

'Yes, thank you, Jeremy,' she replied, reflexively. Being polite was important.

'Yes, thanks for nothing,' Jackie muttered, once he was out of earshot.

CHAPTER 46

The early evening light had a particular clarity after the afternoon's heavy rain. Craving some fresh air, Clare made her way out on to the hotel terrace. She was joined there by Pippa, who had changed her clothes since returning from the afternoon expedition. She now wore a different plum-coloured, pleated dress, with dark pink sandals. She seemed to have lost her abrasive edge, and stood companionably beside Clare, before suggesting they walk together a little, towards the harbour path.

'Some distances are quicker by footpath than by road,' she added, as they made their way along the terrace and on to the track, 'as well as more beautiful.'

'Yes, you're right,' Clare agreed. 'But those coastal paths are steep. I think it's up and down all the way from here to Kynance. I wouldn't fancy the whole route.'

'Dan and Gareth made it back quickly yesterday, but, then again, Gareth is sporty, isn't he? And Dan is fit, too, in more ways than one. You must have noticed.'

Clare only grinned in reply.

Pippa was setting quite a pace, so Clare stopped to admire

the view, giving herself a moment to catch her breath as she looked out to sea. Pippa waited, and both women watched as birds drifted in wide circles, high above the ocean.

'Was something on your mind, Pippa?' Clare asked. 'Are you concerned about Michael? Or something else?'

She was probably asking leading questions, but Jackie was the police officer who had to follow protocol, not her.

'I've been thinking about what I said to you earlier . . . and Michael could have taken all sorts of routes – and met up with her, you know,' Pippa half muttered. They continued walking, careful to sidestep puddles that gleamed with the reflected colours of the sun. 'Last year, it was easier not to acknowledge the possibility, but now, with Vincent disappearing too, I must.'

'Yes, you're right – however difficult that may be.'

'Thanks, Clare. Everyone's saying that Jackie is a police officer and that you know her, from before this. Can you speak to her for me?'

'What would you like Jackie to know?' Clare said, trying to sound calm.

'Michael could have slipped away from where we were staying, last year. It's possible. I wouldn't have known if he had arranged to meet up with Victoria, but I swore blind to the police that we were always together. I wanted to make sure he was free from any suspicion. It was impossible that he was guilty of anything. It still feels impossible, to be honest, even though he hurt me.'

'You have confidence in him,' Clare remarked, carefully keeping pace with her companion.

'Yes, I do. But I could be mistaken, couldn't I? Any of us can be mistaken about other people.' Pippa stopped and looked at Clare, as if for reassurance.

'You're right, and I'll talk to Jackie, but you'll need to say something too.'

'OK, I get it.' Pippa looked out at the seascape again. 'There's something about this place that makes me realise I must do what needs to be done.'

As one, the women turned back towards the hotel. As if by magic, there was Jackie, making her way along the path towards them.

'Clare!' she called. 'I was looking for you.

'And we were just talking about you, Jackie. Pippa has something to discuss with you – isn't that right, Pippa? Maybe it's best to strike while the iron's hot.' Clare regretted her turn of phrase; better not to think about striking things, or people, right now.

Pippa came to a standstill, waiting for Jackie to get closer. Then she spoke with a simple directness which impressed Clare. 'I think I need to correct a statement I made last year to the police. Clare said to talk to you about it.'

'OK.' Jackie took this in her stride. 'Let's clarify that. But Clare, if you're OK to go back, Gail and Jeremy were looking for you.'

'Me?' Clare repeated, her voice pitched high, in sudden anxiety. 'Are my family OK?' Immediately, she felt self-conscious about this degree of alarm. Leading this retreat was taking its toll.

'I'm sure they're fine.' Jackie's brisk reassurance was

chastening. 'I imagine it's something about the retreat programme that the hotel team are concerned about.'

'Of course. Thanks. See you later, Pippa.'

She noticed Jackie steer Pippa back away from the hotel again, perhaps heading for one of the seats which were positioned along the clifftop in order to take in the breathtaking views of the bay. The DCI could take it from there.

CHAPTER 47

As she walked back towards the hotel, Clare prepared herself for whatever Jeremy or Gail might say. In light of all the police activity, would the retreat end early? She would be sorry, if so. However difficult things might be, she wanted to see this through. She thought DCI Nick Faux might have been in touch with an update for the hotel management, and perhaps that was what they wanted to tell her.

But it was a stranger who sat with Lucy on the terrace on her return, with his arm slung around Lucy's shoulders. He stood as Clare approached them. He was a tall man, with a pronounced, beak nose and a slight stoop. His dark, heavy jacket somehow added to the impression of a bird of prey. His eyebrows were extraordinarily bushy, too. Yet his sonorous voice was melodious as he introduced himself.

'I'm a newcomer to your party, Reverend Clare, and I'm delighted to meet you. How do you do.' He bowed slightly as he shook her hand. 'Bill Mackie, Lucy's husband.' There was an old-fashioned formality about him. 'With the events of the day, I decided it was time to join you, to be with Lucy. So, here I am.'

Had the A30 been full of husbands heading to Morva to be reunited with their wives? He and David might have driven in convoy.

'It's lovely to meet you. How was your journey?'

'So-so – coming out of London was slow, as were parts of the A303, but I took the A38, which worked well. I cut through that way, not straight on to the A30, but instead dropped down to the coast, via the 390.' Bill warmed to his theme, continuing the detailed explanation of the intricacies of his route, adding the reasons for the choices he had made and describing the precise siting of speed cameras, while Clare attempted to look interested.

'Great, it certainly sounds as if you had things sussed,' she replied, hoping to betray no trace of irony. 'I hope you'll join us for the Epilogue, later, if you'd like to do so? It would be lovely to have you with us.' After all, there was space in the group, with Vincent gone. Clare wondered when they would be given confirmation about what had happened to him. Perhaps his wife had been informed by now, poor woman.

Clare excused herself politely as she left Lucy and Bill, and opened the door into the hotel lounge.

'Clare, I've been looking for you.' Jeremy was hovering in wait for her and pulled her aside as soon as she entered. 'Let's go into the snug – it's more private in there,' he said, keeping his voice low.

He steered her up the stairs, but instead of heading for the bar, he opened a discreet side door into a small, cosy room. Its wallpaper was dark and patterned with peacocks with exotic plumage. Two purple sofas faced one another on either side of a small fireplace, and there were bookshelves laden with an assortment of board games, magazines and novels for guests to use – Clare wished she had discovered this place before.

Jeremy closed the door behind him and took a seat on one of the sofas, gesturing for Clare to sit on the other side. Jeremy's purple trousers almost exactly matched their fabric, and his green, almost iridescent shirt picked up some of the colours of the feathered birds on the wallpaper. The enclosed space felt very different from the airy openness of the lounge, Clare thought.

'Is everything all right, Jeremy?' she asked.

'Yes, well . . .' Jeremy said. 'DCI Faux will be coming back later tonight, to speak to you and Gail, and perhaps everyone at the retreat.'

'I see,' Clare said. If those were Nick Faux's plans, it meant she was unlikely to see the children this evening, and she was disappointed about that. 'Was that all?' she asked.

Jeremy rested his elbows on his knees and leaned forward, his hands cupping his forehead as if to help him focus. 'Not quite,' he began. 'This is difficult, Clare, but I need your help,' he said, addressing the floor.

Clare saw that his hair was thinning on the crown of his head. He seemed more vulnerable, with his jaunty persona laid to one side. 'What's wrong, Jeremy?' she asked, sympathetically.

'I'm so used to telling no one, and that's how I've coped.' He looked up, and his face appeared to have aged since they entered the room, which he now seemed to be using as a confessional. 'But, with Jackie asking questions and Nick Faux investigating here again, I'm worried. I have to trust someone, and I don't know what to do.'

'Sure, please tell me, if you think I can help, Jeremy.' Clare fought to keep her voice even and told herself there was no reason for alarm, whatever he might say. She prayed for steadiness.

Jeremy sighed. 'The thing is, my name wasn't always Jeremy. That's not who I used to be.'

'OK.' Clare kept still.

Jeremy sat up straighter and continued in a quiet monotone, as if reading a prepared script: 'When I was younger, I was involved in all sorts of stuff you wouldn't want to hear about, Clare. And I'm ashamed of it, too. It was easy money. I was young and stupid – in with the wrong sort. I lost contact with my family over it. I'm sure you know the kind of story.'

Clare nodded; she could imagine it. 'That sounds tough.'

'It was lucrative, Clare. I had a fast car, all the trappings. But eventually I got caught.' Jeremy frowned and cleared his throat.

Clare gave him time; it was obviously difficult for him to carry on and he needed to gather himself. There was a chessboard on the bookshelf, its pieces shaped like medieval combatants. On one side, they wore green, as if representing Slytherin, while their opponents were in Gryffindor red. Anna and Tom would love this room and its contents; she would have to bring them here.

'It's a long story,' Jeremy said.

'There's no rush, as far as I'm concerned,' Clare reassured him, as best she could.

'I was recruited, Clare – that's the long and the short of it. Recruited to gather evidence and to build the case which convicted my bosses and peers. It was serious stuff, and what I had to say, my evidence in court, helped put them away for long stretches. Years.'

Jeremy's speech accelerated and he became more animated, gesturing with his hands as he spoke.

'After I grassed, it was traumatic – people were out to get me. I couldn't tell anyone about this, Clare. I had to enter witness protection, and I was given a whole new identity. I had to start all over.' His voice cracked on the last sentence.

'That sounds incredibly challenging,' Clare said. She couldn't begin to imagine what it must have been like for him, having to leave his identity and entire life behind.

'It was terrifying – and lonely, too, coming to a different part of the country and not knowing anyone. But, after a while, I began to feel safe . . . until all of this stuff happened, with Victoria first, and now Vincent.' He paused and shook his head. 'I think Vincent knew about my background, somehow. He kept asking me stuff and dropped hints. But I never touched him, I swear on my life, Clare. I know what Nick Faux and his lot will do, if they find out I'm not who I say I am. Once they've got a villain in the mix, that's me done for.'

'How long have you worked here, Jeremy? And been out of any trouble? Surely things are different with you, now. This case was some time ago and you've had a new identity for a while.'

'I've tried to keep clean, anyway.'

He looked down, and Clare wondered what she wasn't being told.

'Do you think I should tell Nick Faux about my background, Clare?' He raised his head and looked at her, vulnerable, seeking consolation. 'I don't know whether to wait until he comes at me with it.' His gaze intensified. 'And I wonder whether you – and your mate, Jackie – might help me out a bit?'

'In what way, Jeremy?' She thought the chances of Jackie helping him were less than zero, but she wasn't going to say so. Jackie would think he was an ex-con out to manipulate her.

Before he could elaborate, the heavy door to the room opened and Gail hurried in, her heels clicking on the wooden floor.

'There you are,' she exclaimed. 'Have you told Clare that the police are coming back this evening?'

'Yes, Gail. All sorted – all fine, on that front.'

He stood and, to Clare's amazement, the serious, frightened man she'd spoken to had disappeared. Jeremy the jovial events manager was back, confessional over.

'Good.' Gail was terse. 'We have an extra arrival – Lucy's husband. Have you met him?'

Clare seemed to be included in Gail's query, so she answered that she had, and that she had invited him to join the group for the Epilogue.

'That's fine, then.' Gail seemed satisfied with her response. 'Let's sort that out with him ASAP, Jeremy, and his dinner arrangements, too. Thank you for your flexibility, Clare. I'll see you later.'

Gail turned to leave, and, obediently, Jeremy followed his boss from the room. Clare wondered what crimes Jeremy had been involved with. Being part of a criminal network could mean drugs, people trafficking and prostitution, theft or extortion. Perhaps all of those things. And now, here he was, established in a picturesque setting, and described by Nadiya as 'a good man'. She was eager to vouch for him, and Clare wondered why.

CHAPTER 48

Clare joined the rest of the retreat group on the terrace, where they were admiring the sunset together. The was a slight breeze, but no one opted to go inside yet, and there was still a while to go before dinner.

They welcomed Pippa when she returned along the cliff path, and Clare was pleased to see that the tête-à-tête with Jackie had reached its conclusion. Pippa sat herself between Dan and Astrid, avoiding being next to Lucy or Bill. Gareth was quick to offer to buy her a drink.

Clare sat quietly, thinking about Jeremy's revelation and its implications. Nadiya may have spoken warmly about him, but Rachel seemed less enthusiastic. Maybe he was irksome as a boss – Clare could easily understand that being the case. She realised the team's dynamics were complex, but presumed that no one knew about Jeremy's past. It would have been extremely dangerous for him, if they did. And what might he have done to protect that secret?

Someone had put that jacket and journal amongst the hotel's lost property, ready to be discovered. It made sense to Clare that Victoria would have carried her diary with her last year, rather than leaving it in the room she shared with her sister, who might have been tempted to read it. Conceivably, Victoria had dropped the journal – or her assailant, if there had been an assailant, could have taken it. But what had happened to it after that?

Rachel's colleague, who had discovered the jacket and journal in the hamper, had been told by Nadiya not to take it to Jeremy, but to give it to Rachel instead. Nadiya had wanted the jacket and journal to come to Rachel's attention – and thereby to Clare's notice, too. The hotel team knew about their link.

Nadiya had played a pivotal role, and she was also determined to present Jeremy in a positive light. Why was that?

The rest of the group seemed content to remain on the terrace and discuss the weather forecast, while Dan listened politely to Bill describing his driving route again. Clare left them to it and went in search of Nadiya. She had a hunch, and she wanted to check it out.

She was in luck. Clare breathed a prayer of gratitude as she saw that head of turquoise hair coming towards her along the main hotel corridor; Nadiya was alone. It was easy to waylay her, and to guide her to the newly discovered snug, where they would be undisturbed.

'Nadiya, I think you don't want any trouble, for anyone,' Clare began, seating herself on one of the purple sofas and indicating the one opposite, where Jeremy had sat earlier.

'Yes, of course. I don't want trouble,' Nadiya repeated nervously, perching on the edge of her seat and staring at Clare.

'I think perhaps you found something, a year ago.' This

was quite a risky conjecture, and an intuitive one. But Clare had hit the bullseye.

'How do you know?' Nadiya asked, astounded.

'I think you found a jacket, and perhaps you had no idea what it meant. Until later. Or perhaps you thought that Jeremy, or another person, might have found it, and then they wanted to leave it well alone. However it happened, you had Victoria's jacket and notebook, and you kept it, rather than destroying it or handing it in. It must have been very difficult.'

The note of sympathy was effective.

'Very difficult,' Nadiya echoed, chewing her lip.

'I think you knew it might help with finding out what had happened to Victoria?' This was all guesswork, but Nadiya nodded.

Clare noticed for the first time how chapped the skin was on the back of Nadiya's hands, and the patch of angry red eczema on her right forearm. The hard work of serving the hotel's guests took its toll. One of Nadiya's fingers was still taped.

'Perhaps you found it after Victoria was missing,' Clare hazarded. 'You are always tidying.'

'It was late. That night. I took it home and forgot next morning.'

'Of course, and then you must have been so worried.'

'Yes. Everyone was crazy about where she was. I was afraid. When I remembered the jacket, it was days later. Then I saw the notebook. Read it. I was afraid for me, and for others. It is easy to suspect people, people who have done nothing.' Nadiya picked at the white surgical tape on her hand.

'Yes, it must have been very worrying. So, you kept it hidden? At home?'

'You know everything. You are priest, I think?'

'Yes, and I guessed, Nadiya. I see how hard you work and how much you care for people. You wanted us to know that Jeremy is a good man.'

Nadiya was silent at this, gazing at Clare, waiting for her to continue.

'But I think you realised it would be good if the police had the journal, or if I had it, and read it. And this year's retreat was the chance to do something to help, without getting anyone else in trouble. Or being in trouble yourself.'

'I will be in trouble, now.' Nadiya scratched at the inflamed skin on her forearm.

Clare winced and couldn't stop herself from leaning across to still her, placing her hand on Nadiya's arm. 'Some trouble, perhaps. Not a lot. What time did you find it? Was it when you were going home, late? And where was it?' Clare kept going; she wanted to discover all that she could, while Nadiya seemed able to trust her.

'Yes. Sometimes, I wait to collect my son – he works late. Jeremy was kind to him, you know. He found him a job, in the pub. So, sometimes, I am finishing here late, alone. I sit outside, above the sea; I watch the stars. The lights of ships in the sea. It is peaceful, beautiful.'

'Yes, I can hear the waves from my room, if I leave the window open. Where do you sit, Nadiya?'

'On the first bench, on the coast path. Towards harbour, that way. Then I go to my car.'

'Is that what you did, that night?'

'Yes, I sat. In the quiet. Except for noise of the sea – you are right. The jacket was there.'

'On the bench?'

'On the ground. I put it on the bench.'

'You didn't take it inside?'

'I was tired. It would have got wet, maybe, so I took it home, to bring back in morning. I was on breakfast shift.'

'But you forgot it?' Clare knew she was prompting, asking Nadiya leading questions – Jackie would have a fit. But she wanted to keep going, and she was right, Nadiya would tell her, she knew it.

'Yes, I forgot. Then, too late.'

'Too risky?'

'Too late. Police had gone. Guests had gone. Nothing to do. Too late.'

Clare was dubious about that. It seemed more likely that this was a convenient realignment of the actual timeline, but what mattered now was that the evidence had come to light, eventually.

'Thank you so much, Nadiya. Thank you for telling me this. I think the diary Victoria wrote will help us find out what happened to her – and, thanks to you, it has been found.' Better to skim over the intervening period of it being kept hidden. For now, anyway. 'And knowing where you found it, and when, will be very helpful, too.'

'The police know I worked late, know I was there. They asked many questions. About my son, too. It was difficult.'

'Yes, it sounds very difficult. Did you see Victoria, that

night?' Clare tried to sound matter of fact. 'Or anyone else – on the path, maybe?'

'Nothing to see. Nothing to say.' Nadiya was resolute. 'I told them, nothing. No one.'

Clare wondered about that, but decided not to pressurise her any further. Not now, anyway. Helping her to talk to DCI Nick Faux was next on the agenda, and, according to Gail and Jeremy, he would be arriving later. He would have plenty to investigate, and she and Jackie had made a start for him.

'Nothing to say,' Nadiya repeated. 'I must go, now. Work to do for dinner.'

'Of course, and thank you, Nadiya.' Clare respected this woman, with all that she was managing. Even telling Clare this much must have taken great courage. And placing the jacket and journal in that wicker basket, too. Clare hazarded a guess that Nadiya had wanted to keep Jeremy out of things, perhaps not wanting to cause him trouble, whether or not she had any knowledge of his shady past. But Nadiya would need to tell others her story now, too – there was no avoiding that.

'I think Nick Faux, or maybe Jackie, will need to hear what you have told me, and I can talk to them too.' Clare tried to be reassuring about that, smiling and nodding.

'Thank you, Clare. You help me,' Nadiya said, and Clare suddenly felt uneasy. Supposing she had rushed to conclusions? Was she somehow helping Nadiya too much? Or, conversely, had she exerted too much pressure on her, pushing her into constructing a false narrative of events, which would obstruct rather than assist Nick Faux's enquiry?

Well, she had tried her best, and it was for the police to

follow up on this new information. DCI Nick Faux might be preoccupied with Vincent and what had happened to him, but the mystery of Victoria's disappearance was beginning to yield its secrets.

CHAPTER 49

When Clare emerged from the snug, she went directly to the bar and ordered a Diet Coke from the young barman, who as usual was assiduous in offering her ice and lemon to go with it. Soon, the retreat would be over and she'd be able to savour a gin and tonic again; but, for the time being, total sobriety was the order of the day. She needed her wits about her with Nick Faux joining them later, and there were crimes to solve. Clare also knew that the more sober she was, the more tactful she was likely to be, which had to be a good thing.

It seemed an age since she had sat in the warm sunshine of their first evening here, relishing a long, cool gin and tonic and discussing with Vincent the fateful collision of the *Titanic* and an iceberg. It felt surreal that something so untoward had happened to the journalist himself since then – another fateful collision of circumstance, perhaps. Despite everything, Clare realised part of her was still hoping he might wander into the lounge, ready to join them for a drink before dinner.

She thought he had probably used his relationship with Gail to access material advertising the retreat, and had sent it on to the others to encourage their attendance. Jackie seemed to think he had a police contact of some kind – conceivably, that was how he had discovered Gareth and Pippa were involved with the investigation, too. He was going to get quite a story out of such a gathering – and he also seemed to enjoy the drama of stirring things up between people.

Clare turned to see the younger members of the group coming inside to the lounge. Astrid looked a little the worse for wear, nursing what must have been the latest in a succession of pre-dinner drinks. This one was a cocktail of luminous green, which she held in both hands while laughing a little more loudly than usual at something Gareth said, but which Clare didn't catch.

Gareth was flushed in the face; he reclined across one of the larger sofas opposite the bar, a smile playing across his features. Perhaps he was tipsy, too. Dan was speaking to Pippa about his father's illness, explaining that his dad was currently in remission. Clare could hear snippets of that conversation and saw the sincerity with which Pippa listened attentively to the earnest young man, whose brow furrowed as he spoke unselfconsciously about his concern for his parents. Clare speculated that Dan's father's ill health explained why he had been alert to the signs of Michael's discomfort and the attempts which the older man made to mask any symptoms he was experiencing.

'Hey, Pippa!' Gareth called, interrupting Dan. 'What's your favourite cocktail? Astrid says you'd like a vodka base – is she right? She's having a Green Hawaiian. Do you want to try one?'

'I'm fine, thanks,' Pippa replied, smoothing her glossy hair and returning her attention to Dan. He wore a T-shirt which advised, *Think outside the box*. Clare was trying to do so.

Gareth turned his focus back to Astrid instead, sitting himself up straight and offering to get her a coffee if she needed to sober up a bit before it was time to eat. Clare thought that would probably be a good idea, but reminded herself that she was their retreat facilitator, not their mum.

She took her Diet Coke to an outside table on the terrace. A few other hotel guests were also enjoying the colours of the evening sea and sky, including Jackie, who was sitting alone.

Clare suggested they take a stroll, and the two of them walked along the building's frontage and stood admiring the landscape which stretched westward, bathed in evening light and shadows. There was a gentle breeze, but it continued to be pleasantly warm, with no indication that rain might ensue. Dan had mentioned that the forecast was for poor weather to come rolling in overnight, and that it might last for most of the next day. Clare hoped it would clear up before the children's morning ride, if David had managed to book one for the following day, although they would probably enjoy it even if they got drenched. She must remind David to take their thickest waterproof jackets to the stables, and a second change of clothing, she thought. He would probably remember, but she'd like to check.

Jackie was gratifyingly impressed when Clare told her about Nadiya's admission.

'It was just a guess, really,' Clare said, attempting to look modest.

'Don't do yourself down – it was a good one. You persuaded

her to admit to finding that jacket, and exactly where it was, too. That's really useful information, Clare – we're finally getting somewhere with this. And Nadiya orchestrated things to ensure that you heard about the journal from Rachel. That's significant, too.'

Clare felt the glow of approbation and recounted the news that Michael had some health issues and had decided to tell Victoria about them last summer.

'I believe they did arrange to meet, but Michael didn't tell anyone that, as he thought suspicion would fall on him, after Victoria went missing.'

'Too right. Though, he was subject to Nick Faux's investigation anyway, even without that admission.' Jackie watched as some walkers made their way across a field in the distance, their two pale dogs running hither and thither ahead of them across the green landscape.

'Yes, indeed. And Michael is adamant that he didn't actually see Victoria that night, but of course he could be misleading us.' Clare looked back to make sure there was no danger of being overheard.

'Absolutely. Michael's squarely in the frame. If he hurt Victoria, let's hope he gets banged up for it and we can throw away the key.' Jackie was resolute, gazing out to the horizon.

She looked so sanguine, any passer-by might assume she was discussing the patterns of clouds or the beautiful reflection of light shimmering on the water's surface, but Clare felt unnerved by the level of Jackie's vitriol. The DCI normally seemed so composed, but this investigation was personal – Victoria had been her friend.

'I also learned something about Jeremy,' Clare said. She recounted the tale he had told her about his participation in witness protection.

Jackie seemed unsurprised by his admission. 'That explains his sensitivity to Vincent probing into his background,' she said. 'It also raises the possibility of Vincent having threatened Jeremy with something, and of him retaliating.'

Clare nodded. That had crossed her mind, too.

'Well, I've already given Nick Faux plenty to think about, and this is all useful, Clare. Unofficial or not, I'll send him another update, so he'll have all the relevant information before he sees everyone. I'll give dinner a miss and do that now.'

'I can arrange for a tray to go up to your room,' Clare offered. She surprised herself by feeling uneasy that Jackie wouldn't be with them in the dining room; she realised that she felt safer having the DCI nearby. She'd been unaware of how nervous she had become at the hotel. There seemed to be so many undercurrents in play.

CHAPTER 50

Bill raised his hand in salutation as Michael arrived at dinner and sat at the far end of the long table. Clare thought that Lucy had also clocked her former brother-in-law's entrance but chose to ignore it.

Lucy was more animated now that her husband was here; she talked loudly about a visit they had made to Amsterdam, with its canals and cafés.

'I wish I'd taken advantage of the jewellers selling shed-loads of diamonds there; I could have smuggled them home in a bunch of tulips,' she said, and her shrill, slightly manic laugh reminded Clare of the stress this woman was under. It also seemed likely that Lucy had consumed a fair amount of alcohol before dinner.

'The less said about that, the better,' Bill muttered, and Clare affected not to notice the edge of bitterness in his voice. She wasn't sure whether it was the mention of Lucy's spending habits or the reference to smuggling which had riled him. She also wondered why Lucy now seemed unconcerned about Vincent's whereabouts, when only that morning she had been so distressed at his absence.

Astrid sat unobtrusively beside Clare at the table and wasn't touching her wine glass. She had a new reserve since telling Clare about her father, which wasn't unusual, in Clare's experience. Once someone had confided something very personal, it was as if they feared the consequences of having done so and couldn't trust themselves not to stray back into painful reminiscence – or they feared that Clare would insist they did so.

Dan raised his voice and addressed the whole group: 'Has anyone been down to the harbour since this morning?'

There was a clatter of cutlery on plates and continuing conversation, as people either responded to his question or repeated to others what had just been asked.

'I wondered about taking a boat trip tomorrow, if time allows, and whether anyone would like to join me, if so? I believe it's possible to take a boat out from the harbour,' he added, and looked to Clare for confirmation, or permission.

She thought it likely that Nick Faux would prefer to keep the group available for interview tomorrow, rather than wave them off on a pleasure voyage, but did not want to be the one to say so. DCI Faux or his colleagues could explain that for themselves.

Gareth looked concerned at the prospect, too, when Clare caught his eye.

'Would we see seals?' Astrid asked, with unexpected enthusiasm. 'Or whales? There were whale sightings off Cornwall a few weeks ago, weren't there?'

'I'd rather not get up close and personal to a whale.' Lucy shuddered. 'I'll stay safely on land, thanks.'

This reference to danger at sea punctured the atmosphere, and it was suddenly impossible to continue to ignore the question of Vincent's whereabouts and what might have befallen him, not to mention the questions and griefs surrounding Victoria's disappearance.

It was Michael who chose to be direct: 'I'm with you, there, Lucy – and, as everyone knows, you and I have had our differences, and still do. But we may need to support one another through this, if things have gone badly for Vincent, as I think we all realise could well be the case.'

'Don't patronise me,' Lucy muttered, and Bill put a consoling – or possibly a restraining – hand on her arm and tried to hush her. She shook him off and raised her voice, content to take centre stage: 'You had something to do with Victoria's disappearance, Michael, I'm sure of it, and now you want to play some game of helping us cope with Vincent going missing, too. Maybe you'll quote some poetry at us next. Well, I'm not falling for it. I know you, and what a bastard you are.'

Clare was ready to take a lead to stop things escalating, but it was Dan who stood.

'I think we're all rather on edge, and that's no surprise,' he said. 'We're all concerned about Vincent – and Victoria, too, of course. But can we leave this for now, please? Clare, are there plans for this evening that we should know about, maybe? Sorry if I'm ahead of myself in asking.'

As Dan sat down again, Clare realised that this good-looking Heathcliff did show considerable potential for ministry. He'd held the attention of the group without hogging the limelight, had provided a buffer to protect Michael from further verbal attack and had also intervened to prevent any immediate retaliation from him.

'We'll have our usual Epilogue together later, yes. Thanks, Dan,' she replied.

'What about Jackie? Where is she? Is she investigating us all? We know she's police.' Astrid's interest in seals and whales had been superseded by her concerns about Jackie's whereabouts and activities. 'And I saw you two talking on the terrace earlier, Clare. We all did.' She said this as if accusing them of criminal conspiracy.

Gareth looked shocked at Astrid's hostility, while Dan's face betrayed his embarrassment.

'I believe Jackie has no official role here,' Clare said, using her most soothing vicar voice, as the whole group stared at her. 'But you're right, Astrid, she is a police officer.' Clare had no problem in keeping calm; the group needed steadiness, not more drama.

'She knew Victoria.' Lucy's voice was dull, but the impact of her words caused several group members to gasp, or to turn their heads in surprise.

'She knew Victoria?' Pippa echoed. 'Why didn't she say?'

'That's for her to answer, not me.' Lucy shrugged, absolving herself of responsibility.

'Has she been spying on us? Have you?' Astrid was on the attack again. Those cocktails she had consumed earlier might have been playing a part in this.

'We've been set up,' Gareth said, and Pippa nodded in agreement.

Initially, Clare didn't notice Jackie's approach, and nor did Astrid. Gradually, silence fell, as everyone turned their attention to the DCI, who stood behind Clare's chair. Clare was relieved not to have to answer Astrid, now that Jackie was here. The sooner the police took over this whole ghastly business, the better, as far as she was concerned.

CHAPTER 51

'Good evening, everyone,' Jackie said, looking round at the assembled diners, and Clare recognised the more formal tone of her voice and the difference in her stance. 'I gather you are now aware of my job as a police officer, although I joined the retreat in a personal capacity. As I think you are also now aware, I had a neighbourly relationship with Lucy's sister, and earlier today it was appropriate to mention that to Lucy.'

The DCI was wearing a smart green jacket over her jeans, and when she spoke she addressed the group with a detached, professional courtesy. 'My apologies for any difficulties my reticence may have caused you,' she continued, looking around the table at each person in turn. 'To date, I haven't been professionally involved in any police investigation regarding what happened to Victoria. DCI Nick Faux is leading that ongoing enquiry, and we have all been asked to convene this evening, so that he can meet with us. The Leven Room is available, and we are asked to be there at eight thirty – half an hour before our usual Epilogue.'

Thanks for the heads up, Clare thought, while also feeling

relieved that the police were getting on with this tricky investigation, and that she wasn't responsible for it.

She looked at Astrid. The colour had drained from her cheeks and she seemed shrunken, her shoulders hunched, her face downcast. Then, she flicked her eyes up and met Clare's gaze. Her vulnerability was startling. Obviously, she had realised that Clare would have to tell the police about her father's death and Vincent's involvement with his case, and she was terrified. There was no appeal for silence in her look, just fear of what she and Clare both knew might be revealed.

Meanwhile, Michael looked sickened. He stared at his plate, on which the food had barely been touched. Clare thought he would be regretting his candour earlier that day in the Cadgwith church, about arranging to meet with Victoria, with all the implications of that admission. Then, she noticed that Pippa was watching him, too, with a strange smile of satisfaction on her face. What was that about?

The DCI continued, 'If possible, please refrain from further discussion amongst yourselves until DCI Faux from Devon and Cornwall Police has had the opportunity to meet with you all. Thank you. Excuse me.'

So, that was it. Jackie turned on her heel and left them to finish their meal. Clare realised that she was expected to speak next; Dan and others were looking to her to take charge.

'OK, everyone, I'm very sorry about the last-minute change of plans, but, as DCI Jackie has said, the police want to speak to us all this evening, so let's be prompt and convene at eight thirty.'

'Did you know Jackie's real identity?' Gareth asked, clearly articulating something which the entire group wanted to know.

'Jackie and I have met before this,' she said, with a quickening urge to tell them that Jackie and David, Clare's husband, had spent a youthful summer madly in love, and that she was still sick as a parrot at the thought of it. She quelled the impulse, and instead said something vague about respecting Jackie's wish to come on the retreat as an individual, rather than as a police officer. That was only partly true, and Clare felt uncomfortable saying it.

'Are you saying that you and Jackie decided to keep it quiet, that she's a police officer?' queried Bill, indignant on his wife's behalf.

'Give it a rest, Bill,' Lucy said, pushing her hair back from her forehead, as if to clear away difficult thoughts. 'It doesn't matter now, and nothing will bring Vic back. Perhaps this Nick Faux will do more to find out what actually happened to her, with Jackie here.'

'I think it is time that every one of us told the truth.' Michael's voice was gravelly and deep. 'We all have things we can offer to help piece together what happened to Vicki, and to Vincent. We probably all noticed something that could be relevant, and we can let the police work out what's significant.'

As Michael spoke, Bill reached for his wine glass, knocking over a tall pitcher of water standing next to it. He swore as a gush of water spread across the table, and Lucy scraped her chair back noisily to avoid being splashed. Astrid also got up, mopping at her lap with a napkin, as Gareth lifted the jug with its remaining contents, to stem the flow.

The disruption provided a natural opportunity for others to stand and for the group to begin to disperse. Tomorrow was due to be their final day together on the 'Refresh and Renew' retreat, and Clare felt about as refreshed and renewed as the heap of sodden napkins piled on the table. If most of those around the dinner table emerged from the retreat relatively unscathed by the trauma of attending, that would be a result.

CHAPTER 52

Some guests headed to their rooms after dinner, but not all. As Clare passed the door to the lounge, Bill stepped out into the corridor, blocking her way.

'I have concerns, Clare,' he said, leaning over her and speaking low. 'Given the events of the day, and of last year, what is the police assessment of any danger or threat to my wife, or to others?'

Clare was sympathetic, but told him that she had no advice from DCI Faux to offer about that.

'That's disappointing. If we are expected to remain at the Morva, I think some police protection should be made available, at the very least.'

Lucy joined them, standing behind her husband and looking at Clare expectantly.

Clare tried to be supportive, and to ignore the mischievous temptation to offer them Mia, her golden retriever, as a canine bodyguard. Although the dog might be eager to help, she would be utterly ineffective in protecting anyone or anything. Maybe that was unfair; Mia had played her part in the apprehension of a violent individual last year. Mostly by barking and jumping about in random excitement, admittedly, but she had meant well.

Neither Bill nor Lucy was reassured by Clare's attempts to allay their concerns, not least because Clare had nothing specific to offer. No one could guarantee that there would be no further disturbances; it seemed as if anything was possible.

'It's disturbing for all of us,' Lucy declared, then surprised Clare by adding, 'It's difficult for the hotel staff, too. Jeremy has been looking keyed up and anxious, and Rachel, that friendly young woman at reception, seemed very tense earlier this evening.'

Clare thanked them for their forbearance and went to find Rachel. She gathered that David had been in touch and had successfully booked a ride for the children for the following morning. That was good to know.

'I hear that news is out about Victoria's journal, or that the police have it, now,' Rachel added, looking sombre. Perhaps Nadiya had also confided in her, following her admission to Clare.

'Yes, and it's better that way.' Clare decided to be positive. 'And they're also aware about who paid Lucy's bill last year. The police need to have every piece of information that we can give them.'

'Maybe –' Rachel was more hesitant – 'but the fallout for some of us could be awful.'

'How do you mean?' Clare was not going to let that hint pass.

'I think visitors have no idea what it is like, trying to

make a living here, Clare.' Rachel raised her chin, her cheeks flushed. 'Sorry, I know you mean well, but no one can afford anywhere to live. We have to work crazy hours just to get by, while visitors sip cappuccinos and cocktails, wear nautical outfits and think they're experiencing the real Cornwall – staying in tarted-up cottages which lie empty for most of the year.'

'Yes. I'm sorry.' It was better to say little, and to listen. Rachel wasn't usually so blunt, and this was raw.

'People who've got jobs can't afford to lose them, and so what if they cut corners, or make a bit on the side? We need to do what we can.' Rachel shook her head, exasperated at the challenges her community faced, and the inability of outsiders to understand them.

'Sure, it must be so difficult.' Clare waited to see if Rachel would say more, then decided to prompt her, to keep on track. 'I wonder whether people here have been caught up in things they'd rather the police didn't know about?' She tried a stab in the dark. 'Like Nadiya? Or Gail?'

'What do you mean?' the receptionist parried.

'Someone thought that one of the hotel guests might have accessed stuff to give them a boost while they were here, and I wondered if people sold it, maybe. Or maybe were involved in distribution, or something.' It sounded vague, but Rachel would know what she was getting at.

'If that were true, I wouldn't know anything about it,' Rachel asserted, unconvincingly, and looked away as she did so.

Clare thought it would be more accurate to say that she opted to know nothing about it. 'I think the police need to get a full picture, and then they can work out what's relevant. Two people are missing, Rachel, and the likeliest explanation is that they're dead.'

'OK, so maybe your friend Jackie needs to take a closer look at what Gail's business background might be,' Rachel murmured, 'but you didn't hear it from me, Clare. OK?' She bent over the computer screen on the reception desk, as if suddenly absorbed by it.

This mention of Gail was big. Clare tried to emphasise her willingness to keep things discreet by nodding and not speaking.

'But she's a good boss, she's quite hands off – leaves a lot of things to Jeremy and me.' Rachel spoke softly, still staring at her screen rather than facing Clare directly.

'Yes, I thought that.' This was safer ground. 'And Jeremy keeps himself out of the shadier stuff?'

'Right.'

Nick Faux would need to hear all this, Clare thought. She didn't want to press Rachel further, or to ask for any more names. The implication about Gail was enough. Her past would be relevant, and Clare was increasingly sure that she and Vincent had been an item.

'Thanks, Rachel. And I'm sorry about all this.'

'It's not your fault. And whoever hurt Victoria or Vincent must be stopped.'

'Yes, we want no more of this. Bill and Lucy are worried

about safety, and I don't blame them. Look after yourself, too, Rachel, won't you.'

'Don't worry, I do, Clare. I do.'

'OK, thanks.' Clare had an uneasy feeling that she might be sensible to do likewise.

CHAPTER 53

At eight thirty on the dot, the group arrived en masse at the Leven Room to meet DCI Nick Faux. Clare watched them as they filed in, like a crocodile of schoolchildren, entering the room two by two, then tentatively picking their seats. Nick Faux and his younger colleague had rearranged the chairs into a horseshoe shape in the middle of the room – making it easier for them to watch everyone. Clare had tried to help with the furniture moving but had been waved away; the room was police territory now.

As seats were taken and anxious glances exchanged, Gail, Jeremy, Nadiya and Rachel sidled in, hovering uncertainly. Clare smiled a welcome. She was pleased to see the hotel team here, and it also emphasised that DCI Faux was including them in the ongoing investigation.

'Please sit, everyone,' Nick Faux said, waving the staff forward into the empty seats beside Clare. 'Good evening. I'm Detective Chief Inspector Nick Faux, and I and my fellow officer Detective Constable Teasdale are grateful to you for joining us. I believe many of you already know DCI Jackie Carter, from the Dorset police service, who happens to be staying here at the hotel at this time.' He spoke with energy and authority, and his shorter, rotund colleague nodded affirmatively at every sentence uttered.

Everyone was focused on what the DCI was saying, anticipating the awful news, and Clare was grateful that, when it came, he didn't try to sugar-coat it.

'I am very sorry to inform you that a hotel guest, Vincent Hyde, was discovered with life-threatening injuries earlier today, and that it was not possible to save him. He died where he was found.'

Someone made a whimpering sound, quickly suppressed, and Clare herself found it difficult to breathe. However much this news had been expected, and whatever the news reports had suggested, it was still a brutal shock to hear Vincent's death confirmed. He had sat with them all in this very room, had splashed in the pool with some of them, too. He'd discussed fateful catastrophes with Clare while sharing a drink on the sunlit terrace, only two days ago.

'Mr Hyde's family have been informed, and their local police service are offering appropriate support.'

Presumably that would be in Devizes, Clare thought, with Wiltshire police.

'We will need to trace Mr Hyde's movements, and at present it is unclear how his injuries were caused. There is, I regret to say, the possibility that they were not accidental. Because of this, we will need to hear from each of you about your contact with Mr Hyde and any relevant information you may have to give us, to assist in our enquiries.'

DCI Faux explained that they would be interviewed

individually, and he regretted that this meant they would need to remain on site for the remainder of the evening, and during the following day.

'I understand that the retreat holiday ends tomorrow afternoon. However, it's essential that you all remain here and are available to assist with our enquiries. I'm grateful to the Morva management –' he nodded towards Gail – 'who have confirmed they are able to offer a further night's accommodation to anyone who has not already booked to stay on tomorrow night, after the retreat finishes. I regret any inconvenience this delay to your departure may cause, but I'm confident that you will understand the gravity of the situation, and the need for your forbearance.'

Bill now spoke, raising his hand as he did so, but not waiting for Nick Faux's acquiescence before beginning: 'Am I to understand that, as yet, you are not linking this unfortunate incident with the disappearance of my sister-in-law, a year ago? If not, if I may say so, that seems the most extraordinary oversight.'

Clare realised that he was trying to keep his tone respectful, but there was no mistaking the intensity of his feeling, however polite his words might be. She leaned forward enough to see that he'd screwed up his face, making his bushy eyebrows seem even more prominent and aggressive.

'We're considering all options, of course, but must avoid reaching any premature conclusions,' Nick Faux replied, obviously unintimidated and well versed in handling people's responses to extreme situations. 'All relevant information, including the missing-person enquiry into Ms Armstrong's disappearance, will be considered appropriately and with rigour.'

'How can we have confidence in your investigation, when last year you discovered precisely nothing?' Lucy's voice rose, filled with anger.

Clare saw Astrid place a conciliatory hand on her neighbour's arm, patting her gently. Lucy shook her off and continued to focus on the DCI.

'My concern is that you ensure you don't miss anything which is relevant to Victoria's disappearance. Is there any suggestion that Vincent may have known something about what happened to my sister?' Lucy demanded.

'That's a significant question, but one which we will address to each of you as individuals,' Nick said calmly.

Clare was impressed by how unperturbed he seemed by Lucy's outburst.

'We will begin in twenty minutes,' he said. 'My colleague, Detective Constable Teasdale –' he waved to indicate the young man next to him – 'will let you know the outline of approximate timings of those interviews, which will take place in the small room beside the lounge – called the snug, I believe. Thank you for your attention and cooperation.'

And that was it. No opportunity for discussion, and little sense of urgency, either. Nick Faux walked out, taking his colleague with him.

'Is this usual?' Clare turned to ask Jackie, perplexed. 'He's just . . . gone?'

'It's one way of doing it.' Jackie had her impassive face on, but Clare knew her well enough to deduce that she was far from impressed by her counterpart's approach.

Jeremy positioned himself in front of the group and began

answering queries about whether guests would be able to retain the same room, now that they had to stay for an additional night. Clare noticed that Gail left him to it, slipping away with Rachel, who was presumably returning to her post at reception. Gail was an expert in keeping a low profile, but Clare suspected the hotel manager had her own feelings about Vincent's death to process, and that she chose to do so in private.

'When did anyone see Vincent last?' Lucy asked, loudly, before any more of the group could disperse. 'I think he went missing sometime after dinner and before the Epilogue, yesterday. This is so terrible. I feel sick.'

'Did you see him at all this morning, Gareth,' Pippa asked, 'when you were out for your run? I thought you came back up from that direction, before heading off towards the harbour.'

'I don't know what you mean,' Gareth said. 'Where exactly did you see me?'

'Perhaps it would be helpful to say these things to DCI Faux,' Jackie interjected, with a note of authority. 'He can clarify and coordinate the information we each have to contribute.'

That was nicely done, Clare thought. Jackie stepping in would prevent anyone tailoring their answers to fit in with what others said. Clare was surprised that Nick Faux hadn't been more explicit about asking everyone not to discuss the case with one another. She thought that Gareth had mentioned meeting Dan down at the harbour, but Nick Faux and his team could piece the timings of everything together.

'Will we still have an Epilogue this evening? I hope we can.'

Dan was scratching his head and shaking it, too. He looked bewildered by the night's turn of events.

'Yes, that will be good to do, but a bit later, tonight.' Clare spoke with confidence, knowing that was what people needed now. 'I'll play some music in here and we'll have candles lit from ten until eleven or so, for people to come and sit, whenever you want to, during that time. If I'm with DCI Faux myself at any point, you can simply continue without me. While I'm here, we may have some very brief readings and reflection, interspersed with the music.'

'Thank you, Clare – that sounds good. We're all rather shocked by this news about Vincent.' Dan was a reliable lieutenant on the retreat front. 'Would you like the chairs put back into a circle again?'

As soon as Clare acceded to his suggestion, Michael and Pippa began to move their seats back to their former positions, while Lucy leaned down to gather up her bag and jacket before standing.

'There's something you should know, Lucy. And I'm sorry I didn't tell you before.' Michael stood at a respectful distance from his former sister-in-law, but, even so, Bill edged himself between them, protectively.

'What?' Lucy now stood eerily still, as she waited for Michael to continue.

'I did see Victoria. That last day.'

Everyone stopped what they were doing, as if the room were collectively holding its breath.

'Where?'

'I was in the little church at Cadgwith. She looked in, but

only for a moment. We didn't have long; Pippa was on her way up the path, from the village—'

'Why didn't you say anything?' Bill interrupted. 'What happened between you?'

'I asked if we could talk. I had some news I wanted to give her.' Michael gulped and swallowed, as if reliving the moment. 'She told me to meet her on the bench above the beach, beside the hotel. Late, so it would be after you were asleep.'

That was consistent with Victoria's journal, Clare realised. Was he telling the truth?

'So, you met her and killed her.' Lucy spoke with a strange detachment.

'And tried to pay us off. And I thought you were my mate.' Bill's face reddened and his neck bulged with anger. Clare had never seen someone show their teeth like that, as if ready to fight.

'Pay us off?' Now, Lucy looked shocked, no longer standing as if carved in stone, but turning sharply to her husband and frowning in disbelief.

'It was nothing. Just a budget issue. I didn't want to bother you. Because we stayed here for so long – or you did – it was a steep bill. Michael covered it.' Bill was almost dismissive of Lucy. He was still focused on Michael, as if ready to strike.

'You asked him to do that?' Lucy's fury was now concentrated on her husband.

Clare saw Jackie move slowly towards them, ready to intervene if things escalated, which looked increasingly likely.

It was Pippa who asked the more pressing question, ignoring

the issue of who had covered Lucy's bill: 'So, did you come here, that night, Michael? Is that what all this is about?' She spoke with a mixture of satisfaction and hostility. Of course she was angry, but perhaps she was also pleased to have been proved right in her suspicions about his movements that night.

Michael hung his head. Clare had seldom seen anyone look so ashamed.

'I'm sorry, Pippa. I should have said. To you, to everyone. But what was the point? It would have meant the police focused on me, not on what really happened.'

'You mean they would have known it was you.' Lucy's voice dripped with venom. 'You would have been caught, if it hadn't been for Pippa's alibi.'

Michael stood with his palms open, as if in surrender, facing Lucy directly as he answered her. 'That's your assumption, and it would have been theirs, too. Yes, I came, and yes, I sat on the bench next to the path, where it drops more steeply. But Vicki never came. I sat for a while, and I thought she had decided against it. I couldn't blame her.'

There was hollow desolation in his voice. No wonder Michael had sought refuge in Hardy's poems of lament. Clare imagined him sitting there, waiting for the woman who never came. It was certainly a Hardyesque scene. But, according to Nadiya, Victoria's journal had been left by a bench on the level path en route to the harbour, not on the downward path to the beach. It was possible that Michael had waited in the wrong place, she supposed. In their hasty conversation in the Cadgwith chapel, had he and Victoria been at cross purposes about their rendezvous?

Before Clare had an opportunity to ask, Jackie intervened.

'This information is relevant to DCI Faux's ongoing investigation. Rather than discussing it here, in front of everyone, it would be best to give your own full account directly to him, Michael,' she insisted sternly.

That was impressive self-control. Clare knew that Jackie would be itching to interrogate Michael herself – indeed, she would be itching to question everyone, in forensic detail. But Jackie would do things by the book, because then Nick Faux was more likely to build a solid case and get a conviction. Things were not looking good for the ex-husband; Jackie had her sights on him, all right. Yet Clare's questions lingered. Was Michael telling the truth? And had he simply waited for Victoria in the wrong place?

CHAPTER 54

Jackie was pulsating with frustration at Nick Faux's missteps. He hadn't even left the hotel guests under the watchful eye of one of his officers. It was lucky that she had been there to hear Michael's revelation, and others' responses. And it was thanks to her presence that they had been prevented from colluding any further on their versions of events, too.

When she hurried to speak with the Cornish DCI at his new base in the snug, to inform him about this latest development, he listened attentively enough, but offered no encouragement for her to try to elicit further information – quite the reverse.

'I appreciate this input; there are a number of lines of enquiry which my team will pursue,' Nick Faux said, while also directing the rearrangement of furniture in the small room with a wave of his arm. One officer was shifting a sofa further back against the wall; another was clearing shelves of paraphernalia, presumably to make space for police equipment in this hastily established base.

Jackie was succinct: 'This admission from Victoria Armstrong's ex that they had a rendezvous planned on the night of her disappearance is significant and may also have a bearing on the Vincent Hyde case.' She had Nick Faux's full attention, now. 'The retraction of his alibi, previously provided by Pippa Carpenter, may account for his sudden decision to admit to his movements that night.'

'Yes, thank you – and for the notes you have already submitted to the team, which we'll consider carefully.' DCI Nick Faux looked Jackie in the eye. 'You'll understand I need to make it clear that I will be moving the investigation forward from now on, which means you must refrain from any further discussion or involvement with witnesses or suspects. Are we clear about that, DCI Carter?'

'Of course.' Compliance was the best way forward, even if Jackie had to grit her teeth to give it. 'I fully appreciate the position and will steer clear of investigation.'

She could understand Nick Faux not wanting to risk his case being compromised, but excluding her entirely was self-defeating. Last year, she had asked Clare for her input in the Greenwood case, despite the vicar's unofficial role. And that input had proved useful.

Now, she was being kept away from a police enquiry, and she didn't like it. She wanted to burrow down, to question and scrutinise Michael's account properly. What precisely had he seen? Where had he been? And for how long? She would find the inconsistencies in his story and get the real details out of him, if this was her case.

Jackie would have to satisfy herself with talking things through with Clare, as her police colleagues were reluctant to engage with her. She sought out the vicar, going up to Clare's room and knocking sharply on the door.

'Just a moment!' Clare's voice sang out, and through the door Jackie could hear the murmurings of the vicar ending a phone conversation, presumably with her husband.

'Sorry – please, come in,' Clare said, as she finally opened the door, and it was a relief to be in that private space together, with no risk of being overheard.

'How did Nick Faux take what you had to tell him?' Clare asked. She now sat cross-legged on the bed, having gestured to Jackie to seat herself on the sofa, next to the picture window.

Jackie chose to be non-committal; she didn't want to undermine her professional loyalty to her counterpart, despite wanting to talk frankly with Clare. At least Clare had zero involvement in Victoria's disappearance, and Jackie was one hundred per cent confident that she was innocent of any ill intent towards Vincent. Jackie also trusted her not to repeat what she told her, except perhaps to David, and she trusted her former boyfriend, too.

However, Clare took Jackie by surprise; rather than simply listening to Jackie's speculation, she had made an important realisation of her own.

'Remember what Michael said about the bench he sat on being beside the steep path? I think Victoria was waiting for him along the path in the other direction, near where you talked to Pippa, and where Nadiya found the jacket and journal. On the path that goes towards the harbour, not the one that drops down to the beach at the cove below the hotel.'

'OK.' Jackie nodded her head as she took a moment to consider the point. 'If that was the case, it was a big misunderstanding. What are the implications?' She wanted to hear Clare's conclusions.

'If that happened, maybe Pippa saw he was there, realised that he had arranged to get together with Victoria, and flipped? Supposing she had taken something which impacted her judgement – her reaction might have been extreme, and violent.'

'If she found out, Pippa might have been upset about the two of them making plans to meet, but that's a stretch,' Jackie said. 'But the two paths . . . maybe that does explain why Victoria was outside for quite a while that night. She was waiting for him – and maybe she wandered down to the harbour and saw that Gail or her contacts were up to something there, retrieving packages or something else incriminating. If it is Gail who's involved – but the underhand stuff here has to be organised by someone, and she seems the most likely suspect.'

'Gail? Right.' Clare took her time to consider her answer, then continued, 'And, if it was Gail I heard on the phone that first day, she said something about being under pressure from suppliers. Sure, she could have been talking about food deliveries or bed linen for the housekeeping team . . . but she could also have been referring to something very different.'

Jackie frowned, then added to Clare's suggestion: 'I'm interested in her past history with Vincent, in London; I think Nick Faux should dig into that. If she worked in hospitality, she'd have been a good source of news stories, or perhaps the two of them share a shadier past. Or maybe it was just Gail involved in dodgy stuff. If she realised that Vincent was on to her involvement with crime here, and what had happened to Victoria, she might have decided to deal with him, too.' Jackie knew they were working well together, firing ideas off one another.

Clare picked up the baton: 'Maybe she was involved in drugs or whatever, that could easily be true. But supposing what happened to Victoria and Vincent had nothing to do with that.' She paused. 'I think Vincent used Gail to contact people to get them to come to the retreat, so that he could write about it. This whole time, I've been bothered by the question of why so many people who knew Victoria have ended up here. Gail wouldn't want trouble at her hotel, but, if Vincent was after a story, he could have used her and some police tip-off to access their details and send them invitations. She was incredibly unhappy with the person on the phone; it seemed more than just business.'

Jackie wanted to explore every angle, as she would do with her team. She raised another possibility: 'Lucy might not be as innocent as she'd like us to think, either. And how does Bill feature?'

'We know they had some financial issues – Victoria wrote about how Lucy mustn't sponge off their dad anymore, or off her. Maybe that was what they argued about,' Clare suggested.

Jackie thought the vicar was asking some pertinent questions, and she wasn't a bad sounding board, given the absence of the DCI's regular team.

The sky was darkening as they talked. Out at sea, lights flickered and glimmered, marking the passage of vessels in the shipping lane.

'I'll go down and see if anyone wants to chat,' Clare said. 'And I'll start sorting the candles in the Leven Room – once lit, they can't be left unattended. A fire at the Morva is all we need. This isn't Manderley, and we aren't going to have a dramatic denouement in a blazing building. No Mrs Danvers moment, thank you.'

'I don't know – whoever hurt Victoria can blaze away in an inferno, as far as I'm concerned, and I'll happily chuck on some extra petrol to help them burn.'

Jackie wasn't usually as frank as this in expressing her views about what such murdering scum deserved. She was lowering her guard, where Clare was concerned, and perhaps that wasn't a good thing. But Jackie wanted justice for whoever had harmed Victoria. And retribution.

CHAPTER 55

With the later start time, it was dark by the time the Epilogue finished, although lights placed along the edge of the grass still illumined the hotel garden. The door to the Leven Room was open, and Clare could hear the sound of the waves as she sat alone in there, with the candles burning low. The tide must be coming in. Or maybe, because the hotel was quieter now, the noises of the sea's rhythms were more noticeable. The sounds of ebb and flow weren't precise; there were pauses, as well as changes in volume, as waves broke on to the shore or retreated more gently.

Some of the retreat group had sat with her in the quietness, while others had been occupied with giving their statements to Nick Faux and his colleagues, upstairs. Clare noticed that some people wept, as they sat. She felt too exhausted for tears, but her heart was heavy. One by one, everyone had eventually drifted away, perhaps to go to their rooms to try to sleep, or to sit outside in contemplation. Some would no doubt gather in the lounge bar, for company.

The bartender would be on duty for a while longer. Clare wondered whether to get a drink herself, but simply sat on, in the peace of the room. She prayed for everyone who had been in there that day and on previous days. She prayed for Vincent's wife – it still felt too soon to think of her as a widow. She wondered about Gail, and what she might be experiencing now. Clare prayed for her, too – and for Rachel, and all the hotel staff.

Jackie moved so quietly that Clare didn't notice she was there until the DCI sat down beside her. Neither woman spoke as they listened to the repeating sound of waves in the distance and the occasional murmur of conversation from the terrace above.

'How are you doing?' Clare asked eventually, her voice low.

'Nick Faux has left, with all his team.' Clearly, Jackie was fixed on the investigation, not on herself. 'They've had an initial interview with everyone and will be back tomorrow to follow up.'

'That was quick.'

'It was just an initial overview, identifying areas to look into more deeply.' Jackie was bland, but Clare suspected that she thought the enquiries to date were too superficial, even if she was unwilling to say so. The DCI was less inscrutable than she might realise. Clare's own interview had been brief in the extreme.

'Is the beach still closed off?' she asked.

'No point; the forensics team did their stuff earlier, and the tide has been in and out several times since Vincent went missing.'

'I thought I'd go down and take a look.' Clare didn't mention that she wanted to pray for Vincent there, in the place where he'd died. Jackie already thought she was weird, there was no need to add to that impression. Clare would continue to pray for whoever had killed him, too, and she thought Jackie would be even less impressed by that.

'Yes, it would be useful to check exactly what you can see from the benches beside that steep path down to the beach. At night, how much can you see from the hotel terraces?' Jackie said. Nick Faux might be leading this investigation, but she was clearly determined to do what she could.

'I'm not sure. Can you see the benches to the far side of the hotel, where Victoria's journal was found?' Clare was mulling over possibilities. 'Surely, they're too far along, and it's dark now. I wonder whether Victoria did leave her jacket there, and walked further down that way, towards the harbour. If the night was warm, she might have taken it off and forgotten it. But if she'd left willingly, I don't think she'd have forgotten to take her journal. The whole point of keeping it with her was to stop anyone else reading it.'

'That's a good point. I hope Nick Faux considers that possibility, too.' Jackie's tone of voice implied that she doubted he would. 'Though, it might be better for you to leave beach wandering until tomorrow. We don't need any accidents. I think I'll just have a quick look at the benches, to take stock of what's visible.'

This made Clare all the more determined to make the trip down the newly opened path – no way would she be corralled by Jackie, thanks. Especially as Jackie was planning on doing some exploring herself.

Footsteps approached from outside, and Dan appeared in the doorway, silhouetted by the lights from the garden lamps.

'Everything OK, Clare?' he asked, leaning into the room, holding on to the doorframe with one arm raised. She found his care a touch oppressive rather than supportive, but he was young and eager to please.

'All good, thanks, Dan,' she said. 'I hope you're doing OK?'

'All right, I suppose. Not the easiest evening, but thanks. Pippa has been quite upset. Astrid talked with her and kept her company for a while, I think.'

Perhaps Dan hadn't noticed Jackie, or perhaps he was simply willing to be candid with everyone. 'Bill and Michael sort of squared up to one another in the corridor, but Lucy calmed them down.'

'Did you hear what they were saying?' Clare asked, realising that Jackie would thank her for it.

'No. Gareth wanted a word, so I had a drink with him. He was a bit stressed about having to stay another night, but thankfully Jeremy's sorted that. I've booked on to stay another day, too.'

As he explained accommodation arrangements, Jackie quietly rose and left by the internal door. Clare was sure the DCI would take advantage of the opportunity to begin her exploration of sight lines and viewing points without being hampered by Clare's presence and would be content to leave her to Dan's conversation.

'In spite of everything, it's nice here,' he said. 'I'm hoping to walk along the coast over the weekend, using the Morva as my base. I think I'll travel back on Sunday, in time for evening service, then go for pizza with some of the guys from church. It's a good way to finish the weekend. I'm due back at work next week.'

'What do you do?' Clare asked, on conversational autopilot.

'I work for Customs and Excise.'

Now she was more alert.

'It's a bit like auditing,' Dan explained. 'Checking up on money being where people say it is, that kind of thing.'

'It sounds interesting. I didn't see you as a tax collector.'

'It's not the most popular job. But Jesus had tea at Zacchaeus's house, and people hated him.'

'You're right. And Zacchaeus said he'd repay all the money he had extorted from people and would give loads more away. I hope he did.'

'It's interesting to think about what happened to people after they met Jesus – what happened to Lazarus, or Martha? I wish we knew.'

'Yes, perhaps we will, one day. One of the perks of getting older is seeing some of the stories of people's lives unfolding. The happier ones, anyway.'

'Yes, Vincent spoke about that. Maybe I ought to have told Nick Faux.'

'What did Vincent say?' Clare kept her tone conversational.

'In the minibus, heading for Kynance, he talked about our identities, and how our beliefs and attitudes can be transformed over time. I agreed with him. I see people being changed. My dad kicked the cat in the kitchen, after he was converted. Then he said sorry. He'd never have apologised for anything before. He and my mum started giving money away, too. A bit too much, sometimes. But then, I'm in finance, so I get worked up about budgets and pensions. Mum says I should have more faith.'

'Faith and budgets aren't mutually exclusive.' Clare smiled. 'Although, I'm better at spending money than earning it, that's for sure. What else was said in that chat about life stories? It sounds interesting.' Would Dan realise she thought it might have been more than that?

'Not much – we got a bit distracted, as there was a tricky manoeuvre for the minibus then.'

'Right.' And Jeremy would have been all ears when Vincent was discussing identities and life histories. Perhaps it had affected his driving.

'I suppose we talked a bit about people's assumptions about one another. Because I like trains, I'm a bit of a geek. Because Gareth runs fast, people underestimate his intelligence – that sort of thing.'

'I wish I'd been there – it sounds interesting. Thanks for telling me, Dan.'

'Thanks for the Epilogue, and for your care for us. Let me know if there's anything I can do to help, won't you.'

'I will, thanks. Goodnight.'

'Shall I close the door?'

'I'll do it, thanks.'

Dan meant well, but she was relieved to see him go. She was ready to close up for the evening and head for the beach.

CHAPTER 56

Clare began the descent to the cove gingerly, but gained in confidence as her feet seemed to find their grip quite easily and there was enough moonlight to follow the route down. The predicted rain hadn't materialised and it was a lovely night for a walk: the air had a softness to it and the sounds of nature enveloped her. The smells of salt, seaweed and the countryside were stronger than during the day, but perhaps that was because her other senses were more alert now that there was less to see. A sheep baaed, and another replied to it, or joined in with whatever complaint or comment was being made.

Clare hadn't anticipated meeting any members of the group once she was on the downward path and away from the proximity of the hotel. But it wasn't long before she encountered Jeremy, who was breathing heavily as he made his way up towards her. She heard him before she saw him, so was less startled than he was by their near collision.

'Sorry, Clare!' he gasped, when he realised who he had nearly walked into. 'I'm trying to hurry; it'll be time to close the bar soon. But it's a steep climb, that's for sure. I wanted to pay my respects.' He stood with his hands on his hips, then hitched up his trousers with a familiar gesture. 'I guess that's why you are going down, too? Taking time to do so feels appropriate, given Vincent's association with us all at the Morva. He was a regular, and this dreadful loss impacts everyone. Thank you for being here, Clare, at this sad and difficult time for the hotel community, and for our guests.'

Clare wasn't entirely convinced by his laborious explanation for being out at this hour, but nodded along.

'I thought I'd catch some air,' she said, and then made an effort to be more truthful. 'And I wanted to pay my respects, too – you're right, Jeremy. That's lovely that you've done so.'

'It's a natural impulse, I think, and we're not the only ones. I thought I saw someone else down there, too. We all want to remember Vincent in different ways, I suppose. Watch your step, won't you.'

They bade one another goodnight and Jeremy continued upwards, almost jogging as he disappeared. Clare had no reason to hurry, so she stood for a moment longer, then was distracted by the rustle of movement in the hedgerow to her right, which interrupted the louder noises of the sea below. It was probably a rodent scuffling, or perhaps a bird, if any were still awake at this hour. Anna would know – she was the family's go-to expert on all things ornithological or wildlife-related. Clare only knew that owls went out hunting in the dark – and, as yet, there was no sound of any hooting.

She continued down, pleased that she was able to keep her footing when navigating the section of the path near the stream, and, after turning left, she reached the beach itself.

At the end of the path, the squat, functional building she'd noticed before stood sentinel, its grimy windows reflecting the moonlight. Sometimes, that light dimmed, dispersed by the moving patterns of clouds overhead, which also obscured some stars and then revealed them again, parting and passing on by.

Shale crunched beneath her feet as Clare made her way towards the water. There was less beach exposed tonight than had been the case when she'd met Lucy down here on that first afternoon.

And then, just like the first day, she saw Lucy again. This time, she stood on the shore, looking out at the inky dark water, which was ridged with white as its waves tumbled towards her and then were sucked back, before reaching forward again, but not quite so close.

Clare was discomfited to discover her there, alone. Not wanting to disturb her, she headed for the cluster of rocks where she had found her that first day, when the jet from Culdrose had accelerated over their heads.

Her mind wandered to tales of smugglers, and of landing craft bringing their cargo of contraband ashore, whether in modern, plastic containers or the wooden barrels and packing cases of the past. She felt a flicker of alarm, but consoled herself with the thought that, with all the police activity today, surely there was no danger of anyone landing illicit goods tonight.

As she approached the rocks, she spotted Bill. He sat there, watching Lucy from afar, but stationed within calling distance. Clare was relieved that he had been keeping watch.

'Hello, Bill. It's warmer than I thought it would be,' Clare said. As far as platitudes went, this was up there with the best of them.

'Do you think Nick Faux has any chance of catching him? Michael, I mean?' Bill was not interested in idle chat. He stood, and his words tumbled out in a rush. 'I was a fool not to see it, but I thought he was a good bloke – decent. He seemed to be. Lucy and I have a certain lifestyle, certain expectations, and Michael covered for me more than once – he was generous like that. That clouded my judgement, I think. Sometimes, we get in a tight spot financially; there have been issues with clients and cash flow. Lucy didn't know, but it's true that Michael covered the bill last year. I was in a tight spot, but I won't make that mistake again.'

'I'm sure the police will explore all possibilities,' Clare said. She wondered what it was exactly that had landed Bill in financial trouble.

Bill shook his head. 'I don't suppose you know any more than we do about what really happened to Vic, or to Vincent,' he said, more quietly. 'Lucy was disappointed that neither you nor Jackie had come clean about things, though.'

'Yes, I'm sorry, that must have been a shock.'

'Not so much of a shock as having Vincent disappear, and then to be part of a murder enquiry.'

'If it was murder,' Clare corrected him half-heartedly.

'I think it's pretty obvious, don't you? Someone did this Vincent in, then left him to die – or to be drowned, maybe; no one is telling us the grisly details. You've been involved with murder before, Astrid says.'

'Only by coincidence. How did she know?'

'I think everyone does. Someone checked you out, and Jackie.'

At this, Clare sank down on to a large flat rock. She immediately regretted her choice when she felt water beginning to soak through her clothing.

'I hope we find out more tomorrow,' Bill continued. 'Anything's better than being left not knowing what happened to Vincent. Whoever it was, it'll be better for Lucy to know.'

'You're right.' Clare wanted to be supportive. 'And perhaps tracking down who hurt Vincent will lead the police team to solve Victoria's disappearance, too. I think we have to be open to possibilities and not assume it was Michael.'

'Do you have other ideas?'

'Yes, I do.'

At this, Clare thought she heard a dislodged rock or stone tumble on to the beach from the stack of boulders on the far side of where she was seated. Bill seemed to take the noise as a cue to rejoin Lucy. Perhaps he was concerned about leaving her alone for too long.

Clare didn't want to encroach on them, so stayed where she was. She had an impulse to make herself smaller and drew herself further on to the rock, pulling up her feet and wrapping her arms around her legs to gather herself into a hunched ball. As she rested her chin on her knees and stared out at the sea, she felt vulnerable and alone.

CHAPTER 57

Clare stood to stretch her stiffened limbs. In thinking about the letter she would write to Vincent's wife, she had spent longer huddled on that damp rock than she had intended. Bill and Lucy were long gone. The sky had grown darker, the clouds had thickened and the tide was further out now. It was time to leave.

She began to pick her way round the outcrop of rocks and back towards the path, feeling increasingly uneasy about her solitude. Jackie had cautioned against visiting the cove so late, and unaccompanied.

Then Clare realised that she wasn't alone. She could make out a hooded figure in the distance, moving along the shoreline, seeming to make a sweeping search of the beach. They turned their body this way and that, as if scouring the expanse of sand cradled beneath the cliffs. Her skin prickled. It occurred to her that the figure might not be seeking anyone else, but might be checking that the beach was deserted, except for her. And this was the place where Vincent had died. What kind of fool had she been, coming down here alone?

She remembered the sound which had disturbed her

conversation with Bill. Someone had been listening and spying on them, just as Victoria had been watched. They would know that Clare was serious about finding out what had happened to Victoria, and to Vincent. And Vincent had been killed for asking questions.

Clare shivered and took out her phone. Her fingers were clumsy. There was no signal. Nothing. No time to message, anyway. She needed to think, and to move.

She took a deep breath. Don't overreact, she told herself. Nothing will happen to you. Just make your way back to the hotel and everything will be fine. But it was a warm night, so why was that figure so muffled up?

And, if they knew that Clare was there and that no one else was down at the cove, they could simply wait for her to emerge. If she took the usual path, there would be no avoiding that ominous figure; they could hide by the abandoned building before she reached it, or be ready to ambush her at another striking point.

Clare knew that, to get away, her only chance was to get ahead – quietly and fast. Not up the expected path. There must be another way.

She would clamber on round these rocks and somehow scramble upward, up the cliff itself. There must be a continuation of the coast path somewhere above her, and she could reach it if she climbed. She mustn't risk revealing her position with any light from her phone, so she stuffed it deep into her pocket, and prayed as hard as she had ever prayed – for help, strength, survival. No way was she not going to be with Tom and Anna tomorrow. She mustn't think about them, or David. She must simply move, and quietly.

Move, move, move. She clambered and scrambled over rocks, scarcely noticing grazes or bruising, trying to breathe smoothly and without any gasps to give her away. She was managing to find her way upwards, levering herself over a rock face at one point, gripping some sharp gorse as she got higher, not daring to look downwards or behind her. Perhaps she was wrong and there was no danger, but her body told her otherwise. Seeing that figure methodically making its way along the shore, checking the whole beach, had told her all she needed to know.

She knew who it was, too, hooded or otherwise – strong and fast moving. There was no possibility of outrunning them; this was her only chance of escape.

Clare was panting, now – she couldn't help it. Her breath came in ragged, shuddering snatches of air. Perhaps she was sobbing, but she must keep going. There was some semblance of a path – or an animal track, at least – snaking its way up between rocks and patches of earth and tufty scraps of grass. She made herself hold still for a moment in order to gather her strength, and there was no sound of anyone behind her. She strained her ears to check, but all she heard were the waves in their relentless dance with the shore. She didn't dare risk looking, she had to keep her focus upward, and she mustn't think about height or the risk of falling.

'*Father above me, Son beside me, Spirit within me, the Three all around me*,' she repeated, silently, as she moved forward again. She hoped that 'around me' included the space beneath her, too, as she prayed for encircling protection. She didn't dare look down.

Finally, agonisingly, she reached the top of the cliff face and lurched herself forward over the edge of the highest rock and lay spreadeagled on sloping grass. The feel of its cool dampness and the smell of its freshness had never been so sweet. Her heart thudded in her chest. She was exhausted, spent. But she mustn't linger, she had to get away – and not by any expected route.

'Clare, what are you doing? I saw you climbing. It looked so risky – with no ropes, either.' Gareth's voice was full of concern as he approached her from along the cliff path.

So, it was him, and he had managed to cut off her route. Clare scrambled to her feet, terrified to see him and afraid that she would betray that fear. But perhaps she could still bluster her way out of this.

'Yes, I was just making my way back,' she began. Maybe she was wrong about him. Maybe everything would be OK. But then the clouds parted and she caught the expression on Gareth's face, his eyes hard and steely – murderous.

Should she run?

Before she could process the thought, she discovered she was doing exactly that, and she was moving faster than she'd ever thought possible. She had a mad sense of disappointment that David would never know about this burst of speed, as she hurled herself forward, away from Gareth, and further away from the hotel and any hope of safety.

'You won't get far,' Gareth called, and she heard his footsteps gaining on her.

Then another figure rushed past her on the clifftop, directly towards him.

Clare stopped running and turned to look. Gareth had halted his pursuit and now had a rock in his hand, which he was threatening Jackie with. The DCI dodged his movements, rolling herself away from him and away from the cliff edge.

'Drop the weapon, Gareth,' she said. 'It's too late for that, now.'

'What do you mean?' Gareth asked. 'What weapon? I was just carrying this; it's serpentine, look.' He held the rock up, as if bewildered at Jackie's command, and it did have a glistening edge, glinting in the light. He began to move away from her – towards where Clare now half stood, half crouched, breathing heavily.

'I never touched Vincent,' Gareth said, as he edged closer to Clare. 'I was never here when Vicki was meeting Michael, either, whatever you bitches think.'

'Don't move!' Jackie warned. 'I said, *don't move*!' she shouted again, as Gareth lunged towards Clare.

Jackie leapt forward, pulling Gareth to the ground as Clare twisted away. In the dim light, she could make out their dark shapes rolling back and forth as Jackie wrestled with him, Gareth swearing as they struggled. Suddenly, Jackie rocked herself back and slipped out of his grasp, then moved towards him again with a lunge, and was that a twist or a kick of her foot? Clare was not entirely sure what she saw as Gareth screamed and fell, toppling over the cliff edge and down, with a sickening series of thuds.

But Clare knew that she must be certain, absolutely certain, that she had seen Gareth reach to attack Jackie and that she had sidestepped him as he fell forward and over the edge. She must be sure that it had not been possible to save him. There must be no doubt, and she would never tell anyone anything else, not even David.

'Jackie, are you OK?' she asked, rushing forward and reaching down to hug her. 'You were so brave. Thank you. I saw him. I saw him fall. There was nothing you could have done. I know that. I'm sure of what I saw.'

Jackie stayed crouched and still, then stood and didn't speak, shrugging Clare off and dusting herself down. She wiped her face with her hand, and Clare saw the wetness of blood on it. Gareth must have hit her in the face.

Clare fished in her pocket for one of David's large hankies, which were useful for various purposes, and offered it to the DCI in silence.

'Thank you, Clare,' Jackie said, and it was unclear whether that was for the means to mop up her battered face, or for the certainty of Clare's account of what had happened. Either way, Jackie's gratitude sounded heartfelt.

CHAPTER 58

At the hotel, Gail was surprisingly solicitous, making hot drinks for Clare and Jackie while DCI Faux and his team did their stuff, calling in the coastguards and others to retrieve Gareth, or what might remain of him after his shattering fall.

Clare was bruised, but otherwise uninjured, yet she couldn't stop shaking – she was amazed at how Jackie kept it together. Having cleaned herself up, the DCI was already typing her account of events into her phone, only stopping to answer calls and to give more precise instructions to Nick Faux's colleagues as they headed towards the cove.

At least all the other retreatants were in their rooms and undisturbed by the drama of the night. Clare knew she couldn't face them, yet.

'How did you know where to find me?' Clare asked, once she'd stopped shivering.

'I met Bill and Lucy on their way up to bed, and Bill told me that you were still down there,' Jackie explained. She managed to combine talking to Clare with tapping on her phone. The woman was a machine, in pursuit of justice.

'Did you have any idea about Gareth?' Clare asked. She

clutched her hot drink as the images and fear reared up in her mind and body, threatening to overwhelm her.

'Not initially.' Jackie shook her head. 'Did you? What made you suspect?'

'I didn't know . . . not until the very end, anyway. But I had an inkling. Everyone discounted Gareth, as his relationship with Victoria had apparently been so short-lived,' Clare said, 'and, in a way, Victoria had discounted him, too, in her journal. She had planned on a future with a child, not with him.

'But the way he blamed Michael . . . and could get so caught up in someone new like Astrid so quickly,' Clare remembered. 'It made me think that he was eager to deflect blame and sometimes he was very intense. The sort of person that might become obsessive. He also seemed familiar with the coastal terrain, despite saying he'd never been here before, and Pippa saw him out early once, near where Vincent was found. And I think he heard me talking to Bill and knew I was investigating – just like Vincent had been.'

Jackie's phone buzzed with an incoming call from Nick Faux, and she left the room to take it in private. Clare was content to stay on the sofa in the snug, her knees drawn up to her chin. She was still in shock, processing the implications of the night.

Whatever Gareth's alibi might have been when Victoria disappeared, the police had been duped. Somehow, he had been here – Clare thought he could have arrived by boat and run up from the harbour. She had noticed his disquiet at the prospect of the group taking a trip out from there, when Dan had suggested it.

None of them would ever know what happened to Victoria that night, Clare thought, but at least they would know who had done it. Clare shuddered and wrapped herself tighter in the blanket which Gail had given her.

Suddenly, the door burst open and a golden retriever bounded in. Mia snuffled up to her, delirious with joy at being reunited. Clare buried her face in Mia's golden fur as the dog nestled as close to her as she could. Mia was tender and gentle; she knew what was needed. She licked Clare's sore hands.

'Jackie messaged,' David said, sitting down next to Clare and somehow managing to embrace his wife and their dog, too. He buried his face against her shoulder, suddenly wordless.

'What about Anna and Tom? You didn't leave them?'

'They're already tucked up in your room upstairs. We'll have to use the sofa bed; they're in the double. They're thrilled. I've promised them a room-service hotel breakfast as well as their ride in the morning.'

'What did you tell them about me? Are they OK?' Clare asked.

'No need to worry – they're fine.'

David was obviously in no rush to tell her more, and at that moment she was just glad he was here, and that she was safe – and that she would be with the children again, very soon.

'Thank God you're all right,' David said, and rested his face against Clare, while stroking her hair.

'Jackie saved me. She was amazing.'

'You're amazing. And I never want you anywhere near a crime of any kind, ever again.'

‘That makes two of us.’

Mia wriggled herself to be even closer to David, as well as to Clare. The dog leaned in against the two of them and thumped her tail on the floor in delight.

CHAPTER 59

Tom was sorry to be too tall for Nugget now, but was cheered by his promotion to riding Perran unaided, despite her larger size and liveliness.

'She kicks if anyone gets too close, Mum,' he announced, proudly. 'Except for her daughter, that's the chestnut mare that lady is riding.'

Clare's own daughter was perched on top of a piebald thunderbolt, but had somehow stayed on board when it sidestepped and skittered its way across the stable yard as she mounted. It was now calmer, kept at a respectful distance from the other horses, but Clare was not deceived. There was a glint in the creature's eye and Anna would have her hands full.

'It's OK, Mum – I'll be fine.'

Was her daughter telepathic? Maybe it was just another instance of Clare's poker face not being up to scratch. She had decided not to ride with them this morning; she was too jittery after last night's escape.

Anyway, she and David needed to return to the Morva after they'd dropped the children off at the stables. Rachel had arranged for Anna and Tom to spend the whole day with the horses, under the watchful eye of her sister, and to have an afternoon ride, too. Rachel herself would also be at the hotel, as Nick Faux needed everyone to be available today. He and DC Steven Teasdale were interviewing everyone separately, and piecing events together in the light of Gareth's actions.

'He believed you'd realised it was him,' Nick Faux had told Clare, the previous night. 'That has to be the explanation for his attack on you.'

'Maybe he only knew that for sure when I tried to get away from him,' she said, thinking of how the expression on Gareth's face had changed on the clifftop. 'So, then he thought he had to get rid of me—'

'Don't say that,' David interrupted. 'It sounds as if you're blaming yourself for getting away. That was exactly what you had to do.'

'Yes, thank you, David.' Nick Faux was obviously only just tolerating David's presence. 'And it was fortuitous that DCI Carter was there, just in the nick of time.'

As Clare walked slowly with David behind the troop of horses along the muddied track, she wondered what else Nick Faux might have to tell them, later that morning. When they reached the gate to the first field, they waited as the riders went through, then stood to watch as they set off diagonally across the grass.

Anna's mount was reaching up its head and shaking it, adding an occasional sudden sidestep or attempted spin, making it very clear it was eager to be off and at speed. Tom's bulky ride, the intimidating Perran, turned her head ready to bite if Anna's horse got too close, and shifted herself, ready to kick out, too.

The young woman in charge was used to all this and very capable; her younger assistant nosed her own horse between Tom's and Anna's, much to Clare's relief. Their children would have a great time, with plenty of stories to tell their parents that evening.

Standing by the gate and resting her arms on it, Clare told David more about the retreat group, and what she and Jackie had surmised about them.

'Michael became more open as the days went on, and his willingness to admit to coming to the Morva last year changed things. I think Gareth became more nervous that he'd been spotted and probably assumed I knew more than I did.'

Clare rested her chin on her hands as she talked, crouching slightly to do so. She was exhausted, but being here with David was helping her cope with what had happened.

'Perhaps me going to the beach and checking out the bench spooked him, too. He'd taken a huge risk attacking Vincent there; I guess Vincent had begun to set his sights on him as Victoria's murderer, or Gareth assumed that he had. His anger was all-consuming, I saw it. When I tried to get away, he was a predator with prey, fixed on catching me.'

'It's terrifying, and you were incredible, getting yourself up that cliff.'

'It isn't so steep, not all the way. And I had plenty of adrenaline – it was all so crazy.'

'Thank God Jackie headed down to find you; she thought

you would probably be checking out that cove, and then Lucy said you went down there.'

It sounded as if Jackie hadn't let on that she had advised against Clare doing so. That was decent of her, Clare thought. They were watching one another's backs.

Clare had been crystal clear with Nick Faux in explaining how Jackie had intervened to stop Gareth's attack on her, and had then defended herself, with no possibility of preventing Gareth's fall. Clare was unwavering and explicit in her description of Jackie's actions, choosing not to dwell upon, let alone voice, Jackie's earlier declarations of animosity towards whoever had harmed Victoria. Nor on her desire for retribution. There must be no doubt about what had happened on that clifftop, or what Clare had seen.

She and Jackie had focused on Dan's view that Gareth had seemed familiar with the terrain around the harbour and pathway when they walked back from Kynance together. Jackie believed Gareth and Victoria had walked down towards the harbour, and that Victoria had left her journal and jacket behind at the bench near the beginning of that route from the hotel. Had Victoria deliberately left her things there, if her relationship with Gareth had already become fractious? They would never know precisely what had happened between the missing woman and this murderous man.

David was mulling over Clare's words. 'And you think Gareth considered Vincent a threat, once everyone discovered he was a journalist?' he asked.

'Yes, and it was Vincent who engineered bringing everyone back to this retreat. Gail's admitted to Nick Faux that Jackie and I were right – Vincent hadn't only been having an affair with her, but also used her to advertise the retreat to people connected with Victoria. I suppose Gareth must have believed that Vincent would discover what had happened to Victoria, and he felt threatened. Maybe the conversation in the minibus, about knowing people's pasts, also alerted him to the danger Vincent posed, and all the questions he was asking, too.'

Clare paused, remembering the two men's behaviour, and how unaware she had been of their true feelings and motivations.

'When Gareth arrived, it must have been a massive shock to discover that others on the retreat had known Victoria, too. And what arrogance he had, to show up at all, and to assume he'd got away with it.' Clare shook her head.

'So, fearing discovery, Gareth attacked Vincent on the beach and left him to die,' David finished. 'Maybe he assumed he was dead, or that the tide would take him, and that it would cover traces of the violent assault, too.'

'Yes. And, when I saw him last night, I knew. Before then, he'd seemed so innocent, but I was becoming uncertain about him. Suspicious, even. And it turns out his alibi wasn't as rock solid as the police thought.'

Clare frowned as she recounted how Gareth's parents had vouched for him. They had assured Nick Faux's colleagues that their son had been staying with them and his brother, at their home in Wales, on the night Victoria went missing, and on the following night too. Presumably, they had wanted to keep Gareth safe from any accusation of involvement in a crime and had believed him to be blameless.

Clare hoped they regretted their naïve complicity. Vincent's death could have been prevented if Gareth had been more fully investigated when Victoria disappeared. Yet Gareth had remained under the radar, despite his guilt. And now his bereaved family were suffering his loss, as well as the impact of his crimes.

It had been foolish of him to return to the Morva, but Jackie said that killers often had a certain sort of hubris. They wanted to return to the scene of the crime and gloat over getting away with it. Though they would never know exactly what had happened to Victoria now, Jackie believed that Gareth had attacked her the night she went to meet Michael.

The misery resulting from Gareth's hatred and violence strengthened Clare's resolve to turn away from evil and to try to live out her faith with more integrity, in ways of love and mercy. Jackie had little interest in religion, as far as Clare was aware, but she was valiant in the service of what was good, in utter opposition to Gareth and his kind.

It was thanks to Jackie that Clare was still here, leaning on this gateway, with her husband beside her, their children happily beginning their holiday with no greater grief on their minds than their parents' refusal to allow Mia anywhere near the horses in the yard. Clare did not dwell on any uncertainty about Jackie's actions on the clifftop; it was better that way.

Similarly, it would be up to Nick Faux to follow up concerns about any illegal activities at the Morva or its surrounds, in which Gail might or might not be involved. Clare preferred not to ask herself what Rachel might have known, or suspected, about that, or why Nadiya had been so determined to protect Jeremy from suspicion.

For now, her responsibility was to console the others as best she could at this outcome of events, with all that it implied about what had happened to Victoria, a year before. There would be closure of some kind, although much remained unknown. She had messaged her archdeacon to ask for prayers today and would do her best for the group, with everything they would be facing.

In the meantime, it was time to let the dog out of the car for a run before returning to the hotel, where she would resolve things as far as possible with DCI Faux and his team, and support the retreat members and hotel staff as best she could. But first, Clare would savour this moment and breathe in the peace of it.

EPILOGUE

A Year Before

In the dawning light, if anyone had been down on the coast path near the harbour, they would have marvelled at the beauty of the scene: the expanse of sky with early tints of dawn, the light stretching more widely across the horizon, moment by moment. They probably wouldn't have noticed where a body had been dislodged from the rocks by the tide. Foam surged and sapped back and forth over the lifeless legs, which were being shifted by the momentum of the water.

Gulls were beginning to move; an occasional call accompanied their first swinging flights down from the cliffs in gliding arcs. The body was carried backwards, further from the land. Seaweed formed dark masses beneath the water, interspersed with lighter areas of sand on the seabed below. The body continued to move away from the shore. Its coloured clothing contrasted with the deep green of the sea, its red dress darkened by the water. The swell of the waves nudged it from side to side, the currents pulling it out to deeper waters beyond.

If there had been a dawn walker on the cliff path, perhaps

they would have noticed the dead woman floating below. Someone out early with their dog might have spotted her. If there had been an early morning delivery for the café, perhaps someone would have looked out and seen – an alarm could have been raised and the body's drift seawards arrested.

The gulls swooping across the bay thickened. The hedges and fields behind the cliff face became patterned with the movement of wildlife, and gradually the outlines of stocky red-brown cattle became fully formed figures, standing in formation across the tufted grass and grazing there.

Before the area was peopled, the body was beyond view. Perhaps an offshore seal nudged it, or a gull veered away from it in flight. No one saw.

ACKNOWLEDGEMENTS

Thank you for reading this book and I hope you have enjoyed it. Since I began writing about Clare's sleuthing adventures, it has been lovely to hear from readers and also to meet some of you at bookshop and library events – and in parishes where I take services. It is very good to meet you and to swap recommendations of other books, too – there are so many great crime novels to choose from. My warm thanks to all the booksellers and librarians who make it possible to try lots of them!

I am very fortunate to be published by Quercus. Thank you to all the team there for their hard work and care, including Florence Hare, Vanessa Phan, Stefanie Bierworth, Myrto Kalavrezou, Katy Blott, Laura Hunt, Kyla Dean, Megan Schaffer, Andrew Smith and Fran Hambling. So many people are involved in the production of a book – my warm thanks to Penelope Price for her copy-editing, and to all who have been involved in producing the audio version, including Carrie Hutchinson and Helen Keeley.

Rebecca Carter is such an astute, tactful and experienced agent, I am fortunate to work with her and the team at

Rebecca Carter Literary – Tilda Butterworth, and also Margaret Halton and Alex Chernova, who look after translation rights. Simon Appleby and his colleagues at Bookswarm created and maintain my author website (www.revpennystephens.com) – my warm thanks to them and to my son, Ben, who helps load material on to it.

Family, friends and neighbours have been so generous in encouraging and supporting me as I write, and it means a lot – thank you. Clergy friends and colleagues have been very kind, and some have provided anecdotes for me to fictionalise and add to the novels. Other crime-fiction writers have been similarly generous in their encouragement – my particular thanks to Elly Griffiths, Lesley Thomson, Fiona Cummins and Laura Marshall.

My family are unstinting in their support – my daughter Eleanor and son-in-law Matthew, my son Ben and husband Jonathan – I can't thank you enough for all the backing you give me, day by day. This book is dedicated to my wonderful nieces and nephews, but of course it is also for you, with lots of love and happy memories of cream teas, beach explorations and other adventures with you, in Cornwall and elsewhere.

RAISING READERS
Books Build Bright Futures

Dear Reader,

We'd love your attention for one more page to tell you about the crisis in children's reading, and what we can all do.

Studies have shown that reading for fun is the **single biggest predictor of a child's future life chances** – more than family circumstance, parents' educational background or income. It improves academic results, mental health, wealth, communication skills, ambition and happiness.[1]

The number of children reading for fun is in rapid decline. Young people have a lot of competition for their time. In 2024, 1 in 10 children and young people in the UK aged 5 to 18 did not own a single book at home.[2]

Hachette works extensively with schools, libraries and literacy charities, but here are some ways we can all raise more readers:

- Reading to children for just 10 minutes a day makes a difference
- Don't give up if children aren't regular readers – there will be books for them!
- Visit bookshops and libraries to get recommendations
- Encourage them to listen to audiobooks
- Support school libraries
- Give books as gifts

There's a lot more information about how to encourage children to read on our website: **www.RaisingReaders.co.uk**

Thank you for reading.

hachette UK

[1] OECD, '21st-Century Readers: Developing Literacy Skills in a Digital World', 2021, https://www.oecd.org/en/publications/21st-century-readers_a83d84cb-en.html

[2] National Literacy Trust, 'Book Ownership in 2024', November 2024, https://literacytrust.org.uk/research-services/research-reports/book-ownership-in-2024